WRITER
&
CRITIC
AND OTHER ESSAYS

Works by Georg Lukács published by The Universal Library

ESSAYS ON THOMAS MANN
GOETHE AND HIS AGE
STUDIES IN EUROPEAN REALISM

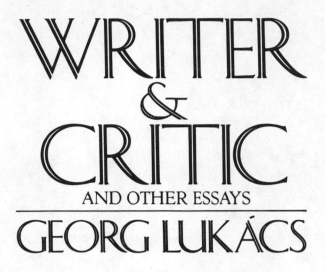

WRITER & CRITIC

AND OTHER ESSAYS

GEORG LUKÁCS

Edited and translated
by
Arthur D. Kahn, Ph.D.
Chairman, Department of Classics
Brock University, Ontario, Canada

The Universal Library

Publishers GROSSET & DUNLAP *New York*
A NATIONAL GENERAL COMPANY

© THE MERLIN PRESS LTD. 1970

LIBRARY OF CONGRESS CATALOG NUMBER: 73-158769
ISBN: 0-448-02500-0 (Hard)
ISBN: 0-448-00259-0 (Soft)

UNIVERSAL LIBRARY EDITION, 1971
BY ARRANGEMENT WITH THE MERLIN PRESS LTD.

1974 PRINTING

PRINTED IN THE UNITED STATES OF AMERICA

Contents

Preface

THE essays assembled in this book originally appeared in Moscow and Budapest during the thirties and forties, that is, under the Stalin and Rakosi regimes. It is not hard to see today that the main direction of these essays was in opposition to the dominant literary theory of the time. Stalin and his followers demanded that literature provide tactical support to their current political policies. Accordingly, all art was to be subordinated, both in the positive and negative sense, to these needs. Only acceptable characters and situations, ideas and emotions were to be introduced, only material adapted to their policies and nothing going beyond these policies. As everyone knows, no open polemics were possible during that period. Yet I did protest consistently against such a conception of literature. A revival of Marx and Lenin's views regarding the complicated dialectic, rich in contradiction, between the political and social positions of writers and their actual works, ran counter to Zhdanov's prescriptions. In expounding such and similar views through analyses of a Balzac or a Tolstoy, I not only offered a theory in opposition to the official line but also by clear implication a critique of the official literature. As many documents attest, those I criticized were well aware of what I was doing.

The examples I adduced to contrast with the great works of the past were not selected from socialist literature alone but from works of decadent bourgeois schools as well. The reason was not simply tactical. During the thirties my Russian friends and I were not the only ones critical of the artistic qualities of socialist literature. There was, in addition, no small group who were prepared to cut themselves off from the Russian realistic traditions (that is, the traditions of Tolstoy, Chekhov, Gorki and Sholokhov) and were seeking a solution to their

7

aesthetic problems in an appropriation of the Joycean style. They even considered the naturalism in fashion at the time, the "new objectivity" with its technique of journalistic montage, as a possible effective new direction. My critical studies thus were directed against two fronts: against the schematic deadliness and impoverishment of socialist literature and against those movements seeking salvation in following Western avant-garde schools. When I think back to this period now, more than thirty years later, I find this struggle on two fronts even more profoundly justified than I did then. For if certain exponents of the artistic avant-garde now represent themselves as inveterate anti-Stalinists, they can do so only because their work of that period has properly fallen into oblivion. In fact, it did not differ at all philosophically and politically from the crass naturalism and schematism of the Stalinist "construction novels".

I sought, on the other hand, to revive the realist tradition of richness in content and form and to combat the barren schematism of the official literature not only in regard to its technique and its artistic approach but also in regard to its fundamental principles regarding the representation of people and life and to open the way through my criticism to a new great literature capable of encompassing life in the age of socialism.

Such was the rationale for the essays assembled here. If they are to reappear now a quarter century later in a new language, this rationale must be understood even though an understanding of this rationale alone cannot justify their reappearance. In fact, however, the problems which they treat have not lost their significance and may have even more meaning now than at their original publication.

My friend Arthur Kahn, who has painstakingly translated these essays, was, in my opinion, entirely correct in eliminating from the text polemics pertinent at the time of publication in order, by this pruning, to expose more effectively what is of lasting significance. As a result of this editing, the text presented in this volume is entirely relevant to current problems. Indeed the contemporary significance of these essays is attested by the current reactions to these and similar essays. I do not intend to multiply these arguments with rejoinders. Time will rule upon them.

In all seriousness, essays like these have contemporary relevance only if my conception of a two-front struggle actually rested on an enduring and important complex of aesthetic problems. I believe that such a unity and continuing timeliness are not difficult to demonstrate, for these essays constitute an indictment of the impoverishment in artistic content and in fictional representation both in western avant-garde movements and in what is customarily called socialist realism. Involved are not simply artistic questions. The author of these essays subscribes to Goethe's observation: "Literature deteriorates only as mankind deteriorates." In various essays I have exposed the social bases for the frustration of man's noblest aspirations, contrasting the brutal manipulations of the Stalin period and its aftermath with the more refined manipulations of contemporary capitalism and its democracy.

Our investigation leads in another direction. One should not seek the sources of literary problems in the unreliable phenomena of everyday life. Internal discrepancies in artistic form are manifestations of distortions in life patterns and result from unresolved (and therefore especially compelling) social contradictions.

To characterize the contemporary artistic deterioration briefly, one might say that literature has lost that richness in dimension which provides the unfailing attraction and timeless effectiveness of earlier literatures. It makes little difference whether the multidimensionality of the outer and inner worlds or of their uninterrupted interaction is reduced ultimately to an internalized monotonous stream of associations in monologue or whether an autonomous external, self-sufficient world emerges in the trend toward lifeless objectivism, a world which can have no relation to men and with which they can have nothing in common, where every meaningful interaction between an individual's inner life and his environment is precluded by the very mode of representation. The contemporary movements displace one another, faster or slower, more or less completely, but a common principle remains: each particular technique creates a corresponding single-dimensional world, and this single-dimensionality excludes and eliminates all other aspects of life as irrelevant and unworthy of the mode of representation.

At first sight, this single-dimensionality seems to be merely a question of artistry and technique, and from a superficial artistic and technical point of view such is the case. Underlying the problem, however, are questions of ideology, often unconscious but sometimes explicit. The philosophy of Karl Jaspers, long widely disseminated, is based on the premise that man is essentially unknowable. In modern literature outstanding and even famous writers, whether acquainted with Jasper's thought or not, base their creative work on this view of man. One need only point to Frisch or any of the exponents of the "nouveau roman", all of whom, despite superficial differences, share this view.

In this essay we can merely touch upon this question. Of greater significance, in any event, are the artistic consequences. Artists have long been aware of the problem. Reporting a conversation he had had with Cézanne at an exposition of the latter's paintings, Osthaus, a director of an art gallery, declared: "He pointed out precisely how far he had succeeded in providing a suggestion of depth and where his painting had failed, where the colour had remained mere colour without providing any sense of perspective." In this instance, admittedly involving a simple, specific question, the great master's declaration of war against single-dimensionality in artistic expression is clear. But as one studies Cézanne's conversations and letters, one sees that distance was far from the only dimension the master expected to achieve with colour. The rendering of the many-sidedness and many levels of visible reality as well as of what is not directly visual but is transmitted through various mediations is what Cézanne was accustomed to call "realization". For him the function of drawing and colour in the total work as well as in the details, was to render visual the essential aspects of all sides of reality. For Cézanne to say that colours remained nothing but colours was a sharp criticism. It is signifi-

cant that he repeatedly declared that Gauguin had made the
problem too easy for himself. What would he have said about
Matisse or Mondrian?

It is not too difficult to apply the lesson of Cézanne's artistic
intentions to literature. The multidimensionality of colour in
painting has its analogue in the multidimensionality of word
and phrase. With its forms of organization, its science and its
techniques of manipulation, modern life moves relentlessly toward reducing the word to the mechanical simplicity of a mere
sign. That means a radical departure from life, for the dynamism of everyday language derives precisely from its always
being either less or more in vocabulary and syntax than mere
signs : less in that in its ambiguity it skirts the essence of the
object being discussed, more in that in its very imprecision it
articulates the concrete essence of an entire concrete complex.
The reduction of words to mere signs is, of course, a technical
necessity in certain fields, like military codes, where not only
the word but even the manner of articulation freeze to a
mechanical explicitness. The introduction of manipulated
symbolism into the theory and practice of literary language
inevitably produces a false polarization because of the inherent
tendency of signs to eliminate multidimensionality. On the one
hand, the articulation, like that which is to be expressed,
obtains almost the dry precision and lack of ambiguity of
science. On the other hand, the signs achieve a far-fetched,
ingenious single-dimensionality in the words and sentences
themselves, and in the delineation of an object the atmosphere
and multidimensionality disappear with the loss of ambiguity
in language. Ambiguity in daily speech presupposes the intensive inexhaustibility of man (the subject) and of the objective
world encompassing him. That is why poetry created from
living speech does not grow stale and why its words do not
suffer devaluation to small change. New relationships of subject and object constantly emerge, and in the process of innovation in life experiences in new and intrinsically significant
situations, the most ordinary and trite expression undergoes a
rebirth, conveying new thoughts and feelings. One need merely
refer to the final scene in Goethe's *Iphigenie*, where such

expressions as "go away" and "farewell" are sufficiently suggestive to effect a profound catharsis.

Semanticists pretend that such problems are merely problems of language. Actually they arise out of life and bear the birthmarks of profundity or triviality according to their source. If I may cite Goethe again, this time in regard to the writer's mission: Goethe chose as the epigraph for his *Elegies*: "And if man falls speechless in his torment, God give me to say what I suffer." But speech and silence do not merely reflect the difference between the average man and the poet but even more a fundamental opposition within literature itself. For a mere imitation of anguish is as mute as the anguish itself if the speech is not elevated to a poetic articulation of the essence of the anguish in its uniqueness, concreteness and universality. But the virtuoso single-dimensionality in the modern use of language contemptuously rejects just such an achievement. The simultaneous impoverishment and sickly over-cultivation of language are products of a distortion in man's relationship to himself, his fellows and to the objects of his environment. Since he considers himself and his peers as unknowable and views the world of objects merely as a complex of manipulations simultaneously manipulated by man and in turn manipulating him, subject and object lose all substance, all solidity. Thus the bifurcation of language into false extremes is the inevitable consequence of a writer's view of life.

Of course, there is no more uniformity in this view of life than in the world it views and in the intellectual and emotional reactions to this world. Every true writer develops his own emphasis and his own organization of life experiences. Every new direction differs sharply from previous and succeeding directions. Yet the general characteristics distinguishing today's dominant currents from those of the much disparaged nineteenth century are easily defined. There is, of course, a distinction between the two eras but not as clear-cut and fundamental as many literary critics pretend. The intellectual climate producing the peculiar character of contemporary literature is itself the outgrowth of tendencies long germinating within bourgeois society. At first glance, the present seems to have effected abrupt changes, but beneath these changes the preceding generating movement can be perceived. If we investigate the particular trends of the nineteenth century, we note that as early as Schopenhauer a characteristic antinomy had emerged in bourgeois life: boredom and intoxication. It obtained further theoretical elaboration in Nietzsche and reached a culmination in literature at the turn of the century. Names long forgotten like J. K. Huysmans or Gabriele d'Annunzio represented stages in the development which people combated as radical innovation or honoured as the acme of art. If we attempt a similar synthesis of the dominant trends today, we find an apparent opposition of neopositivism and existentialism in theory and of artificially manipulated alienation and shock in the emotional substratum.

What is important in both cases is that the apparently unbridgeable antithesis disguises a deep inner association and reciprocal extension and support. One overcomes ennui as little through intoxication (one is even impelled back into its sphere) as one is liberated by shock from manipulated alienation, for shock merely groups, concentrates and conserves the characteristic moral features of this alienation. In both cases it is a question therefore of constantly repeated emotional revolts concealing, for all practical purposes, the desire *quieta non movere*, to leave inviolate the bases of this pair of opposites. The Italian writer Italo Svevo, whose fame rests on his association with Joyce, expressly declared that protest is the shortest road to resignation.

Schopenhauer forged the required ideological weapons: when the social bases of particular decisive issues are conceived as cosmic, the man affected by their consequences obtains absolute absolution in fashionable and impressive terms for even having dared to think about possible modification of or resistance to their consequences. From this rejection of any "profligate optimism", a nexus of ideologies extends to Heidegger's "Geworfenheit" (propulsion by destiny) and to the ideology of the "condition humaine"—all preaching resignation to inhuman social conditions, a resignation that may be expressed as rejection, protest or, minimally, as escape, but never results in a real, effective ethical confrontation of the individual with his destiny. Intoxication does indeed eliminate boredom as little as shock eliminates manipulated alienation; each establishes an emotional transition to the restoration of the other.

This observation brings us back to Goethe, to "falling speechless" and "telling what I suffer". In modern art there is sufficient noise about expressionism and futurism and even about the anti-literature of the absurd. If one analyzes the content and ignores the self-advertising, it becomes clear that the shrillest yelling conveys nothing more than an inner speechlessness. I know that many have resented my characterizing the modern "isms" as naturalism (as distinct from realism). The point at which realism passes into naturalism is not at issue; it is not a question whether a grey, everyday existence or a fantastic unreality is represented, but whether the more profound *how* of an event is articulated or remains silent. A bloodcurdling ghost story may remain pure naturalism if it fails to disclose any levels beyond the triviality of everyday existence, if it does not articulate the essential relevance in an event and in the reaction to the event. On the other hand, the most commonplace setting can transmit essential truths about life. Chekhov is no naturalist; Beckett is. The photographic character of naturalism is not to be sought simply in a direct objective rendering of colourless workaday existence, such as might have been achieved with some justification in Zola's day, though even then Huysmanns always remained inherently a naturalist while Maupassant in his outstanding short stories went far beyond naturalism. With present-day techniques anything from the atom bomb to the interior monologue can be photographed, and it is ultimately the writer's approach to reality that determines whether he produces a painting or a photograph, an articulate statement or a mute babbling.

There does not seem to be a relationship between the assumption of the "condition humaine" as the ideological base of the social process and the development of the predominant single-dimensional technical virtuosity. But though marching separately, they strike together, impelling literature into varied forms of naturalism. For each in its own fashion reduces fiction to mere direct imitation of an isolated aspect of the social and historical totality and to a mere immediate reaction of an individual (who himself is naturally many-faceted) to such an artificially isolated aspect. The single-dimensional technique suffices, of course, to produce shock, but shock in itself prevents a penetration into the deeper concrete reality of the relationship of the particular individual to his particular reality. Shock prevents any illumination of the power in appropriate human reactions to concrete alternatives in life. It prevents the mobilization of this power as well as the articulation of these reactions. If this voice is silenced, a work sinks into the morass of lifeless naturalism regardless of any skilful contriving and ingenious tinkering.

Generally, this is no mere literary morass. There is a literary question involved indeed in the fact that catharsis presupposes a genuine mastery of reality and of seriously investigated alternatives while intoxication, boredom and shock in the last analysis merely reproduce and perpetuate alienation. But more than a literary question is involved. Resignation before degrading circumstances the Age of Enlightenment labelled philistinism, against which the best creative works of Diderot and Rousseau, Lessing and the youthful Goethe were directed. This struggle culminated effectively in the great French Revolution. Only in the blind reaction of the French Restoration, above all in romanticism, was philistinism redefined incorrectly as merely a stupid response to genuine art. Now resignation to degrading circumstances implicit in the aesthetic pseudo-protest came to be glorified, and philistinism was transformed into a limited concept. Mere aesthetic scoffing at philistinism results in its perpetuation both in the ironist and in the object of his irony.

The leading democratic writers of the nineteenth century often criticized this distortion and the aristocratic pretension it implied. Gottfried Keller declared that "the bohemian petit bourgeois is not a bit wittier than the solid citizen". Of course, the exemplifications of both poles have changed, but the trenchancy of Keller's remark remains. One is often tempted to assert today that the most disagreeable non-conformist is no less a smug philistine than the self-advertising conformist, complacent and dyed-in-the-wool; and that the champion of "sexual freedom" who despises as "old-fashioned sentimentality" such a love as that between Robert Browning and Elizabeth Barrett is no less a philistine than the most prudish blue stocking.

As Matthew Arnold correctly observed, literature is "criticism of life". The question, however, is whether life is criticized from above or from below, whether the criticism reveals insights and illuminations more profound than the superficial image mankind has of itself at a particular time. If we think of genuine and great literature, these comments seem obvious. Undoubtedly, Balzac and Stendhal provide a clearer, more penetrating and more comprehensive exposition of the general problems of the Restoration than could be gained by ordinary, superficial observation at the time. For a long time literature has accepted the premise that the immediate present prescribes the kind and level of questions to be posed and answers to be achieved. A plausible observation but actually profoundly false. Consider the documents of our own immediate past. We possess magnificent testimonies of deliberate and unselfconscious heroism. One need only recall the collections of the last letters of anti-fascists condemned to death or documents like Fuçiks's prison diary or Niekisch's autobiographical *Hazardous Life*.

What about literature? Until very recently one would have had to respond with silent embarrassment, for aside from a few great names nothing approaches the nobility of these documents. But then not long ago Semprun's *Great Journey* appeared. This is not the place to speak of the extraordinary qualities of this novel. One must at least note, however, that Semprun depicts no less vividly the horrors of fascism in their inhumanity and apparent triumphant power than the direct and indirect chroniclers of the period. But he is not satisfied with mere description of the "human condition" under these circumstances. He creates people mounting active resistance to the horrors. Artistically, it is not important how effective such resistance could be (at the time, not effective at all) but how such activity modifies the total picture of the period.

For the psychology of the "human condition", single-dimensionality is inevitable—a single-dimensionality of fear, the single note of many writers since Kierkegaard and the inevitable correlative to the inhuman objective world. (Of course, fear does not hold an absolutely privileged status. Now that the obvious horror of the Hitler period has disappeared and the new theme of artificial alienation predominates, nausea can replace fear. But the common denominator remains: both attitudes of resignation preclude any active resistance and thus guarantee single-dimensionality in the technique of representation.) Conscious resistance breaks the magic circle restricting and degrading men. When fear is no longer the sole inevitable reaction, an integrated human being full of contradictions can mobilize his inner reserves and make a stand against a total social environment. Then the forces which in a given moment may coalesce to transform men into mere objects and to implant fear as their sole spiritual content suffer defeat in a particular collision within the continuous network of ever-changing alternatives determining the maintenance or loss of human integrity. Instead of the monotony of the "eternally victorious" alienation, of the single-dimensional fear, an inner, deeply impelling drama emerges of the struggle for human dignity at the very moment of the external triumph of the most brutal inhumanity. And the inner life of struggle (for externally no struggle is possible) breaks the single-dimensionality and provides a dynamic and impelling wholeness to life.

Although, of course, fascism is not the problem of today but of yesterday and the day before yesterday, the spirit behind the literary representation of life is still the important question. And it must be pointed out in regard to the key issue today, the issue of the artificially induced alienation, that yesterday before this danger had scarcely emerged to the proportions it has attained today, writers were already offering resistance. The best novels of Sinclair Lewis like *Babbitt* and *Arrowsmith*, the later tragedies and tragi-comedies of O'Neill and the last

novel of Thomas Wolfe, *You Can't Go Home Again*, demonstrate the possibility of a wider scope in the representation of
alienation than that between the poles of manipulated alienation and shock.

The writer of this essay cannot pretend to a familiarity with
contemporary writing in the United States. He can therefore
merely call attention to an example of chance reading which
he thinks may be symptomatic, Styron's *Set This House On
Fire*. Here alienation provides the theme but not simply as
"human condition". One protagonist becomes alienated because of his wealth, the other because of his poverty. And if
Styron offers a romantic murder as an escape from alienation
for the humble character, he nevertheless does show that even
for such a controversial and humble individual a way does
exist to break out of alienation though at the risk of self-
destruction. Styron reveals his artistic skill in underscoring this
possibility with great vigour while demonstrating that it is only
one of the possibilities and that the moral seriousness and the
ethical determination in the will for self-preservation can effect
a practical catharsis for an individual even in the midst of the
current general alienation.

It is this approach and not mere random and superficial
similarities in style that links significant writing in our time
with the great literature of the past. Yet history, theory and
criticism operate in the opposite direction, striving to
rediscover superficial, technical or at best atmospheric echoes
of the present in the past. In such searches for analogies,
mannerism was squeezed dry with the revival of such painters
as Arcimboldi, who composed portraits of fruit, animals, pots
and pans, etc. Such fads deserve no comment. If anyone
objects that a firmer basis for the aesthetic principles of
Dadaism can be found, we wish him luck. The reason for
Cézanne's admiration of Tintoretto is not to be mentioned in
the same breath with such pettifoggery.

What we are discussing is altogether different. Problems of
the impulse to artistic expression are not to be discussed so
flippantly. Every true work of art arises out of the particular
and real alternatives of its time. The means for the dynamic

rendering of these alternatives is what we are accustomed to call style, which requires a two-fold investigation. One must consider first the *what* of the human content in the alternatives and in the meaningful responses to these alternatives; and second, the *how* in the artistic expression, the way in which the human reactions to the world are articulated and fixed aesthetically. By "realization" Cézanne meant the indissolubility of the *what* and the *how* in works of art.

Today people repeatedly condemn any serious emphasis on the *what* as inartistic. The reproach is justified only where the *what* is divorced from the artistic *how* and rendered autonomous. It can never be autonomous, however, except when life itself compels the articulation—as in the letters of the anti-fascists condemned to death. But that is an expression of life and at best the raw material or impulse for art, not art itself. In Goethe's sense, only in Semprun's novel do we have the "say what I suffer" for the Hitler period.

It would be still more incorrect to make the artistic *how* formally and semantically autonomous. What exalts Shakespeare above his contemporaries is his indissoluble unity of the *what* and *how*; any separation of the two is unimaginable in his art.

When we speak of concreteness, we mean the concrete integrity of the subjective and objective world in life as well as in literature. Many writers literally take up "the issue of the day" and attempt direct responses to particular questions in their environment. Not without some justification, for such an approach often aids them to set their particular problem, which had often remained unrealized, in a realistic perspective and to define it without exaggerated abstraction, that is, to integrate it into the continuum of human development. The question is always to achieve the unity of the *what* and the *how* within the context of the times and in terms of men's success and failure in confronting the great challenges of the day.

Here again all the rubble of restrictive prejudices must be cleared away. On the one hand, some say that the problems confronting us are unprecedented, without any connection to the past; on the other hand, the old copybook philosophy holds that there is something "eternally human" apart from or beyond any actual evolution of mankind, divorced *a priori* from this evolution. Both views fail to recognize that what we call humanity is the product of a long historical process, the result of an evolution over the course of millenia moving in a contradictory dialectic full of digressions and retrogressions. Only today are we finally able to apprehend the general contours of this problem complex. Viewed in this perspective, every historical event is both integrally and uniquely new and also a product of the historical development. Marx's vigorous emphasis of this principle is well-known. Less well-known is his placing equal emphasis on the unevenness of the development and above all on the fact that often what is objectively progressive materializes in forms in which its essential quality not merely disappears but even is transformed into its opposite.

The great figures of literature from Homer to Thomas Mann were not, of course, Marxists. Yet without exception the direction of their work reveals an understanding of this evolutionary process; because of this understanding they are able to accomplish the true mission of literature. Long ago Aristotle defined the artist's task when he declared that even in verse Herodotus would be an historian and not a poet since a poet is concerned not with what has actually happened but with what is possible. The possible, considered both positively and negatively, the maximally possible—in our understanding of Aristotle's great insight after more than two thousand years— represents the issue of the moment confronting the human species—intensified to the maximum of its inner dynamics and dialectic. Literary forms develop from the theoretical and practical exploration of these concrete maximal potentialities to the ultimate. Not in the sense of mere formal techniques, for the transformation of a history or chronicle into verse might actually result in unprecedented innovations in prosody without producing true literature, but in the sense of true form, in the sense of the genuine creation of form, in the sense of the integration of the *what* of the social and historical question with the *how* of the formal artistic response. Of the unity of content and form Hegel said: "Content is nothing but the transformation of form into content, and form is nothing but the transformation of content into form." That is why the genuine categories of literary forms are not simply literary in essence. They are forms of life especially adapted to the articulation of great alternatives in a practical and effective manner and to the exposition of the maximal inner potentialities of forces and counterforces. Of course, these do not emerge spontaneously as literary forms. It is precisely in this respect that the genius of the great poet is required. Thus in introducing the second actor, Aeschylus accomplished something more than a formal innovation. The new dramatic conflict in dialogue revealing the profoundest essence of personality with a richness of sense and sensibility had its origin undoubtedly in the unfolding of Athenian polis democracy. Aeschylus' genius lay "simply" in his discovering the maximal literary expression for the maximal revelation of life. Dramatic dialogue became infinitely varied in the course of time, but the interrelationship of life content and dialogue form remained constant within the changes introduced over thousands of years (Goethe's "Dauer im Wechsel").

I believe that in any serious analysis of literary forms and even of formal elements, this unity of continuity and of ever-renewing uniqueness will always be discovered. Though the pedants of modernism screw up their noses at Lessing, his insight into the ultimate identity of dramatic form in Sophocles and Shakespeare is one of the most important achievements toward an historical and systematic theory of genres. The paucity of such syntheses in this field of theory sets in perspective the significance of his achievement. That historical evolution brings forth entirely new forms does not mean a denial of the validity of forms expressing continuity and stability within the development. Consider such Aristotelian terms as catharsis and recognition. It would perhaps also amaze admirers of such modern fictional techniques as interruptions in continuity and interweaving of foreshadowing and flashback to learn that the principle of the non-chronological, continuous epic representation of time can be traced back in practice to Homer and in theory to Horace's "Ars Poetica", to the opposition of "ab ovo" and "in medias res". Of course, over the years there have been endless variations (representing no essential changes in principle or effect) depending upon the achievement of the unity of the *what* and the *how*. Similar formal solutions in some cases have arisen organically out of the material and in other cases have been merely the products of subjective wilfulness.

I do not pretend that in writing my essays in the two-front battle against the literature of crass and of sophisticated manipulation, I had grasped the theoretical principle involved clearly and consciously. The thoughts I have sketched here took long to crystalize. Yet they are implicit in the earlier essays and afford a theoretical unity to this collection of diverse and independent studies. As for the effectiveness of these essays— because of their fundamental premise, their author became an outsider to the official literatures both of the socialist countries and of the "Free World", rejected by all dominant movements. In both parts of the world people are of the opinion—even if they do not say so openly—that literature and art really can be manipulated and that content and form can be manufactured to order according to the needs of the day.

I reject this view and its consequences though understanding as an historian their origin and their dissemination. That does not mean, however, that I believe that things will remain as they are. Much has been happening. What was considered fixed and unshakeable at the end of the Second World War, by the end of the sixties, if not actually tottering, is under serious and mounting criticism. Since the Twentieth Congress of the Soviet Communist Party criticism of Stalin's distortions of the teaching and methods of Marx, Engels and Lenin can no longer be completely repressed. Simultaneously, in the capitalist countries, in the United States itself, the ideological resistance to the dogma of the American Way of Life is intensifying. These movements are hampered not only by the continuing fierce resistance of the old entrenched circles but also by the internal weaknesses, lack of clarity and contradictions in the opposition forces. Yet ultimately, I am confident, the forces for progress will gain the upper hand.

In any event, as I stated in 1957, paraphrasing Zola : "La vérité est lentement en marche et à la fin des fins rien ne l'arrêtera." In this development the view that art is to be evaluated in terms of its significance to mankind will enjoy wider and wider acceptance.

I am aware, too, that at present the proponents of a "liberalization" of Stalinist dogmatism or of the conformism artificially imposed in the West and masquerading as non-conformity are more in fashion, and they view this perspective with scepticism. I do not share their attitude and take comfort, so far as I need comfort, in the words of the young Marx : "No people despairs even if its hopes have for a long time been vain; in the end, after many years, with sudden wisdom it will fulfil all its sacred aspirations."

Budapest, March 1965
revised April 1970

Art and Objective Truth

The Objectivity of Truth in Marxist-Leninist Epistemology

THE basis for any correct cognition of reality, whether of nature or society, is the recognition of the objectivity of the external world, that is, its existence independent of human consciousness. Any apprehension of the external world is nothing more than a reflection in consciousness of the world that exists independently of consciousness. This basic fact of the relationship of consciousness to being also serves, of course, for the artistic reflection of reality.

The theory of reflection provides the common basis for *all* forms of theoretical and practical mastery of reality through consciousness. Thus it is also the basis for the theory of the artistic reflection of reality. In this discussion, we will seek to elaborate the *specific* aspects of artistic reflection within the scope of the general theory.

A valid, comprehensive theory of reflection first arose with dialectical materialism, in the works of Marx, Engels and Lenin. For the bourgeois mind a correct theory of objectivity and of the reflection in consciousness of a reality existing independent of consciousness, a materialist, dialectical theory, is an impossibility. Of course, in practice, in bourgeois science and art there are countless instances of an accurate reflection of reality, and there have even been a number of attempts at a correct theoretical posing and solution of the question. Once the question is elevated, however, into a question of epistemology, bourgeois thinkers become trapped in mechanistic materialism or sink into philosophic idealism. Lenin characterized and exposed the limitations of both directions of bourgeois thinking with unsurpassed clarity. Of mechanistic materialism he declared: "Its chief failure lies in its incapacity to apply dialectics to the theory of images, to the process and evolution of knowledge." Philosophic idealism he went on to characterize thus: "Contrarily, from the standpoint of *dialectical* materialism, philosophical idealism is a *one-sided*, exaggerated, extravagant . . . development, a pompous inflation of one aspect, of one side, of one frontier of knowledge to a sanctified absolute divorced from matter, from nature. . . . Single-dimensionality, one-sidedness, frigidity, subjectivism and subjective blindness, *voilà*, the epistemological roots of idealism."

This double-faceted inadequacy of bourgeois epistemology appears in all areas and in all problems of the reflection of reality through consciousness. In this connection we cannot investigate the entire realm of epistemology or trace the history of human knowledge. We must limit ourselves to a few important aspects of the epistemology of Marxism-Leninism which are especially significant for the *problem of objectivity* in the *artistic reflection of reality*.

The first problem to deal with is that of the direct reflections of the external world. All knowledge rests on them; they are the foundation, the point of departure for all knowledge. But they are *only* the point of departure and not all there is to the process of knowing. Marx expressed himself with unmistakable clarity on this question, declaring: "Science would be superfluous if there were an immediate coincidence of the appearance and reality of things." And in his study of Hegel's logic, Lenin analysed this question and arrived at this formulation: "Truth is not to be found at the beginning but at the end, more particularly within the process. Truth is not the *initial impression*." Following Marx he illustrated this observation with an example from political economy: "Value is a category which deprives goods of their materiality, but it is *truer* than the law of supply and demand." From this introductory observation Lenin goes on to define the function of abstract terms, concepts, laws, etc., in the total human comprehension of reality and to define their place in the over-all theory of reflection and of the objective knowledge of reality. "Just as the simple incorporation of value, the single act of exchanging goods, includes in microcosm, in embryo, *all* the principal contradictions of capitalism—so the simplest generalization, the initial and simplest formulation of *concepts* (judgments, conclusions) implies man's ever-expanding apprehension of the *objective* macrocosm." On this basis he is able to state in summary : "The abstractions of matter, natural *law*, value, etc., in a word, *all* scientific (accurate, seriously considered, not irrational) abstractions reflect nature more profoundly, more faithfully, more *completely*. From active observation to abstract thought and from there to practical activity—such is the dialectical path of apprehending truth and objective reality."

By analysing the place of various abstractions in epistemology, Lenin underscores with the greatest precision the dialectical dichotomy within them. He says : "The significance of the *universal* is contradictory : it is inert, impure, incomplete, etc., but it is also only a *stage* in the cognition of the concrete, for we never apprehend the concrete completely. The infinite sum of general concepts, laws, etc., provides the concrete in its completeness." This dichotomy alone clarifies the dialectic of appearance and reality. Lenin says : "The phenomenon is *richer* than the law." And he goes on to comment on a definition of Hegel's : "That (the word 'passive') is an excellent materialist and remarkably apt description. Every law deals with the passive—and that is why a law, every law, is restricted, incomplete, approximate."

With this profound insight into the incompleteness of the intellectual reproduction of reality, both in the direct mirroring of phenomena as well as in concepts and laws (when they are considered one-sidedly, undialectically, outside the infinite process of dialectical interaction), Lenin arrived at a materialist elimination of all false formulations of bourgeois epistemology. For every bourgeois epistemology has one-sidedly emphasized the priority of one approach to apprehending reality, one mode in the conscious reproduction of reality. Lenin concretely presents the dialectical interaction in the process of cognition. "Is the perceptual image *closer* to reality than thought? Both

·yes and no. The perceptual image cannot entirely comprehend motion; for example, it cannot comprehend speed of three hundred thousand kilometres per second, but *thought* can and should do so. Thus thought derived from perception mirrors reality." In this way the idealistic depreciation of the "lower" faculties of cognition is overcome through dialectics. With the strict materialism of his epistemology and his unwavering insistence on the principle of objectivity, Lenin is able to grasp the correct dialectical relationship of the modes of human perception of reality in their dynamics. Regarding the role of fantasy in cognition, he says: "The approach of human reason to the individual thing, obtaining an impression (a concept) of it is no simple, direct, lifeless mirroring but a complicated, dichotomous, zigzag act which by its very nature encompasses the possibility that imagination can soar away from life. . . . For even in the simplest generalization of the most elementary universal idea (like the idea of a table) there lurks a shred of imagination (vice versa, it is foolish to deny the role of imagination in the most exact science)."

Only through dialectics is it possible to overcome the incompleteness, the rigidity and the barrenness of any one-sided conception of reality. Only through the correct and conscious application of dialectics can we overcome the incompleteness in the infinite process of cognition and bring our thinking closer to the dynamic infinity in objective reality. Lenin says: "We cannot imagine motion, we cannot express it, measure it, imitate it without interrupting its continuity, without simplifying, vulgarizing, disintegrating and stifling its dynamism. The intellectual representation of motion is always vulgarized and devitalized and not only through thoughts but through the senses as well and not only of motion, but of any concept at all. And precisely in this is the essence of dialectics. *Precisely this essence* is to be expressed through the formula: unity, identity of opposites."

The union of materialist dialectics with *practice*, its derivation from practice, its control through practice, its directive role in practice, rest on this profound conception of the dialectical nature of objective reality and of the dialectic of its reflection in consciousness. Lenin's theory of revolutionary practice rests on his recognition of the fact that reality is always richer and more varied than the best and most comprehensive theory that can be developed to apprehend it, and at the same time, however, on the consciousness that with the active application of dialectics one can learn from reality, apprehend important new factors in reality and apply them in practice. "History," Lenin said, "especially the history of revolution, was always richer in content, more complex, more dynamic, subtler than the most effective parties, the most class-conscious vanguard of the most progressive classes ever imagined." The extraordinary elasticity in Lenin's tactics, his ability to adapt himself swiftly to sudden changes in history and to derive the maximum from these changes rested on his profound grasp of objective dialectics.

This relationship between the strict objectivity in epistemology[1] and its integral relationship to practice is one of the significant aspects of the materialist dialectic of Marxism-Leninism. The objectivity of the external world is no inert, rigid objectivity fatalistically determining human activity; because of its very independence of consciousness it stands in the most intimate indissoluble interaction with practice. In his early youth Lenin had already rejected any mere fatalistic, abstract, undialectical conception of objectivity as false and conducive to apologetics. In his struggle against Michailowsky's subjectivism he also criticized Struve's blatantly apologetic "objectivism". He grasped the objectivism in dialectical materialism correctly and profoundly as an objectivism of practice, of *partisanship*. Materialism implies, Lenin said in summarizing his objections against Struve, "so to speak the element of partisanship within itself in setting itself the task of evaluating any event directly and openly from the standpoint of a particular social group".

[1] Objectivity not in the sense of a pretension to non-partisan tolerance of all positions but in the sense of the conviction of the strict objectivity in nature and society and their laws.—*G.L.*

II

The Theory of Reflection in Bourgeois Aesthetics

This contradictory basis in man's apprehension of the external world, this immanent contradiction in the structure of the reflection of the eternal world in consciousness appears in all theoretical concepts regarding the artistic reproduction of reality. When we investigate the history of aesthetics from the standpoint of Marxism-Leninism, we discover everywhere the one-sidedness of the two tendencies so profoundly analysed by Lenin : on the one hand, the incapacity of mechanical materialism "to apply dialectics to the theory of images", and on the other hand, the basic error inherent in idealism : "the universal (the concept, the idea) as a *peculiar entity in itself.*" Naturally, these two tendencies rarely appear as absolutes in the history of aesthetics. Mechanical materialism, whose strength lies in its insistence upon the concept of the reflection of objective reality and in its maintenance of this view in aesthetics, is transformed into idealism as a result of its incapacity to comprehend motion, history, etc., as Engels so convincingly demonstrated. In the history of aesthetics, as in epistemology generally, objective idealists (Aristotle, Hegel) made heroic attempts at overcoming dialectically the inadequacy, one-sidedness and rigidity of idealism. But since their attempts were made on an idealistic basis, they achieved individual astute formulations regarding objectivity, but their systems as a whole fall victim to the one-sidedness of idealism.

To expose the contradictory, one-sided and inadequate approaches of mechanical materialism and idealism, we can cite in this discussion only one classical illustration of each. We refer to the works of the classics because they expressed their opinions with a straightforward, honest frankness, quite in contrast to the aestheticians of the decadence of bourgeois ideology with their eclectic and apologetic temporizing and chicanery.

In his novel *Les bijoux indiscrets*, Diderot, a leading exponent of the mechanistic theory of the direct imitation of nature, expressed this theory in its crassest form. His heroine, the spokesman for his own points of view, offers the following critique of French classicism: "But I know that only truth pleases and moves. Besides, I know that the perfection in a play consists in such a precise imitation of an action that the audience is deceived into believing that they are present at the action." And to eliminate any doubt that he means by this deception the photographic imitation of reality, Diderot has his heroine imagine a case where a person is told the plot of a tragedy as though it were a real court intrigue; then he goes to the theatre to witness the continuation of this actual event: "I conduct him to his loge behind a grille in the theatre; from it he sees the stage, which he takes to be the palace of the Sultan. Do you believe that the man will let himself be deceived for a moment even if I put on a serious face? On the contrary." For Diderot this comment represents an annihilating aesthetic judgment on this drama. Clearly, on the basis of such a theory, which strives for the ultimate in objectivity in art, not a single real problem of specifically artistic objectivity can be resolved. (That Diderot does formulate and resolve a whole series of problems both in his theory and more especially in his creative work is beside the point, for he resolves them solely by departing from this crude theory.)

For the opposite extreme, we can examine Schiller's aesthetics. In the very interesting preface to his *Braut von Messina*, Schiller provides an impressive critique of the inadequacy of the aesthetic theory of imitation. He correctly poses the task of art—"not to be content simply with the appearances of truth," but to build its edifices "on truth itself". As a thorough idealist, however, Schiller considers truth not as a more profound and comprehensive reflection of objective reality than is given in mere appearance; instead he isolates truth from material reality and makes it an autonomous entity, contrasting it crudely and exclusively with reality. He says: "Nature itself is only an idea of the Spirit, which is never captured by the senses." That is why the product of artistic fantasy in Schiller's eyes is "truer than reality and more real than experience". This idealistic attenuation and petrification

of what is normal and beyond immediate experience under-
mines all Schiller's correct and profound insights. Although in
principle he expresses a correct insight when he says "that the
artist cannot utilize a single element of reality just as he finds
it", he carries this correct observation too far, considering only
what is immediately at hand as real and holding truth to be
a supernatural principle instead of a more incisive, comprehensive reflection of objective reality—opposing the two
idealistically and absolutely. Thus from correct initial insights
he arrives at false conclusions, and through the very theoretical
approach by which he establishes a basis for objectivity in art
more profound than that provided by mechanical materialism,
he eliminates all objectivity from art.

In the contemporary evolution of aesthetics we find the
same two extremes : on the one hand, the insistence on immediate reality; on the other hand, the isolation from material
reality of any aspects reaching beyond immediate reality. As a
result of the general turn in ideology in bourgeois decadence,
however, to a hypocritical, foggy idealism, both theoretical
approaches suffer considerable modification. The theory of the
direct reproduction of reality more and more loses its mechanical materialist character as a theory of the reflection of the
external world. Direct experience becomes even more strongly
subjectivized, more firmly conceived as an independent and
autonomous function of the individual (as impression,
emotional response, etc., abstractly divorced from the objective
reality which generates it). Naturally, in actual practice the
outstanding realists even of this period continue to create on
the basis of an artistic imitation of reality, no longer, however,
with the subtlety and (relative) consequence of the realists of
the period of bourgeois ascendency. More and more, theories
become permeated with an eclecticism of a false objectivism
and a false subjectivism. They isolate objectivity from practice,
eliminate all motion and vitality and set it in crass, fatalistic,
romantic opposition to an equally isolated subjectivity. Zola's
famous definition of art, "un coin de la nature vu à travers un
tempérament", is a prime example of such eclecticism. A scrap
of reality is to be reproduced mechanically and thus with a

false objectivity, and is to become poetic by being viewed in the light of the observer's subjectivity, a subjectivity divorced from practice and from interaction with practice. The artist's subjectivity is no longer what it was for the old realists, the means for achieving the fullest possible reflection of motion of a totality, but a garnish to a mechanical reproduction of a chance scrap of experience.

The resultant subjectivizing of the direct reproduction of reality reaches its ultimate extension in naturalism and enjoys the most varied theoretical exposition. The most famous and influential of these theories is the so-called theory of "empathy". This theory denies any imitation of reality independent of consciousness. The leading modern exponent of this theory, Lipps, declares, for example: "The form of an object is always determined by me, through my inner activity." And he concludes, "Aesthetic pleasure is objectivized self-gratification." According to this view, the essence of art is the introduction of human thoughts, feelings, etc., into an external world regarded as unknowable. This theory faithfully mirrors the ever-intensifying subjectivization in artistic practice apparent in the transition from naturalism to impressionism, etc., in the growing subjectivization of subject matter and of creative method and in the increasing alienation of art from great social problems.

Thus the theory of realism of the imperialist period reveals an intensifying dissolution and disintegration of the ideological preconditions for realism. And it is clear that with the undisguised reactions against realism, idealistic subjectivism attains a theoretical extremism unknown to earlier idealism. The extreme idealistic rigidity is further intensified insofar as idealism under imperialism has become an idealism of imperialist parasitism. Whereas the great exponents of classical idealism sought an effective intellectual mastery of the great problems of their time, even if in their idealism their formulations were distorted and inverted, this new idealism is an ideology of reaction, of flight from the great issues of the era, a denial of reality by "abstracting it out of existence". The well-known, influential aesthetician Worringer, founder and theoretician of the so-called "theory of abstraction", derives the need for abstraction from man's "spiritual space-phobia" (*geistige Raumscheu*), his "overwhelming need for tranquillity" (*ungeheures Ruhebeduerfnis*). Accordingly, he rejects modern realism as too imitative, as too close to reality. He bases his theory on an "absolute will to art", by which he means "a potential inner drive completely independent of the object . . . existing for itself and acting as will to form". The faddish pretension of this theory to the highest artistic objectivity is characteristic of the theories of the imperialist period; they never come out in the open but always mask their intentions. In his characterization of the "struggle" of the Machians against idealism, Lenin exposed this manœuvre of imperialist idealism. The theory of abstraction, which subsequently provided the theoretical base for expressionism, represented a culmination of the subjectivist elimination of all content from aesthetics; it is a theory of the subjectivist petrification and decay of artistic forms in the period of capitalist degeneration.

III

The Artistic Reflection of Reality

The artistic reflection of reality rests on the same contradiction as any other reflection of reality. What is specific to it is that it pursues another resolution of these contradictions than science. We can best define the specific character of the artistic reflection of reality by examining first in the abstract the goal it sets itself, in order then to illuminate the preconditions for attaining this goal. The goal for all great art is to provide a picture of reality in which the contradiction between appearance and reality, the particular and the general, the immediate and the conceptual, etc., is so resolved that the two converge into a spontaneous integrity in the direct impression of the work of art and provide a sense of an inseparable integrity. The universal appears as a quality of the individual and the particular, reality becomes manifest and can be experienced within appearance, the general principle is exposed as the specific impelling cause for the individual case being specially depicted. Engels characterized this essential mode of artistic creation clearly in a comment about characterization in a novel: "Each is simultaneously a type and a particular individual, a 'this one' (*Dieser*), as old Hegel expressed it, and so it must be."

It follows then that every work of art must present a circumscribed, self-contained and complete context with its own *immediately* self-evident movement and structure. The necessity for the immediate obviousness of the special context is clearest in literature. The true, fundamental interrelationships in any novel or drama can be disclosed only at the end. Because of the very nature of their construction and effect, only the conclusion provides full clarification of the beginning. Furthermore, the composition would fail utterly and have no impact if the path to this culmination were not clearly demarcated at every stage. The motivating factors in the world depicted in a literary work of art are revealed in an artistic sequence and climaxing. But this climaxing must be accomplished within a direct unity of appearance and reality present from the very beginning; in the intensifying concretizing of both aspects, it must make their unity ever more integral and self-evident.

This self-contained immediacy in the work of art presupposes that every work of art evolve within itself all the preconditions for its characters, situations, events, etc. The unity of appearance and reality can become direct experience only if the reader experiences every important aspect of the growth or change with all their primary determining factors, if the outcome is never simply handed to him but he is conducted to the outcome and directly experiences the process leading to the outcome. The basic materialism of all great artists (no matter whether their ostensible philosophy is partly or completely idealistic) appears in their clear depiction of the pertinent preconditions and motivations out of which the consciousness of their characters arises and develops.

Thus every significant work of art creates its "own world". Characters, situations, actions, etc., in each have a unique quality unlike that in any other work of art and entirely distinct from anything in everyday reality. The greater the artist, the more intensely his creative power permeates all aspects of his work of art and the more pregnantly his fictional "world" emerges through all the details of the work. Balzac said of his *Comédie Humaine*: "My work has its own geography as well as its own genealogy and its own families, its places and its objects, its people and its facts; even as it possesses its heraldry, its aristocracy and its bourgeoisie, its workmen and its peasants, its politicians and its dandies and its army—in short, its world."

Does not the establishment of such particularity in a work of art preclude the fulfilment of its function as a reflection of reality? By no means! It merely affirms the special character, the peculiar kind of reflection of reality there is in art. The apparently circumscribed world in the work of art and its apparent non-correspondence with reality are founded on this peculiar character of the artistic reflection of reality. For this non-correspondence is merely an illusion, though a necessary one, essential and intrinsic to art. The effect of art, the immersion of the receptant in the action of the work of art, his complete penetration into the special "world" of the work of art, results from the fact that the work by its very nature offers a truer, more complete, more vivid and more dynamic reflection of reality than the receptant otherwise possesses, that it conducts him on the basis of his own experiences and on the basis of the organization and generalization of his previous reproduction of reality beyond the bounds of his experiences toward a more concrete insight into reality. It is therefore only an illusion—as though the work itself were not a reflection of reality, as though the reader did not conceive of the special "world" as a reflection of reality and did not compare it with his own experiences. He acts consistently in accordance with this pretence, and the effect of the work of art ceases once the reader becomes aware of a contradiction, once he senses that the work of art is not an accurate reflection of reality. But this illusion is in any case necessary. For the reader does not consciously compare an individual experience with an isolated event of the work of art but surrenders himself to the general effect of the work of art on the basis of his own assembled general experience. And the comparison between both reflections of reality remains unconscious so long as the reader is engrossed, that is, so long as his experiences regarding reality are broadened and deepened by the fiction of the work of art. Thus Balzac is not contradicting his statement about his "own world" when he says, "To be productive one needs only to study. French society should be the historian, I only its amanuensis."

The self-containment of a work of art is therefore the reflection of the process of life in motion and in concrete dynamic context. Of course, science sets itself the same goal. It achieves dialectical concreteness by probing more profoundly into the laws of motion. Engels says: "The universal law of the transformation of form is far more concrete than any individual 'concrete' example of it." This progression in the scientific cognition of reality is endless. That is, objective reality is correctly reflected in any accurate scientific cognition; to this extent this cognition is absolute. Since, however, reality is always richer, more multifaceted than any law, it is in the nature of knowledge that knowledge must always be expanded, deepened, enriched, and that the absolute always appears as relative and as an approximation. Artistic concreteness too is a unity of the absolute and the relative, but a unity which cannot go beyond the framework of the work of art. Objective progress in the historical process and the further development of our knowledge of this process do not eliminate the artistic value, the validity and effect of great works of art which depict their times correctly and profoundly.

There is a second and more important difference between the scientific and the artistic reflections of reality in that individual scientific cognitions (laws, etc.) are not independent of each other but form an integral system. And this context becomes the more intensive the more science develops. Every work of art, however, must stand on its own. Naturally, there is development in art, and this development follows an objective pattern with laws that can be analysed. But the fact that this objective pattern in the development of art is a part of the general social development does not eliminate the fact that a work of art becomes such by possessing this self-containment, this capacity to achieve its effect on its own.

The work of art must therefore reflect correctly and in proper proportion all important factors objectively determining the area of life it represents. It must so reflect these that this area of life becomes comprehensible from within and from without, re-experiencable, that it appears as a totality of life. This does not mean that every work of art must strive to reflect the objective, extensive totality of life. On the contrary, the extensive totality of reality necessarily is beyond the possible scope of any artistic creation; the totality of reality can only be reproduced intellectually in ever-increasing approximation through the infinite process of science. The totality of the work of art is rather intensive: the circumscribed and self-contained ordering of those factors which objectively are of decisive significance for the portion of life depicted, which determine its existence and motion, its specific quality and its place in the total life process. In this sense the briefest song is as much an intensive totality as the mightiest epic. The objective character of the area of life represented determines the quantity, quality, proportion, etc., of the factors that emerge in interaction with the specific laws of the literary form appropriate for the representation of this portion of life.

The self-containment implies first of all that the goal of the work of art is depicting that subtlety, richness and inexhaustibility of life about which we have quoted Lenin, and bringing it dynamically and vividly to life. No matter whether the intention in the work of art is the depiction of the whole of society or only an artificially isolated incident, the aim will still be to depict the intensive inexhaustibility of the subject. This means that it will aim at involving creatively in its fiction all important factors which in objective reality provide the basis for a particular event or complex of events. And artistic involvement means that all these factors will appear as personal attributes of the persons in the action, as the specific qualities of the situations depicted, etc.; thus in a directly perceptible unity of the individual and the universal. Very few people are

capable of such an experience of reality. They achieve knowledge of general determinants in life only through the abandonment of the immediate, only through abstraction, only through
generalized comparison of experiences. (In this connection, the
artist himself is no exception. His work consists rather in
elevating the experiences he obtains ordinarily to artistic form,
to a representation of the unity of the immediate and the
universal.) In representing individual men and situations, the
artist awakens the illusion of life. In depicting them as exemplary men and situations (the unity of the individual and the
typical), in bringing to life the greatest possible richness of the
objective conditions of life as the particular attributes of individual people and situations, he makes his "own world"
emerge as the reflection of life in its total motion, as process
and totality, in that it intensifies and surpasses in its totality
and in its particulars the common reflection of the events of
life.

This depiction of the subtlety of life, of a richness beyond
ordinary experience, is only one side in the special mode of the
artistic representation of reality. If a work of art depicted only
the overflowing abundance of new concepts, only those aspects
which provide new insights, only the subtlety beyond the
common generalization about ordinary experience, then the
reader would merely be confused instead of being involved,
for the appearance of such aspects in life generally con-
fuses people and leaves them at a loss. It is therefore necessary
that *within* this richness and subtlety the artist introduce a
new order of things which displaces or modifies the old abstractions. This is also a reflection of objective reality. For such a
new order is never simply imposed on life but is derived from
the new phenomena of life through reflection, comparison, etc.
But in life itself it is always a question of two steps; in the first
place, one is surprised by the new facts and sometimes even
overwhelmed by them and then only does one need to deal
with them intellectually by applying the dialectical method.
In art these two steps coincide, not in the sense of a mechanical
unity (for then the newness of the individual phenomena
would again be annihilated) but in the sense of a process in

which from the outset the order within the new phenomena manifesting the subtlety of life is sensed and emerges in the course of the artistic climaxing ever more sharply and clearly.

This representation of life, structured and ordered more richly and strictly than ordinary life experience, is in intimate relation to the active social function, the propaganda effect of the genuine work of art. Such a depiction cannot possibly exhibit the lifeless and false objectivity of an "impartial" imitation which takes no stand or provides no call to action. From Lenin, however, we know that this partisanship is not introduced into the external world arbitrarily by the individual but is a motive force inherent in reality which is made conscious through the correct dialectical reflection of reality and introduced into practice. This partisanship of objectivity must therefore be found intensified in the work of art—intensified in clarity and distinctness, for the subject matter of a work of art is consciously arranged and ordered by the artist toward this goal, in the sense of this partisanship; intensified, however, in objectivity too, for a genuine work of art is directed specifically toward depicting this partisanship as a quality in the subject matter, presenting it as a motive force inherent in it and growing organically out of it. When Engels approves of tendentiousness in literature he always means, as does Lenin after him, this "partisanship of objectivity" and emphatically rejects any subjective superimposed tendentiousness: "But I mean that the tendentiousness must spring out of the situation and action without being expressly pointed out."

All bourgeois theories treating the problem of the aesthetic illusion allude to this dialectic in the artistic reflection of reality. The paradox in the effect of a work of art is that we surrender ourselves to the work as though it presented reality to us, accept it as reality and immerse ourselves in it although we are always aware that it is not reality but simply a special form of reflecting reality. Lenin correctly observes: "Art does not demand recognition as *reality*." The illusion in art, the aesthetic illusion, depends therefore on the self-containment we have examined in the work of art and on the fact that the work of art in its totality reflects the full process of life and does not represent in its details reflections of particular phenomena of life which can be related individually to aspects of actual life on which they are modelled. Non-correspondence in this respect is the precondition of the artistic illusion, an illusion absolutely divorced from any such correspondence. On the other hand and inseparable from it is the fact that the aesthetic illusion is only possible when the work of art reflects the total objective process of life with *objective accuracy*.

This objective dialectic in the artistic reflection of reality is beyond the ken of bourgeois theory, and bourgeois theory always degenerates into subjectivism at least in specific points, if not in totality. Philosophic idealism must, as we have seen, isolate this characteristic of self-containment in a work of art and its elevation above ordinary reality, from material and objective reality; it must oppose the self-containment, the perfection of form in the work of art, to the theory of reflection. When objective idealism seeks to rescue and establish the objectivity of art abstractly, it inevitably falls into mysticism. It is by no means accidental that the Platonic theory of art as the reflection of "ideas" exerts such a powerful historical influence right up to Schelling and Schopenhauer. And when the mechanical materialists fall into idealism because of the inadequacy of their philosophic conception of social phenomena, they usually go from a mechanical photographic theory of imitation to Platonism, to a theory of the artistic imitation of "ideas". (This is especially apparent wth Shaftesbury and at times evident with Diderot.) But this mystical objectivism is always and inevitably transformed into subjectivism. The more the aspects of the self-containment of a work and of the dynamic character of the artistic elaboration and reshaping of reality are opposed to the theory of reflection instead of being derived from it dialectically, the more the principle of form, beauty and artistry is divorced from life; the more it becomes an unclear, subjective and mystical principle. The Platonic "ideas" occasionally inflated and attenuated in the idealism of the period of bourgeois ascendancy, though artificially isolated from social reality, were reflections of decisive social problems and thus for all their idealistic distortion were full of content and were not without relevance; but with the decline of the class they more and more lose content. The social isolation of the personally dedicated artist in a declining society is mirrored in this mystical, subjective inflation of the principle of form divorced from any connection with life. The original despair of genuine artists over this situation passes to parasitic resignation and the self-complacency of "art for art's sake" and its theory of art. Baudelaire sings of beauty in a tone of despondent subjective mysticism : "Je trône dans l'azure comme un sphinx incompris." In the later art for art's sake of the imperialist period such subjectivism evolves into a theory of a contemptuous, parasitic divorce of art from life, into a denial of any objectivity in art, a glorification of the "sovereignty" of the creative individual and a theory of indifference to content and arbitrariness in form.

We have already seen that mechanical materialism tends toward an opposite direction. Sticking to the mechanical imitation of life as it is immediately perceived in all its superficial detail, it must deny the special character of the artistic reflection of reality or fall into idealism with all its distortions and subjectivism. The pseudo-objectivity of mechanical materialism, of the mechanical, direct imitation of the immediate world of phenomena, is thus inevitably transformed into idealistic subjectivism since it does not acknowledge the objectivity of the underlying laws and relationships that cannot immediately be perceived and since it sees in these laws and relationships no reflection of objective reality but simply technical means for superficial groupings of sense data. The weakness of the direct imitation of life in its particularity must intensify and develop further into subjective idealism without content as the general ideological development of the bourgeoisie transforms the philosophic materialist basis of this sort of artistic imitation of reality into agnostic idealism (the theory of empathy).

The objectivity of the artistic reflection of reality depends on the correct reflection of the totality. The artistic correctness of a detail thus has nothing to do with whether the detail corresponds to any similar detail in reality. The detail in a work of art is an accurate reflection of life when it is a necessary aspect of the accurate reflection of the total process of objective reality, no matter whether it was observed by the artist in life or created through imagination out of direct or indirect experience. On the other hand, the artistic truth of a detail which corresponds photographically to life is purely accidental, arbitrary and subjective. When, for example, the detail is not directly and obviously necessary to the context, then it is incidental to a work of art, its inclusion is arbitrary and subjective. It is therefore entirely possible that a collage of photographic material may provide an incorrect, subjective and arbitrary reflection of reality. For merely arranging thousands of chance details in a row never results in artistic necessity. In order to discipline accident into a proper context with artistic necessity, the necessity must be latent within the accidental and must appear as an inner motivation within the details themselves. The detail must be so selected and so depicted from the outset that its relationship with the totality may be organic and dynamic. Such selection and ordering of details depends solely on the artistic, objective reflection of reality. The isolation of details from the general context and their selection on the basis of a photographic correspondence with reality imply a rejection of the more profound problem of objective necessity, even a denial of the existence of this necessity. Artists who create thus, choose and organize material not out of the objective necessity in the subject matter but out of pure subjectivity, a fact which is manifested in the work as an objective anarchy in the selection and arrangement of their material.

Ignoring deeper objective necessity in the reflection of reality is manifested also in creative art as annihilation of objectivity. We have already seen how for Lenin and Engels partisanship in the work of art is a component of objective reality and of a correct, objective artistic reflection of life. The tendency in the work of art speaks forth from the objective context of the world depicted within the work; it is the language of the work of art transmitted through the artistic reflection of reality and therefore the speech of reality itself, not the subjective opinion of the writer exposed baldly or explicitly in a personal commentary or in a subjective, ready-made conclusion. The concept of art as *direct* propaganda, a concept particularly exemplified in recent art by Upton Sinclair, rejects the deeper, objective propaganda potential of art in the Leninist conception of partisanship and substitutes pure personal propaganda which does not grow organically out of the logic of the subject matter but remains a mere subjective expression of the author's views.

IV

The Objectivity of Artistic Form

Both the tendencies to subjectivism just analysed disrupt the dialectical unity of form and content in art. In principle it is not decisive whether the form or the content is wrenched out of the dialectical unity and inflated to an autonomy. In either case the concept of the objectivity of form is abandoned. Either means that the form becomes a "device" to be manipulated subjectively and wilfully; in either case form loses its character as a specific mode of the reflection of reality. Of similar tendencies in logic Lenin declared sharply and unequivocally: "Objectivism: the categories of thought are not tools for men but the expression of the order governing nature and men." This rigorous and profound formulation provides a natural basis for the investigation of form in art, with the emphasis, naturally, on the specific, essential characteristics of artistic reflection; always within the framework of the dialectical materialist conception of the nature of form.

The question of the objectivity of form is among the most difficult and least investigated in Marxist aesthetics. Marxist-Leninist epistemology indicates unequivocally indeed, as we have seen, the direction in which the solution of the problem is to be sought. But contemporary bourgeois concepts have so influenced our Marxist theory of literature and our literary practice as to introduce confusion and reserve in the face of a correct Marxist formulation and even a hesitation about recognizing an objective principle in artistic form. The fear that to emphasize objectivity of form in art will mean a relapse into bourgeois aestheticism has its epistemological base in the failure to recognize the dialectical unity of content and form. Hegel defines this unity thus: ". . . content is nothing but the conversion of form into content, and form is nothing but the conversion of content into form." Though this concept seems abstractly expressed, we will see as we proceed that Hegel did indeed correctly define the interrelationship of form and content.

Of course, merely in connection with their interrelationship. Hegel must be "turned upside down" materialistically in that the mirroring quality of both content and form must be established as the key to our investigation. The difficulty consists in grasping the fact that artistic form is just as much a mode of reflecting reality as the terminology of logic (as Lenin demonstrated so convincingly). Just as in the process of the reflection of reality through thought, the categories that are most general, the most abstracted from the surface of the world of phenomena, from sense data, therefore, express the most abstract laws governing nature and men; so is it with the forms of art. It is only a question of making clear what this highest level of abstraction signifies in art.

That the artistic forms carry out the process of abstraction, the process of generalization, is a fact long recognized. Aristotle contrasted poetry and history from this point of view (it should be noted by the contemporary reader that Aristotle understood by history a narrative chronicle of loosely related events in the manner of Herodotus). Aristotle says: "Historians and poets do not differ in the fact that the latter write in verse, the former in prose. . . . The difference lies rather in the fact that the one reports what actually happened, the other what could happen. Thus poetry is more philosophical than history, for poetry tends to express the universal, history the particular." Aristotle obviously meant that because poetry expresses the universal it is more philosophical than history. He meant that poetry (fiction) in its characters, situations and plots not merely

imitates individual characters, situations and actions but
expresses simultaneously the regular, the universal and the
typical. In full agreement Engels declares the task of realism
to be to create "typical characters under typical conditions".
The difficulty in grasping abstractly what great art of all time
has achieved in practice is twofold : in the first place, the error
must be avoided of opposing the typical, the universal and the
regular to the individual, of disrupting intellectually the inseparable unity of the individual and universal which determines the practice of all great poets from Homer to Gorki. In
the second place, it must be understood that this unity of the
particular and the universal, of the individual and the typical,
is not a quality of literary content that is considered in isolation, a quality for the expression of which the artistic form is
merely a "technical aid", but that it is a product of that
interpenetration of form and content defined abstractly by
Hegel.

The first difficulty can only be resolved from the standpoint
of the Marxist conception of the concrete. We have seen that
mechanical materialism as well as idealism—each in its own
way, and, in the course of historical development, in different
forms—bluntly oppose the direct reflection of the external
world, the foundation for any understanding of reality, to the
universal and the typical, etc. As a result, the typical appears
as the product of a merely subjective intellectual operation,
as a mere intellectual, abstract and thus ultimately purely
subjective accessory to the world of immediate experience; not
as a component of objective reality. From such a counterposing
of opposites it is impossible to arrive at a conception of the
unity of the individual and the typical in a work of art. Either
a false conception of the concrete or an equally false conception of the abstract becomes the key to the aesthetic, or at most
an eclectic one-or-the-other is propounded. Marx defined the
concrete with extraordinary incisiveness : "The concrete is concrete because it is the synthesis of many determinants, the unity
within diversity. In our thinking the concrete thus appears as
the process of synthesis, as the result, not as the point of departure, although it is really the point of departure and hence

also the point of departure for perception and conception." In our introductory remarks we noted how Lenin defines the dialectical approach to the intellectual reflection of the concrete in Marxist epistemology.

The task of art is the reconstitution of the concrete—in this Marxist sense—in a direct, perceptual self-evidence. To that end those factors must be discovered in the concrete and rendered perceptible whose unity makes the concrete concrete. Now in reality every phenomenon stands in a vast, infinite context with all other simultaneous and previous phenomena. A work of art, considered from the point of view of its content, provides only a greater or lesser extract of reality. Artistic form therefore has the responsibility of preventing this extract from giving the effect of an extract and thus requiring the addition of an environment of time and space; on the contrary, the extract must seem to be a self-contained whole and to require no external extension.

When the artist's intellectual disciplining of reality before he begins a work of art does not differ in principle from any other intellectual ordering of reality, the more likely the result will be a work of art.

Since the work of art has to act as a self-contained whole and since the concreteness of objective reality must be reconstituted in perceptual immediacy in the work of art, all those factors which objectively make the concrete concrete must be depicted in their interrelation and unity. In reality itself these conditions emerge quantitatively as well as qualitatively in extraordinary variety and dispersion. The concreteness of a phenomenon depends directly upon this extensive, infinite total context. In the work of art, any extract, any event, any individual or any aspect of the individual's life must represent such a context in its concreteness, thus in the unity of all its inherent important determinants. These determinants must in the first place be present from the start of the work; secondly, they must appear in their greatest purity, clarity and typicality; thirdly, the proportions in the relationships of the various determinants must reflect that objective partisanship with which the work is infused; fourthly, despite the fact that they are present in greater purity, profundity and abstraction than is found in any individual instance in actual life, these determinants may not offer any abstract contrast to the world of phenomena that is directly perceptible, but, contrarily, must appear as concrete, direct, perceptible qualities of individual men and situations. Any artistic process conforming to the intellectual reflection of reality through the aid of abstractions, etc., which seems artistically to "overload" the particular with typical aspects intensified to the utmost quantitatively and qualitatively requires a consequent artistic intensification of concreteness. No matter how paradoxical it may sound, an intensification of concreteness in comparison with life must therefore accompany the process of developing artistic form and the path to generalization.

Now when we pass to our second question, the role of form in the establishment of this concreteness, the reader will perhaps no longer consider Hegel's quotation regarding the transformation of content into form and form into content so abstract. Consider the determinants in a work of art we have so far derived exclusively from the most general conception of artistic form—the self-containment of a work of art : on the one hand, the intensive infinity, the apparent inexhaustibility of a work of art and the subtlety of the development by which it recalls life in its most intensive manifestation; on the other hand, the fact that it discloses simultaneously within this inexhaustibility and life-like subtlety the laws of life in their freshness, inexhaustibility and subtlety. All these factors seem merely to be factors of content. They are. But they are at the same time, and even primarily, factors emerging and becoming apparent through artistic form. They are the result of the transformation of content into form and result in the transformation of form into content.

Let us illustrate this very important fact of art with a few examples. Take a simple example, one might almost say a purely quantitative example. Whatever objections one might level against Gerhart Hauptmann's *Weavers* as a drama, there is no question that it succeeds in awakening an illusion that we are not involved merely with individuals but with the grey, numberless masses of Silesian weavers. The depiction of the masses as masses is the artistic achievement of this drama. When we investigate how many characters Hauptmann actually used to depict these masses, we are surprised to discover that he used scarcely ten to a dozen weavers, a number much smaller than is to be found in many other dramas which do not even begin to provide an impression of great masses of people. The effect arises from the fact that the few characters depicted are so selected and characterized and set in such situations and in such relationships that within the context and in the formal proportionality in the aesthetic illusion, we have the impression of a great mass. How little this aesthetic illusion depends on the actual number of characters is clear from the same author's drama of the peasants' revolt, *Florian Geyer*, where Hauptmann creates an incomparably greater cast of characters, some of which are even very clearly delineated as individuals; nevertheless the audience only intermittently has the sense of a real mass, for here Hauptmann did not succeed in representing a relationship of the characters to each other which would give the sense of a mass and would endow the mass with its own artistic physiognomy and its own capacity to act.

This significance of form emerges even more clearly in more complicated cases. Take the depiction of the typical in Balzac's *Père Goriot*. In this novel Balzac exposes the contradictions in bourgeois society, the inevitable inner contradictions appearing in every institution in bourgeois society, the varied forms of conscious and unconscious rebellion against the enslavement and crippling of the institutions in which men are imprisoned. Every manifestation of these contradictions in an individual or a situation is intensified to an extreme by Balzac and with merciless consequence. Among his characters he depicts men representing ultimate extremes : being lost or in revolt, thirsting for power or degenerate : Goriot and his daughters, Rastignac, Vautrin, the Viscountess de Beauséant, Maxime de Trailles. The events through which these characters expose themselves follow upon each other in an avalanche that appears incredible if the content is considered in isolation—an avalanche impelled by scarcely credible explosions. Consider what happens in the course of the action : the final tragedy of Goriot's family, the tragedy of Mme de Beauséant's love affair, the exposure of Vautrin, the tragedy arranged by Vautrin in the Taillefer house, etc. And yet, or rather precisely on account of this rush of events, the novel provides the effect of a terrifyingly accurate and typical picture of bourgeois society. The basis for its effectiveness is Balzac's accurate exposure of the typical aspects of the basic contradiction in bourgeois society—a necessary precondition to the effect but not in itself the effect. The effect itself results from the composition, from the context provided by the relationships of the extreme cases, a context in which the apparent outlandishness of the individual cases is eliminated. Extract any one of the conflicts from the general context and you discover a fantastic, melodramatic, improbable tale. But it is just because of the exaggeration in the individual events, in the characterization and even in the language within the relationships established among those extreme events through Balzac's composition that the common social background emerges. Only with such an extreme intensification of improbable events could Balzac depict how Vautrin and Goriot are similarly victims of capitalist society and rebels against its consequences, how Vautrin and Mme de Beauséant are motivated by a similar incomplete conception of society and its contradictions, how the genteel salon and the prison differ only quantitatively and incidentally and resemble each other in profound respects and how bourgeois morality and open crime shade into each other imperceptibly. And furthermore— through the piling up of extreme cases and on the basis of the accurate reflection of the social contradictions which underlie them in their extremeness, an atmosphere arises which eliminates any sense of their being extreme and improbable, an atmosphere in which the social reality of capitalist society emerges out of these instances and through them in a crassness and fullness that could not otherwise be realized.

Thus the content of the work of art must be transformed into a form through which it can achieve its full artistic effectiveness. Form is nothing but the highest abstraction, the highest mode of condensation of content, of the extreme intensification of motivations, of constituting the proper proportion among the individual motivations and the hierarchy of importance among the individual contradictions of the life mirrored in the work of art.

It is, of course, necessary to study this characteristic form in individual categories of form, not simply generally in composition, as we have done so far. We cannot investigate the particular categories since our task is more general—to define form and to investigate its objective existence. We will select only one example, plot, which has been considered central in discussions of literary form since Aristotle.

It is a formal principle of epic and drama that their construction be based on a plot. Is this *merely* a formal requirement, abstracted from content? Not at all. When we analyse this formal requirement precisely in its formal abstractness, we come to the conclusion that only through plot can the dialectic of human existence and consciousness be expressed, that only through a character's action can the contrast between what he is objectively and what he imagines himself to be, be expressed in a process that the reader can experience. Otherwise the writer would either be forced to take his characters as they take themselves to be and to present them then from their own limited subjective perspective, or he would have to merely assert the contrast between their view of themselves and the reality and would not be able to make his readers perceive and experience the contrast. The requirement for representing the artistic reflection of social reality through plot is therefore no mere invention of aestheticians; it derives from the basic materialist dialectical practice of the great poets (regardless of their frequent idealist ideologies) formulated by aesthetics and established as a formal postulate—without being recognized as the most general, abstract reflection of a fundamental fact of objective reality. It will be the task of Marxist aesthetics to reveal the quality of the formal aspects of art concretely as modes of reflecting reality. Here we can merely point to the problem, which even in regard to plot alone is far too complicated for adequate treatment in this essay. (Consider, for example, the significance of the plot as a means for depicting process.)

The dialectic of content and form, the transformation from the one into the other, can naturally be studied in all the stages of origin, development and effect of a work of art. We will merely allude to a few important aspects here. When we take the problem of subject matter, we seem at first glance to be dealing again with a problem of content. If we investigate more closely, however, we see that breadth and depth of subject matter convert into decisive problems of form. In the course of investigating the history of individual forms, one can see clearly how the introduction and mastery of new thematic material calls forth a new form with significantly new principles within the form, governing everything from composition to diction. (Consider the struggle for bourgeois drama in the eighteenth century and the birth of an entirely new type of drama with Diderot, Lessing and the young Schiller.)

When we follow this process over a long period of history, the conversion of content into form and vice versa in the effect of works of art is even more impressive. Precisely in those works in which this conversion of one into the other is most developed, does the resultant new form attain the fullest consummation and seem entirely "natural" (one thinks of Homer, Cervantes, Shakespeare, etc.). This "artlessness' in the greatest masterpieces illuminates not only the problem of the mutual conversion of content and form into each other but also the significance of this conversion : the establishment of the objectivity of the work of art itself. The more "artless" a work of art, the more it gives the effect of life and nature, the more clearly it exemplifies an actual concentrated reflection of its times and the more clearly it demonstrates that the only function of its form is the expression of this objectivity, this reflection of life in the greatest concreteness and clarity and with all its motivating contradictions. On the other hand, every form of which the reader is conscious as form, in its very independence of the content and in its incomplete conversion into content necessarily gives the effect of a subjective expression rather than a full reflection of the subject matter itself

(Corneille and Racine in contrast to the Greek tragedians and Shakespeare). That content which emerges as an independent entity (like its antithesis, form as an independent entity) also has a subjective character, we have already seen.

This interrelationship of form and content did not escape the important aestheticians of earlier periods, of course. Schiller, for example, recognized one side of this dialectic and acutely formulated it, viewing the role of art as the annihilation of subject matter through form. In this statement, however, he provided an idealistic and one-sided subjectivist formulation of the problem. For the simple transfer of content into form without the dialectical counteraction necessarily leads to an artificial independence of form, to the subjectivizing of form, as is often the case not only in Schiller's theory but in his creative practice as well.

It would be the task of a Marxist aesthetic to demonstrate concretely how objectivity of form is an aspect of the creative process. The comments of great artists of the past provide an almost inexhaustible source for this investigation, an investigation we have hardly begun. Bourgeois aesthetics can scarcely begin any study of this material, for when it recognizes the objectivity of forms, it conceives of this objectivity only in some mystical fashion and makes of objectivity of form a sterile mystique about form. It becomes the responsibility of a Marxist aesthetic in developing the concept of form as a mode of reflection to demonstrate how this objectivity emerges in the creative process as objectivity, as truth independent of the artists's consciousness.

This objective independence from the artist's consciousness begins immediately with a selection of the subject matter. In all subject matter there are certain artistic possibilities. The artist, of course, is "free" to select any one of these or to use the subject matter as the springboard to a different sort of artistic expression. In the latter case a contradiction inevitably arises between the thematic content and the artistic elaboration, a contradiction which cannot be eliminated no matter how skilfully the artist may manipulate. (One recalls Maxim Gorki's striking critique of Leonid Andreyev's *Darkness*.) This objectivity reaches beyond the relationship of content, theme and artistic form.

When we obtain a Marxist theory of genres, we will then be able to see that every genre has its own specific, objective laws which no artist can ignore without peril. When Zola, for example, in his novel *The Masterpiece* adopted the basic structure of Balzac's masterly short story "The Unknown Masterpiece", extending the work to novel length, he demonstrated in his failure Balzac's profound artistic insight in selecting the short story to represent the tragedy of an artist.

With Balzac the short-story form grows out of the essential quality of the theme and subject matter. Balzac compressed into the narrowest form the tragedy of the modern artist, the tragic impossibility of creating a classical work of art with the specific means of expression of modern art—means of expression which themselves merely reflect the specific character of modern life and its ideology. He simply depicted the collapse of such an artist and contrasted him with two other important, less dedicated (therefore not tragic) artists. Thus he concentrated everything on the single, decisive problem, adequately expressed in a tight and fast-moving plot of artistic disintegration through an artist's suicide and destruction of his work. To treat this theme in a novel instead of a short story would require entirely different subject matter and an entirely different plot. In a novel the writer would have to expose and develop in breadth the entire process arising out of the social conditions of modern life and leading to these artistic problems. (Balzac had followed such an approach in analysing the relationship of literature to journalism in *Lost Illusions*.) To accomplish this task the novelist would have to go beyond the bounds of the short story with its single and restricted climax and would have to find subject matter suitable for transforming the additional breadth and diversity in motivations into a dynamic plot. Such a transformation is missing from Zola's work. He did indeed introduce a series of additional motivations in an attempt at providing novelistic breadth to the short-story material. But the new motivations (the struggle of the artist with society, the struggle between the dedicated and the opportunistic artists, etc.) do not arise out of the inner dialectic of the original short-story material but remain unrelated and superficial in the development and do not provide the broad, varied complex necessary for the construction of a novel.

Once sketched, characters and plots show the same independence of the artist's consciousness. Although originating in the writer's head, they have their own dialectic, which the writer must obey and pursue consequently if he does not want to destroy his work. Engels noted the objective independent existence of Balzac's characters and their life careers when he pointed out that the dialectics of the world depicted by Balzac led the author to conclusions in opposition to his own conscious ideology. Contrary examples are to be found in such strongly subjective writers as Schiller or Dostoyevski. In the struggle between the writer's ideology and the inner dialectic of his characters, the writer's subjectivity is often victorious with the result that he dissipates the significant material he has projected. Thus Schiller distorts the profound conflict he had planned between Elizabeth and Mary Stuart (the struggle between the Reformation and the Counter-Reformation) out of Kantian moralizing; thus Dostoyevski, as Gorki once acutely remarked, ends by slandering his own characters.

The objective dialectic of form because of its very objectivity is an *historical* dialectic. The idealistic inflation of form becomes most obvious in the transformation of forms not merely into mystical and autonomous but even "eternal" entities. Such idealistic de-historicizing of form eliminates any concreteness and all dialectic. Form becomes a fixed model, a schoolbook example, for mechanical imitation. The leading aestheticians of the classical period often advanced beyond this undialectical conception. Lessing, for example, recognized clearly the profound truths in Aristotle's Poetics as the expression of definite laws of tragedy. At the same time he saw clearly that what was important was the living essence, the ever-new, ever-modified application of these laws without mechanical subservience to them. He revealed sharply and vividly how Shakespeare, who ostensibly did not follow Aristotle and probably did not even know Aristotle, consistently fulfilled afresh Aristotle's important prescriptions, which Lessing considered the most profound laws of the drama; while the servile, dogmatic students of Aristotle's words, the French classicists, ignored the essential issues in Aristotle's vital legacy.

But a truly historical, dialectical and systematic formulation of the objectivity of form and its specific application to ever-changing historical reality only became possible with a materialist dialectic. In the fragmentary introduction to his *A Critique of Political Economy*, Marx defined precisely the two great problems in the historical dialectic of the objectivity of form in regard to the epic. He showed first that every artistic form is the outgrowth of definite social conditions and of ideological premises of a particular society and that only on these premises can subject matter and formal elements emerge which cause a particular form to flourish (mythology as the foundation of the epic). For Marx the concept of the objectivity of artistic forms here too offered the basis for the analysis of the historical and social factors in the generation of artistic forms. His emphasis on the law of uneven development, on the fact "that certain flourishing periods (of art) by no means stand in direct relation to the general social development", shows that he saw in those periods of extraordinary creative activity (the Greeks, Shakespeare) objective culminations in the development of art and that he considered artistic value as objectively recognizable and definable. Transformation of this profound dialectical theory into relativistic, vulgar sociology means the degradation of Marxism into the mire of bourgeois ideology.

The dialectical objectivity in Marx's second formulation regarding the development of art is even more striking. It is an indication of the primitive level of Marxist aesthetics and of our lag behind the general development of Marxist theory that this second formulation has enjoyed little currency among Marxist aestheticians and was practically never applied concretely before the appearance of Stalin's work on questions of linguistics. Marx said: "But the difficulty does not lie in understanding that Greek art and epic were related to certain forms of social development. The difficulty is that they still provide us with aesthetic pleasure and serve in certain measure as norms and unattainable models." Here the problem of the objectivity of artistic form is posed with great clarity. If Marx dealt in the first question with the genesis of artistic form, form *in statu nascendi*, here he deals with the question of the objective validity of a finished work of art, of the artistic form, and he does so in such a way that he sets the investigation of this objectivity as the task at hand but leaves no doubt of the objectivity itself—of course, within the framework of a concrete historical dialectic. Marx's manuscript unfortunately breaks off in the middle of his profound exposition. But his extant remarks show that for him Greek art forms spring out of the specific content of Greek life and that form arises out of social and historical content and has the function of raising this content to the level of objectivity in artistic representation.

Marxist aesthetics must set out from this concept of the dialectical objectivity of artistic form as seen in its historical concreteness. It must reject any attempt at making artistic forms either sociologically relative, at transforming dialectics into sophistry or at effacing the difference between periods of flourishing creativity and of decadence, between serious art and mere dabbling, to the elimination of the objectivity of artistic form. Marxist aesthetics must decisively reject, in addition, any attempt at assigning artistic forms an abstract formalistic pseudo-objectivity in which artistic form and distinction among formal genres are construed abstractly as independent of the historical process and as mere formal considerations.

This concretizing of the principle of objectivity within artistic form can be achieved by Marxist aesthetics only in constant struggle against bourgeois currents dominant today in aesthetics and against their influence on our aestheticians. Simultaneous with the dialectical and critical reinvestigation of the great heritage from the periods of history when artistic theory and practice flourished, a relentless struggle against the subjectivization of art dominant in contemporary bourgeois aesthetics must be waged. In the end it makes no difference whether form is eliminated subjectively and transformed into the mere expression of a so-called great personality (the Stefan George school), whether it is exaggerated into a mystical objectivity and inflated to an independent reality (neo-classicism) or denied and eliminated with mechanistic objectivity (the stream-of-consciousness theory). All these directions ultimately lead to the separation of form from content, to the blunt opposition of one to the other and thus to the destruction of the dialectical basis for the objectivity of form. We must recognize and expose in these tendencies the same imperialistic parasitism which Marxist-Leninist epistemology exposed long ago in the philosophy of the imperialist period. (In this respect the development of a concrete Marxist aesthetic lags behind the general development of Marxism.) Behind the collapse of artistic form in bourgeois decadence, behind the aesthetic theories glorifying the subjectivist disintegration or petrification of forms, there is to be found the same rot of bourgeois decadence as in other ideological areas. One would be distorting Marx's profound theory of the uneven development of art into a relativistic caricature if on the basis of this Marxist insight one were to mistake this collapse for the genesis of new form.

Especially significant because it is such a widely disseminated and misleading aspect of the trend to the subjectivization of art is the confusion of form with technique which is so fashionable today. Recently too a technological concept of thought has become dominant in bourgeois logic, a theory of logic as a formalist instrument. Marxist-Leninist epistemology has exposed such tendencies as idealist and agnostic. The identification of technique and form, the conception of aesthetics as mere technology of art, is on the same epistemological level as these subjectivist, agnostic ideological tendencies. That art has a technical side, that this technique must be mastered (indeed can be mastered only by true artists) has nothing to do with the question—the supposed identity of technique and form. Logical thinking requires schooling, too, and is a technique that can be learned and mastered; but that the categories of logic have merely a technical and auxiliary character is a subjective and agnostic deduction from this fact. Every artist must possess a highly developed technique by which he can represent the world that shimmers before him, with artistic conviction. Acquiring and mastering this technique are extraordinarily important tasks.

To eliminate any confusion, however, one must define the place of technique in aesthetics correctly, from a dialectical materialist point of view. In his remarks about the dialectics of intentions and subjective intentional activity Lenin gave a clear response and exposed subjectivist illusions about this relationship. He wrote: "In reality human intentions are created by an objective world and presuppose it—accept it as given, existing. But to man it *appears* that his intentions come from beyond and are independent of the world." Technician theories identifying technique with form arise exclusively out of this subjectivist illusion, which fails to see the dialectical interrelationship of reality, content, form and technique or how the quality and efficacy of technique are necessarily determined by these objective factors; or that technique is a means for expressing the reflection of objective reality through the alternating conversion of content and form; or that technique is *merely* a means to this end and can only be correctly understood in this context, in its dependence upon this context. When one defines technique thus, in its proper dependence upon the objective problem of content and form, its necessarily subjective character is seen as a necessary aspect of the dialectical general context of aesthetics.

Only when technique is rendered autonomous, when in this artificial independence it replaces objective form, does the danger arise of subjectivization of the problems of aesthetics, and in a two-fold respect: in the first place, technique considered in isolation becomes divorced from the objective problems of art and appears as an independent instrument at the service of the artist's subjectivity, an independent instrument with which one can approach any subject matter and produce any form. Rendering technique independent can easily lead to a degeneration into an ideology of subjectivist virtuosity of form, to the cult of "perfection of form" for its own sake, into aestheticism. Secondly, and closely related to this, the exaggeration of the relevance of purely technical problems in artistic representation obscures the more profound problems of artistic form that are much more difficult to comprehend. Such obscurantism in bourgeois ideology accompanies the disintegration and congelation of artistic forms and the loss of a sense for the special problems of artistic form. The great aestheticians of the past always put the decisive problem of form in the foreground and thus maintained a proper hierarchy within aesthetics. Aristotle said that the poet must demonstrate his power rather in the action than in verse. And it is very interesting to see that Marx's and Engels' aversion to the "petty clever defecations" (Engels) of contemporary virtuosos of form without content, of the banal "masters of technique" went so far that they treated the bad verse of Lassalle's *Sickingen* with indulgence because Lassalle had at least dared in this tragedy—admittedly a failure and considered so by them—to grapple with real, basic problems of dramatic content and form. The same Marx praised this attempt who in his correspondence with Heine showed that he had so steeped himself in the fundamental problems of art as well as in the details of artistic technique that he was able to offer the great poet specific technical suggestions to improve his poetry.

Marx and Engels on Aesthetics

MARX'S and Engels' studies in literature are in a peculiar literary form. The reader must understand first of all why they are as they are so that he can adopt a proper approach to reading and understanding them. Neither Marx nor Engels ever wrote a special book or even a particular essay on literary questions. In his maturity Marx constantly dreamed of expounding his views on his favourite author, Balzac, in an extensive critique. But this project, like so many others, remained only a dream. The great thinker was so completely involved in his fundamental work on economics until the day of his death that neither this work on Balzac nor one he planned on Hegel was ever realized.

Thus this book[1] consists in part of letters and notes of conversations and in part of isolated quotations extracted from books on various subjects in which Marx and Engels touched on basic questions of literature. The selection and organization were not therefore made by the authors themselves.

This fact does not mean, however, that the fragments assembled here do not provide an organic and systematic view. Indeed we must understand first of all what kind of system this is in terms of the philosophical concepts of Marx and Engels. We cannot, of course, examine the theory of Marxist systematization with any thoroughness in this essay. We will limit ourselves to drawing the reader's attention to two aspects. First, the Marxist system—in contradistinction to modern bourgeois philosophy—never departs from the concept of a total historical process. According to Marx and Engels, there is only one comprehensive science: the science of history, which comprehends the evolution of nature, society and thought, etc. as an

[1] Georg Lukács wrote this essay as a preface for a Hungarian edition of an anthology of the aesthetic writings of Marx and Engels.

integrated historical process and aims at discovering its laws, both general and particular (that is, as they relate to individual periods). This view does not imply—and this is the second characteristic of their system—historical relativism under any circumstances. In this regard, too, Marxism is to be distinguished from bourgeois thinking. The essence of the dialectical method lies in its encompassing the indivisible unity of the absolute and the relative : absolute truth has its *relative* elements (depending on place, time and circumstances); relative truth, on the other hand, so far as it is really truth, so far as it reflects reality in a faithful approximation, has an *absolute* validity.

A consequence of this aspect of the Marxist view is that it does not admit the separation and isolation of individual branches of knowledge so fashionable in the bourgeois world. Neither science as a whole nor its individual branches nor art has an autonomous, immanent history arising exclusively from a peculiar inner dialectic. Their development is determined by the movement of the history of social production as a whole; changes and developments in individual areas are to be explained in a truly scientific manner only in relation to this base. Of course, this conception of Marx and Engels, which is in sharp opposition to many modern scientific preconceptions, is not to be introduced mechanically, as is customary among many pseudo-Marxists and vulgar Marxists.

We will return to this problem for further, close analysis. For the present, we merely want to emphasize that Marx and Engels never denied or misconstrued the relative autonomy existing in the development of particular areas of human activity (law, science, art, etc.). They recognized, for example, how an individual philosophic concept is linked to a preceding one, which it develops, combats and corrects. Marx and Engels deny only that it is possible to explain the development of science or art exclusively or even primarily within their own immanent contexts. These immanent contexts do undoubtedly exist in objective reality but merely as aspects of the historical context, of the totality of the historical process within which the primary role in a complex of interacting factors is played by the economic: the development of the means of production.

The existence, substance, rise and effect of literature can thus only be understood and explained within the total historical context of the entire system. The rise and development of literature are part of the total historical social process. The aesthetic essence and value of literary works and, accordingly, their effect, are part of that general and integrated social process in which man masters the world through his consciousness. In accordance with the first aspect of the Marxist system we discussed, Marxist aesthetics and literary and art history form part of historical materialism; and from the second aspect they represent an application of dialectical materialism. In both respects, of course, they form a special and peculiar part of *this whole*, with definite and specific laws and definite and specific aesthetic principles.

The generalized principles of Marxist aesthetics and literary history are to be found in the doctrines of historical materialism. Only with the aid of historical materialism can we understand the rise of art and literature, the laws of their development and the varied directions they follow in their advance and decline within the total process. That is why at the very outset we must examine certain general, basic questions regarding historical materialism. And not only to establish our scientific foundation but also to distinguish genuine Marxism, the genuine dialectical philosophic view, from its cheap vulgarization; for it is in this area that such vulgarization has perhaps most seriously discredited Marxist doctrine.

It is well known that historical materialism sees the directive principle, the basic determinant of historical development, in the economic base. The ideologies, including literature and art, figure merely as superstructure and thus as secondary factors in the process of development.

Misunderstanding this basic concept, vulgar materialism draws the mechanical, distorted and misleading conclusion that there exists a simple causal relationship between base and superstructure in which the former figures solely as cause and the latter as effect. In the view of vulgar Marxism the superstructure represents a mechanical, causal consequence of the development of the means of production. Such relationships are unknown to the dialectical method. Dialectics reject the existence of any purely one-sided, cause-and-effect relationships; it recognizes in the simplest facts a complicated interaction of causes and effects. And historical materialism insists that in a process so multilevelled and multifaceted as the evolution of society, the total process of the social and historical development emerges in the form of an intricate complex of interactions. Only with such an approach is it possible to confront the problem of ideologies. Anyone who sees ideologies as the mechanical, passive product of the economic process at their base simply understands nothing of their essence and their development and does not expound Marxism but a distortion and caricature of Marxism.

In one of his letters Engels says regarding this question: "Political, legal, philosophical, religious, literary and artistic development rest on the economic. But they also react on each other and on the economic base. It is not that the economic factor is the only active factor and everything else mere passive effect, but it is the interaction with the economic base which always proves decisive in the last analysis."

A consequence of this Marxist methodological orientation is the assignment of an extraordinarily important role in historical development to the creative energy and activity of the individual. According to the basic Marxist concept of historical development, man becomes differentiated from the animals through work. An individual's creative activity is an expression of man's creation of himself, of man's making himself into a man through work; the character, capacity and level of this development are determined by objective natural and social conditions. This conception of historical evolution runs through all Marxist social philosophy and consequently through Marxist aesthetics. Marx declares in one place that music creates a musical sense in men. This concept is again part of the total Marxist concept regarding the evolution of society. Marx concretizes this observation thus : ". . . only through the disclosure of the objective richness within man's natural being will the richness of the subjective human sensibility, an ear for music, an eye for artistic form, be trained for the first time or actually created : in brief, senses capable for the first time of human enjoyment, senses established as essential faculties of man as man."

This concept has great significance not only for understanding the historical and socially active role of the individual but also for understanding how Marxism views the individual periods of history, the evolution of culture, the limits, problems and perspectives of such an evolution. Marx concludes his statement as follows : "The education of the five senses is the work of all previous history. A sense confined within harsh necessity has only restricted sensibility. For starving men civilized eating does not exist, only the mere abstraction : food. It can be absolutely raw and hardly distinguishable from animal fodder. The desperate or anxious man has no sensibility for the finest drama; the hawker of metals sees only the market value of a metal but not its beauty or special qualities. He has no mineralogical sense. Thus the objectivization of human nature, in theoretical as well as practical respects, is necessary for both humanizing man's mind and senses and for creating a human mind corresponding to the full richness present in man and nature."

Man's intellectual activity therefore enjoys a specific relative independence in every field, especially in art and literature. Any of these fields or spheres of activity evolves on its own— through the activity of the individual creative person—out of earlier achievements, which it carries to higher development, even if critically and polemically.

We have already noted that this autonomy is relative and that it does not mean a denial of the priority of the economic base. One is not to conclude, however, that the subjective conviction that every sphere of intellectual life evolves on its own is a mere illusion. This autonomy has its objective basis in the very nature of that evolution and in the social division of labour. Engels wrote in this connection : "People who are involved with this [ideological development, G. L.] belong to distinct spheres within the division of labour; thus they have the impression of cultivating an autonomous field, especially to the extent that they do form an independent group within the social division of labour, and their productions (including their mistakes) exert an influence on the entire social development, even on the economic. But in the last analysis, they remain under the dominant influence of the economic development." And in a further comment, Engels explains how he conceives the economic primacy methodologically : "The ultimate supremacy of the economic development over these fields, too, is a certainty to me, but it takes place within the particular conditions of the individual field : in philosophy, for example, through the influence of economic factors operating primarily in a political guise on the philosophic material at hand, that furnished by the preceding philosophers. The economy does not create anything *a novo*, but determines how the content of the earlier thought will be modified and advanced, accomplishing this indirectly for the most part since it is the political, legal and moral reflexes which exercise the greatest direct effect on philosophy."

What Engels says here about philosophy is fully pertinent to the basic principles of the development of literature. It goes without saying that considered in isolation every development has its own particular character, that one cannot mechanically generalize on an apparent parallelism in two developments and that the evolution of any particular sphere has its own peculiar character and its own laws within the laws of the total social development.

Now if we attempt to concretize the general principle in what we have discussed, we arrive at one of the important principles of the Marxist conception of history. In absolute opposition to vulgar Marxism, historical materialism recognizes that ideological development does not move in a mechanical and predetermined parallel with the economic progress of society. It has certainly never been inevitable in the history of primitive communism and of class societies (societies about which Marx and Engels wrote) that every economic and social upsurge be accompanied by a flourishing of literature, art and philosophy; it is certainly not inevitable that a society on a high social level have a literature, art and philosophy at a higher stage of evolution than a society on a lower level.

Marx and Engels repeatedly and emphatically pointed out this uneven development in the field of the history of ideologies. Engels illustrated this concept by noting that French philosophy in the eighteenth and German philosophy in the nineteenth century emerged in completely, or at least comparatively, backward nations; thus in philosophy these lands could exercise a leading role though economically backward in comparison to the countries surrounding them. Engels stated: "And so it happens that economically retarded nations can play first violin in philosophy: France in the eighteenth century as against England, on whose philosophy the French based their own; later Germany in regard to both."

Marx formulated this concept in general terms in regard to literature but perhaps even more acutely and decisively. He declared: "In art it is recognized that specific flourishing periods hardly conform to the general development of society, that is, of the material base, the skeleton, so to speak, which produces them. For example, the Greeks compared with the moderns, or Shakespeare. People understand that certain forms in art, like the epic, for example, can no longer be produced in the classical form exemplifying an epoch of history, once art production as such emerges; thus within the realm of art itself certain genres are possible only at an underdeveloped stage of artistic evolution. If this is the case with particular art forms, then it is not at all surprising that it should be the case in the relationship of art as a whole to the general development of society."

For genuine Marxists such a conception of historical development precludes any schematic approach, any recourse to analogies and mechanical parallels. How the principle of uneven development is manifested in any field in the history of ideologies in any period is a concrete historical question which a Marxist can answer only on the basis of a concrete analysis of the concrete situation. That is why Marx concluded his statement by saying: "The difficulty lies only in the general formulation of these contradictions. As soon as they are made specific, they are immediately resolved."

Marx and Engels defended themselves during their entire careers against the oversimplification and vulgarization of their so-called disciples, who substituted for the concrete study of the concrete historical process a conception of history based on abstract deductions and analogies and sought to substitute mechanical relationships for complicated, concrete dialectical relationships. One can find notable application of the Marxist approach in Engels' letter to Paul Ernst, in which Engels took exception to Ernst's attempt to characterize Ibsen as a "petit bourgeois" on the basis of the general conception of the "petit bourgeois" that Ernst had arrived at by analogy with the German petit bourgeoisie without investigating the concrete particularities of Norwegian circumstances.

Although the historical investigations of Marx and Engels in the field of art and literature encompass the entire development of society, they directed their attention chiefly, as they did in their scientific investigations of economic development and social struggles, to analyzing the fundamental issues of their time, of modern developments. If we examine the Marxist approach to literature, we see what an important role is assigned to the principle of the uneven development in extrapolating the particularities of any period. Undoubtedly, capitalism represented the highest stage of economic production in the development of class societies. But Marx was also convinced that this mode of production was essentially unpropitious for the evolution of literature and art. Marx was not the first nor the only one to expose this fact. But he was the first to disclose the factors responsible for this state of affairs in their full scope. For one gains insight into such a situation only through a comprehensive, dynamic and dialectical approach. Of course we can merely touch on this question here.

It should now be clear to the reader that Marxist literary theory and history constitute only part of a comprehensive whole: historical materialism. Marxism does not define the fundamental hostility to art of the capitalist mode of production from an aesthetic point of view. Indeed if we were to make a quantitative or statistical study of Marx's comments, something which is impermissible, of course, we might say from the start that such questions hardly interested him. But anyone who has studied *Capital* and Marx's other writings attentively will see that (in context) some of his comments provide a more profound insight into the heart of the question than the writings of anti-capitalist romanticists who busied themselves with aesthetics all their lives. Marxist economics actually relates the categories of economics, the basis of social life, back to where they appear in reality, as human relationships and past these to the relationship of society to nature. Yet Marx simultaneously demonstrates that under capitalism all these categories appear absolutely reified so that their true essence, men's relationships, are obscured. It is this inversion of the fundamental categories of existence that produces the fetishizing of capitalist society. In men's consciousness, the world appears otherwise than it is, distorted in structure, divorced from its actual relationships. Under capitalism a special intellectual effort is required for a man to see through this fetishizing and grasp the actual substance—man's social relations—behind the reified terms which determine daily life (goods, gold, prices, etc.).

Now humanism, that is, the passionate study of man's nature, is essential to all literature and art; and good art and good literature are humanistic to the extent that they not only investigate man and the real essence of his nature with passion but also and simultaneously defend human integrity passionately against all attacks, degradation and distortion. Since such tendencies (especially the oppression and exploitation of man by man) attain such a level of inhumanity in no other society as under capitalism just because of the objective reification we have mentioned, every true artist, every true writer as a creative individual is instinctively an enemy of this distortion of the principle of humanism, whether consciously or not.

It is obviously impossible to pursue this question further here. In an analysis of particular works of Goethe and Shakespeare, Marx emphasizes the dehumanizing effect of money, which deforms and corrupts mankind :

"Shakespeare emphasizes two aspects of money :

"1. It is the visible divinity, the transformation of all human and natural qualities into their opposite, the general distortion and inversion of things; it reconciles impossibilities;

"2. it is the universal whore, the universal procurer of men and nations.

"The distortion and inversion of all human and natural qualities, the reconciliation of impossibilities—the *divine* power—in money derives from its being essentially the alienated, alienating and self-alienating essence of the human species. It is the property of mankind alienated.

"What I cannot do as a *man*, what is beyond my innate capacities, I accomplish through money. Money thus transforms each of these essential capacities into something that it is not in itself, that is, into its opposite."

Marx's statement does not cover all the major ramifications of the question. The hostility toward art in the capitalist mode of production is exemplified in the capitalist division of labour. To understand this contention fully one must refer to the totality of the economy once again. We will investigate only one aspect of our problem, the principle of humanism again, which the proletarian struggle for freedom inherited from earlier democratic and revolutionary movements and evolved to a higher qualitative level : the demand for a free development of a many-sided, integrated man. Contrarily, the hostility to art and culture inherent in the capitalist mode of production brings a disintegration of man, a disintegration of the concrete totality into abstract specializations.

The anti-capitalist romantics also understood this fact. But viewing it simply as fate or misfortune, they sought refuge sentimentally and idealistically in primitive societies and inevitably ended as reactionaries. Marx and Engels never denied the progressive character of the capitalist mode of production, but they were relentless in exposing its inhumanity. They demonstrated that on this road mankind could only create the material bases for the final and real liberation, socialism. But though recognizing the economic, social and historical inevitability of the capitalist social order and decisively repudiating any nostalgia for epochs that had already had their day, Marx and Engels did not relax their criticism of capitalist culture but even intensified their attacks. If they refer to the past, they do not do so in any romantic flight into the past but merely to determine the origin of a struggle for freedom which advanced mankind out of a still more sordid and desperate period of exploitation and oppression, feudalism. Thus when Engels writes of the Renaissance, he directs his comments to the struggles for freedom, to the initial stages of the workers' struggles for freedom; and if he contrasts the mode of production with the later capitalist division of labour, he does not do so to exalt the former but rather to point the way to future liberation. Speaking of the Renaissance, Engels says: "It was the greatest progressive revolution mankind had yet experienced, a time which required giants and produced giants: giants in thought, passions and character, in many-sidedness and learning. The men who laid the basis for the modern hegemony of the bourgeoisie, unlike the modern bourgeois, were anything but narrow. . . . The heroes of that time had not been enslaved by the division of labour whose narrowing one-sidedness we so often note among their successors. What particularly distinguishes them is that they all live and work in the midst of the movements of their time and engage in practical struggle, taking stands and fighting, one with his pen, the other with the dagger, many with both. Thus the universality and power which renders them complete men. Bookworms are the exceptions, either simply second or third-rate people or cautious philistines who don't want to burn their fingers."

Marx and Engels urged the writers of their time to take an effective stand through their characters against the destructiveness and degradation of the capitalist division of labour and to grasp man in his essence and totality. And because they missed in most of their contemporaries this attempt at viewing mankind individually and as a whole, they considered these writers insignificant epigones. In his critique of Lassalle's "Sickingen" tragedy, Engels wrote : "You are fully justified in opposing the paltry individualization of characters so much à la mode today, mere clever pedantry and a hallmark of an epigone literature written in the sand."

In the same letter he explains where the modern writer can obtain this strength, this comprehensive view, this sense of the totality of life. In criticizing Lassalle's drama, Engels reproves him for the political error of overestimating the aristocratic and reactionary Sickingen movement, which was doomed from the outset, while underestimating the great peasants' revolt; but Engels also points out that only with the representation of the multifaceted life of the people could he provide genuine and vivid characters for his drama.

From the foregoing observations it should be clear how the economic base of the capitalist mode of production reacts upon literature—for the most part independently of the author's control. But Marx and Engels hardly underestimated the subjective aspect of creation. In the course of our further discussion we will return for a closer examination of this question. Now we will merely call attention to one particular. The average bourgeois writer, identifying with his class and its prejudices and with capitalist society in general, is fearful of attacking real problems and shrinks from doing so. In the course of the ideological and literary struggles of the late 1840s, the youthful Marx wrote a close critique of Eugene Sue's extraordinarily popular and influential novel then being widely read in Germany, *The Mysteries of Paris*. We will merely note that Marx lashed out at Sue for his cowardice in depicting only the surface of capitalist society and for his opportunism in distorting and falsifying reality. Of course, no one reads Sue any more. But in every decade fashionable writers appear who cater to bourgeois moods of the moment, writers for whom, with appropriate modifications, this critique is fully pertinent.

We have seen our analysis, which began with the origin and development of literature, shift almost imperceptibly to aesthetic questions in the narrower sense. And so we arrive at the second complex of questions in the Marxist view of art.

Marx considered the investigation of historical and social conditions in the genesis and development of literature to be extraordinarily important, but he never contended that literary questions were thereby exhausted : ". . . the difficulty does not lie, however, in understanding how Greek art and epic are linked to certain social forms of development. The difficulty is in understanding why they still provide us with aesthetic pleasure and serve in certain measure as norms and unattainable examples."

Marx approaches the question which he poses himself from both contextual and historical points of view, noting the relevance of the Greek world, the normal childhood of humanity, to the spiritual life of later generations. The investigation thus does not return to the problem of the social origin but advances to the formulation of basic principles of aesthetics, again not from a formalistic point of view but within a comprehensive dialectical context. Marx's reply indeed evokes two great complexes of questions concerning the aesthetic essence of a work of art of any period : what is the significance of such a representation of the world within the evolution of mankind? And how does the artist represent a particular stage within this evolution?

Only with such an approach can we proceed to the question of artistic form. This question can, of course, be posed and answered only in closest relationship to the general principles of dialectical materialism. It is a fundamental thesis of dialectical materialism that any apperception of the external world is nothing but the reflection of a reality existing independently of the consciousness, in the thoughts, conceptions, perceptions, etc., of men. Though in the most general formulation of this thesis, dialectical materialism is in agreement with all other types of materialism and in sharp opposition to any variant of idealism, it is still to be decisively distinguished from mechanical materialism. Criticizing this outmoded materialism, Lenin insisted that it is not capable of conceiving the theory of reflection dialectically.

As a mode of reflection of the external world in human consciousness, artistic creation is subsumed under the general epistemology of dialectical materialism. However, because of the peculiar character of artistic creation, it is a particular, special part often with distinctive laws of its own. In the following remarks, we will touch on some of the particularities of the literary and artistic reflection without attempting, even in broad outline, any exhaustive treatment of this complex question.

The theory of reflection is nothing new in aesthetics. The image, the mirroring, to use the metaphor made famous in the play scene in *Hamlet*, where Shakespeare exposed his own literary theory and practice, is an ancient concept. It was central to Aristotle's aesthetics and has continued to dominate nearly every great aesthetic since—except for the periods of decadence. An account of this historical development is, of course, beyond the scope of this preface. We need merely point to the many idealistic aesthetics (Plato's, for example) which in their own way are based on this theory. More important is the fact that all great writers of world literature have instinctively or more or less consciously followed this theory of reflection in their work and have followed this orientation in seeking to clarify their own artistic principles. The aspiration of all great writers has been the artistic reproduction of reality; fidelity to reality, the unsparing effort to render reality comprehensively and realistically has been the real criterion of literary greatness for every great writer (Shakespeare, Goethe, Balzac, Tolstoy).

The fact that Marxist aesthetics approaches this key question without any pretension to radical innovation surprises only those who, without any basis or real knowledge, associate the ideology of the proletariat with the "radically new", with artistic avantgarde-ism, believing that the cultural liberation of the proletariat means the complete abandonment of the past. The classics and founders of Marxism never maintained such a view. In their judgment, the liberation struggles of the working class, the working-class ideology and culture to be created, are the heir to all mankind has produced of value over the millenia.

Lenin once declared that one of the superiorities of Marxism to bourgeois ideologies lay precisely in its capacity critically to accept the progressive cultural heritage and to absorb whatever was great in the past. Marxism does surpass its predecessors only insofar—but this "only" is of extraordinary significance for methodology and content—as it renders all their aspirations conscious, eliminating all idealistic and mechanistic deviations, relates these aspirations to their effective causes and includes them in a system of consciously defined laws of social development. In the field of aesthetics, literary theory and literary history, we can say in summary that Marxism raises to conceptual clarity those fundamental principles of creative activity which have been present in the philosophic outlook of the best thinkers and the works of the oustanding writers and artists over the centuries.

To clarify some of the more important problems involved here, we have to face the question: what is that reality of which literary creation must provide a faithful reflection? The negative response is required first of all: this reality does not consist simply of the immediately perceptible superfice of the external world, nor simply of accidental, ephemeral, contingent phenomena. While Marxist aesthetics makes realism the crux of its theory of art, it also combats vigorously any kind of naturalism and any direction which is satisfied with a photographic reproduction of the immediately perceptible superfice of the external world. Here again Marxist aesthetics does not propound anything radically new but merely raises to the highest level of consciousness and clarity what has been central to the theory and practice of great artists of the past.

Marxist aesthetics combats with equal vehemence another false extreme in the theory and practice of art, the conception which holds that since copying reality is to be rejected and artistic forms are independent of this superficial reality, artistic forms therefore possess their own autonomy, that perfection of form and striving after perfection are ends in themselves abstracted from reality and that artistic perfection is independent of reality; and thus the artist has the right to transform and stylize reality at will. In this struggle Marxism continues and expands the view of the truly great figures of world literature regarding the nature of art, according to which the task of art is the truthful and accurate representation of the totality of reality; art in this view is as far removed from the photographic copy as it is from what is ultimately mere dabbling with abstract forms.

With such a conception of art, a key question of the epistemology of dialectical materialism is posed: the question of appearance and reality, a question with which bourgeois thought and consequently bourgeois aesthetics has never been able to cope. Naturalistic theory and practice propounds a mechanical, anti-dialectical unity between appearance and reality; in this dubious hodgepodge, reality is inevitably obscured and generally even disappears. The idealistic philosophy of art and the artistic practice of formalist stylization sometimes recognize the contrast between reality and appearance, but through lack of dialectic or through incomplete idealist dialectic see only the antithesis between appearance and reality without recognizing the dialectical unity of opposites in this antithesis. (This problem is obvious in Schiller, both in his interesting and searching aesthetic studies and in his creative practice.) And the literature and theory of decadent periods generally combine both false tendencies: in place of a true investigation of reality, there is a dabbling with superficial analogies as much abstracted from reality as the theories of ideas in the classics of idealism; these empty constructions are then adorned with naturalistic, impressionistic, etc., details, and parts organically related are assembled into a pseudo-unity by means of some mystical "conception of the world".

The true dialectic of reality (Wesen) and appearance rests on their being equal aspects of objective reality (Wirklichkeit), products of reality and not just of consciousness.[1] Yet—and this is an important axiom of dialectical apprehension—reality has various levels; there is the ephemeral reality of the superfice, never recurring, momentary; and there are the more

---

[1] *Wesen* and *Wirklichkeit* are both translated as "reality" in this passage. The former is reality in the dialectic; the latter is reality in general.—*Trans.*

profound elements and tendencies of reality which recur in accordance with definite laws and change according to changing circumstances. This dialectic pervades the whole of reality so that in this context appearance and reality constantly achieve new relationships; that which opposed appearance as reality, as we look beneath the superfice of immediate experience, figures upon renewed examination as appearance, behind which another, new reality arises. And so on to infinity.

True art thus aspires to maximum profundity and comprehensiveness, at grasping life in its all-embracing totality. That is, it examines in as much depth as possible the reality behind appearance and does not represent it abstractly, divorced from phenomena and in opposition to phenomena, but represents instead the dynamic dialectical process in which reality is transformed into appearance and is manifested as a phenomenon and reveals the other side of the process in which the phenomenon in motion discloses its own particular reality. Furthermore, these individual aspects not only contain a dialectical movement, a transference into each other, but also stand in continuous interaction as elements of a continuous process. Real art thus represents life in its totality, in motion, development and evolution.

Since the dialectical conception combines the universal, particular and individual into a dynamic unity, it is clear that this particular dialectics must also be manifested in specific art forms. For in contrast to science which dissolves this activity into its abstract elements and seeks to conceptualize the interaction of these elements, art renders this activity perceptually meaningful as movement in a dynamic unity. One of the most important categories of this artistic synthesis is the type. Thus Marx and Engels allude to this concept first in defining true realism. Engels writes: "In addition to accuracy of detail, realism means, in my opinion, the faithful representation of typical characters in typical situations." Engels, however, also advised that typicality was not to be opposed to individuality by being transformed into abstract generalization. ". . . each is simultaneously a type and a particular individual, a 'this one', [Dieser] as old Hegel expressed it, and so it must be".

The type, according to Marx and Engels, is not the abstract type of classical tragedy, nor the idealized universality as in Schiller, still less what Zola and post-Zola literature and literary theory made of it : the average. What characterizes the type is the convergence and intersection of all the dominant aspects of that dynamic unity through which genuine literature reflects life in a vital and contradictory unity—all the most important social, moral and spiritual contradictions of a time. The representation of the average, on the other hand, inevitably results in diluting and deadening these contradictions, the reflection of the great problems of any age; by being represented in the mind and experiences of an average man, they lose their decisiveness. Through the representation of a type, the concrete, universal and essential qualities, what is enduring in man and what is historically determined and what is individual and what is socially universal, combine in typical art. Through the creation of the type and the discovery of typical characters and typical situations, the most significant directions of social development obtain adequate artistic expression.

We must add another observation to these general remarks. Marx and Engels saw in Shakespeare and Balzac (as against, we may note, Schiller and Zola respectively) the artistic, realistic direction which best conformed to their aesthetic. The choice of these particular outstanding figures reveals that the Marxist conception of realism is not to be confused with any photographic reproduction of daily life. Marxist aesthetics simply asks that the writer represent the reality he has captured not abstractly but as the reality of the pulsating life of phenomena of which it forms an organic part and out of whose particular experiences it evolves. But in our opinion it is not necessary that the phenomena delineated be derived from daily life or even from life at all. That is, free play of the creative imagination and unrestrained fantasy are compatible with the Marxist conception of realism. Among the literary achievements Marx especially valued are the fantastic tales of Balzac and E. T. A. Hoffmann.

Of course there is imagination and imagination, and fantasy and fantasy. If we seek a criterion by which to judge them, we

must return to the fundamental doctrine of dialectical materialism : the reflection of reality.

Marxist aesthetics, which denies the realism of a world depicted through naturalistic detail if it does not express the essential
dynamic forces, accepts the fantastic tales of Hoffmann and
Balzac as among the highest achievements of realistic literature,
since these essential elements are exposed through the very
fantasy. The Marxist conception of realism is realism in which
the essence of reality is exposed perceptually and artistically.
This represents the dialectical application of the theory of
reflection to the field of aesthetics. It is not surprising therefore
that the concept of the type should be emphasized in Marxist
aesthetics. The type, on the one hand, permits a resolution of
the dialectic between reality and appearance not to be found in
any other field; on the other hand, it provides a link to the
social and historical process of which the best realistic art
provides an accurate reflection. This Marxist conception of
realism represents a continuation of what great masters of
realism like Fielding demanded of their own artistic practice.
They called themselves historians of bourgeois reality, of the
private life of their times. But Marx goes further in regard to
the relation of great realistic art to historical reality, assessing
the works of the realists even more highly than they did
themselves. In a conversation with his son-in-law, the outstanding French socialist writer Paul Lafargue, Marx declared
of Balzac : "Balzac was not only the historian of the society of
his time but also the prophetic creator of characters still
embryonic under Louis Philippe, characters who were to
emerge in full maturity only after Balzac's death, under
Napoleon III."

In posing such demands on art, Marxist aesthetics demonstrates its consequent, radical objectivity. In the Marxist view
the definitive quality in great realism is the passionate and
dedicated search to grasp and reproduce reality as it is objectively and essentially. There are many misconceptions in regard
to this tenet of Marxist aesthetics. Many people claim it means
underestimating the role of the creative artist and of the subjective factors in creative effort. People confuse Marx with

the vulgarizers who pretend that the mechanistic and false objectivism of naturalism is Marxism. We have seen that one of the central problems of Marxist ideology is the dialectic of appearance and reality, the recognition and extrapolation of the reality from the network of contradictory phenomena. If we do not believe that the creative artist "creates" something radically new *ex nihilo* but recognize that he discovers a reality existing independently of himself and not accessible to everyone, eluding for a long time even the greatest artists, then the activity of the creative artist not only is not eliminated; it is not diminished in the slightest. If Marxist aesthetics views as the greatest achievement of the creative effort the artist's making us aware of the social process and making it meaningful and experientially accessible and in setting down in his work his own self-awareness and his own awakening to the social evolution—surely the result is no underestimation of the artist's activity but a just and lofty assessment, such as has never previously been accorded.

Here, as elsewhere, Marxism presents nothing "radically new". Plato's aesthetics, the doctrine of the aesthetic reflection of ideas, treats this question. But Marxism once again sets right side up the aesthetic truth which the great idealists had left standing on its head. On the one hand, as we have seen, Marxism does not admit an exclusive opposition between appearance and reality but seeks the reality in the appearance and the appearance in its organic relation to the reality. On the other hand, for Marxism the aesthetic capturing of the reality and of the idea is not a simple, definitive act but a process, an active, step-by-step approximation of essential reality, a recognition of the fact that the most profound essence of reality is never more than a part of the total reality to which the surface phenomena also belong.

If Marxism demands radical, extreme objectivity in aesthetic cognition and representation, it also emphasizes the indispensable role of the creative artist. For this process, this step-by-step approximation of the hidden reality, is accessible only to the greatest and most persevering genius. The objectivity of Marxist science extends even to recognizing the abstraction—the truly meaningful abstraction—not as a mere product of man's consciousness, but further to demonstrating how (especially with the primary forms of the social process, the economic forms) the abstraction is itself a product of social reality. Investigating this process of abstraction with clear-sighted imagination, unravelling its intricacies and concentrating the full complexity within the general process into typical characters and situations is a task which only the greatest artistic genius can attempt.

We see then that the objectivity of Marxist aesthetics does not lead to a rejection of the subjective factor in art at all. However there is still another aspect of this question to be examined. We must note that the objectivity enunciated by Marxism does not imply non-partisanship toward social developments. Marxist aesthetics correctly recognizes that since the great artist does not represent static objects and situations but seeks to investigate the direction and tempo of a process, he must grasp in his art the character of such a process; and such understanding in itself presupposes taking a stand. The concept of the artist as an uncommitted observer above social movements (Flaubert's "impassibilité") is at best an illusion or self-deception; or, more generally, simply an evasion of the basic issues of life and art. There are no great artists who do not express their own attitudes, yearnings and aspirations in their representation of reality.

Does this contention contradict our previous statement that the essence of Marxist aesthetics is its objectivity?

We do not think so. And to eliminate confusion about any apparent contradiction, we will touch briefly on the Marxist interpretation of so-called tendentious art and seek to define the place of such art in Marxist aesthetics. What is tendentiousness? From a superficial point of view, it is the attempt of the artist to demonstrate, propagate or exemplify a political or social view. Interestingly and characteristically whenever discussing such artificial concoctions, Marx and Engels speak with especial irony, particularly when a writer distorts objective reality (compare Marx's critique of Sue above) in order to demonstrate the truth of some thesis or to justify some partisan policy. Marx protested against the attempts even of great artists to use their works or individual characters for immediate and direct expression of their personal opinions; he argued that they thereby prevented their characters from fully exposing their capacities in accordance with the inner and organic dialectic of their own existences. In this regard Marx reproached Lassalle in criticizing his tragedy: "You might have permitted even the most modern ideas to come forth on a much higher level and in their purest form, but as it is, except for *religious* freedom, bourgeois unity provides your principal theme. You would have had to Shakespeare-ize more. I reckon your Schiller-izing, your transformation of your characters into simple mouthpieces of their time, to be your worst weakness."

The repudiation of tendentious literature does not mean that genuine literature is not tendentious. Objective reality is no chaotic jumble but a revolutionary process involving more or less accentuated tendencies moving primarily in a particular general direction. A denial or misinterpretation of this process seriously weakens works of art (see Marx's critique of Lassalle's tragedy).

Thus the proper relationship of an artist to various tendencies of social evolution and especially to the fundamental tendency in the process can be defined. Engels declares of tendency in art: "I am by no means an opponent of tendentious poetry as such. The father of tragedy, Aeschylus, and the father of comedy, Aristophanes, were strongly tendentious, nor were Dante and Cervantes less so, and the greatest merit of Schiller's *Kabale and Liebe* is that it is the first German politically tendentious drama. The modern Russians and Norwegians, who produce excellent novels, are all tendentious. But I think that the tendency must arise out of the situation and the action without having to be revealed explicitly; and the poet is not required to produce a pat solution to the historical conflict he describes, for the reader". Engels is clear that a thesis can only be associated with art and can only promote the production of the greatest works of art when it emerges organically out of the artistic essence of the work, out of the creative design, that is, as we have previously stated, out of reality itself, of which it is the dialectical reflection.

What are the fundamental issues on which the artist must take a stand to be a true artist? The great issues of human progress. No great artist can be indifferent to them. Without passionate commitment he cannot create types or achieve profound realism. Without commitment a writer will never be able to distinguish the essential from the inessential. From the perspective of the totality of social development, a writer who has no enthusiasm for progress and hatred for reaction, who does not love good and repudiate evil, cannot exercise the discrimination essential for great literature.

Once again we encounter an apparent and profound contradiction. It would seem that every great writer must then have a progressive class, philosophical, social and political outlook and that—to formulate the apparent contradiction bluntly—every great writer must be left-oriented politically and socially. However, no small number of great realists in literary history, especially Marx's and Engels' favourite authors, are examples of the opposite. Neither Shakespeare, nor Goethe, nor Walter Scott, nor Balzac was left-oriented.

Marx and Engels do not evade this question; they subject it to profound analysis. In a famous letter to Margaret Harkness, Engels investigated in depth the question as to how Balzac could be a royalist and legitimist in politics and an admirer of the decadent aristocracy while exhibiting ultimately an opposing orientation in his works. "Certainly, Balzac was a legitimist in politics; his great work is an elegy for the inevitable collapse of good society; all his sympathies are with a class whose destruction is fore-ordained. Yet his satire is never sharper, his irony never more bitter than when he sets in motion the very men and women with whom he sympathizes most profoundly —the nobility." And, in contrast, he represents his political enemies, the republican revolutionaries, as the only real heroes of his time. The ultimate consequence of this contradiction Engels summarizes as follows : "That Balzac was forced to act against his own class sympathies and political prejudices, that he saw the inevitability of the collapse of his beloved aristocrats and portrayed them as men who deserved no better fate, that he saw the men of the future where they were actually to be found in his time, I consider one of the greatest triumphs of realism and one of the most magnificent achievements of old Balzac."

Is this a miraculous achievement? Some mysterious fluke of artistic genius transcending the constraints of political orientations? No. What Engels exposes in his analysis is a simple and clear fact, the real significance of which, however, Engels and Marx were the first to discover and analyse. What is involved is the uncompromising honesty, free of all vanity, of truly great writers and artists. For them reality as revealed through painstaking investigation, reality as it actually is, stands above the most cherished preconceptions and most intimate personal aspirations. The great artist's honesty lies in his allowing characters (in whose development the conceptions and illusions on account of which he created them in his imagination are exposed) to evolve freely until all their capacities are revealed and to do so without being in the least concerned that his most profound convictions evaporate in the impersonal dialectic of reality. We can see and study such honesty in Cervantes, Balzac and Tolstoy.

Yet this honesty has its own concrete content. Compare Balzac's legitimitism with that of a writer like Bourget, for example. The latter actually wages war against progress; he would crush republican France under the yoke of the old reaction. He exploits the contradictions and problems of contemporary life in order to propound ideologies long outdated as remedies. In contrast, Balzac is defending human integrity in the great capitalist upsurge which began in France during the Restoration. Balzac saw not only the irresistible power in this process but also that its invincibility was the result of its progressive aspects. He saw that this development, despite its disintegration and deformation of the individual, represented a higher level of evolution than the feudal or half-feudal order it was undermining, at times and in places with the most dreadful effects. Balzac saw that this process brought the disintegration and deformation of man; and in the name and defence of man's integrity, he hated this development. His conscious social and political outlook exemplifies this contradiction, unresolvable for Balzac the thinker. By studying and representing the world with genuine realistic objectivity, he not only arrived at an accurate reflection of the essence of this process in his work but also probed deeply into himself to the roots of his own love and hate. As a thinker Balzac transcended the horizons of Bonald and de Maistre; the creative Balzac sees better, deeper and further than these right-wing political thinkers. With his commitment to man's integrity, he is able to discern the contradictions in the capitalist economic order and the problems of capitalist culture. As a creative artist, Balzac approaches extraordinarily close to the critical picture his great contemporary, the socialist Fourier, had sketched of the rising capitalist society.

In the Marxist conception, the triumph of realism implies a complete break with that vulgar conception of literature and art which appraises creative works mechanically in terms of a writer's political attitudes, according to a so-called class psychology. The Marxist approach we are exploring is exceedingly well-adapted to illuminating complicated literary phenomena, but only when it is applied concretely, in an historical spirit, with genuine aesthetic and social insight. Anyone who imagines it to be a ready-made formula applicable to any literary phenomenon misinterprets the Marxist classics like the vulgar Marxists of the past. In order to eliminate any further misunderstanding in regard to this approach, let me simply add that the triumph of realism, as defined by Engels, does not mean either that the writer's explicit ideology is a matter of indifference or that any work in which a writer departs from his explicit ideology ipso facto represents a triumph of realism. There is a victory of realism only when great realist writers establish a profound and serious, if not fully conscious, association with a progressive current in the evolution of mankind. Thus, from a Marxist point of view, it is inadmissible to set bad or mediocre writers on the pedestal of the classics simply because of their political convictions; and it is equally inadmissible on the basis of Engels' formulation, to seek to rehabilitate partly or entirely reactionary writers because they are more or less accomplished craftsmen.

It was not accidental that we spoke of the defence of human integrity in connection with Balzac. With most great realists this theme provides the impulse to the representation of reality, a representation which varies, of course, in character and emphasis according to periods and individuals. Great art, genuine realism and humanism are inextricably united. And the unifying principle is what we have been emphasizing : concern for man's integrity. Humanism is fundamental to Marxist aesthetics. We stress once again that Marx and Engels were not the first to make humanism the crux of an aesthetic outlook. Here, too, Marx and Engels were continuing the work of the outstanding representatives of philosophic and aesthetic thought and raising it to a qualitatively higher level of development. On the other hand, since they were not the initiators, but the culmination of a long development, they are far more consequent in their humanism.

And this is so, despite the common bourgeois preconception, precisely because of their materialist ideology. Earlier idealist thinkers had defended humanism much as did Marx and Engels, combating in the name of humanism the political, social and moral currents against which Marx and Engels struggled. Yet only the materialist viewpoint provided a key to understanding that the undermining of humanism in the disintegration and crippling of human integrity was an inevitable consequence of the material and economic structure of society. The division of labour of class societies, the separation of town from country and of physical from intellectual labour, the oppression and exploitation of man by man, the specialization of capitalist production (a major factor in the disintegration of the individual)—all are material and economic processes.

Regarding the cultural and artistic effects of these factors idealist thinkers had written with insight and wisdom, in elegiac and ironic tones, but with their materialist view Marx and Engels were able to probe to the root causes. And by probing to the roots, they were able to go beyond mere ironic criticism of the anti-humanism in the development and very existence of class societies and beyond mere nostalgic yearning for some imaginary idyllic past; they were able to demonstrate scientifically how this entire process originated and where it was going and how to defend man's integrity effectively, in actual life, in relation to actual men; how to change the material bases which cause the crippling and deformation of men; and how to awaken men to consciousness and to action as agents of this social and political consciousness—the revolutionary proletariat—in order to create material bases not only for preserving social and political, moral, intellectual and artistic achievements but also for raising them to new, unprecedented heights.

This radical objectivity provides the crux of Marx's thinking. He once contrasted the condition of men under capitalist society and under socialist society thus: "Displacing *all* the physical and intellectual sensibilities, there is the simple alienation of all the senses—the sense of possession. Man must be reduced to this absolute impoverishment before he can again create a new personal richness out of himself. . . .

"The elimination of private property thus represents the complete emancipation of all human sensibilities and qualities; but it is precisely through this emancipation that these sensibilities and qualities become *human*, both subjectively and objectively."

Thus socialist humanism is the core of Marxist aesthetics and of the materialist conception of history. Contrary to bourgeois preconceptions reinforced by the gross, anti-dialectical conception of history of vulgar Marxism, this materialist conception, which probes universally to the roots, does not deny the aesthetic beauty of the blossoms. On the contrary, the materialist conception of history and Marxist aesthetics alone provide the key to an understanding of the unity and organic relationship of roots and blossoms.

On the other hand, the fact that historical materialism sees the real and ultimate liberation of humanity from the deformation of class society only under socialism does not at all imply a rigid, undialectical, schematic opposition to, or the summary rejection of, the culture of class societies or an indifference to their varied cultural achievements and their cultural and artistic influences (as is often the case with the vulgar simplifiers of Marxism). Though the true history of mankind will begin with socialism, pre-history provides the elements in the formation of socialism, and the steps in this evolution cannot be matters of indifference to champions of socialist humanism. Nor to Marxist aesthetics.

Socialist humanism accomplishes the unification of historical and purely artistic knowledge within Marxist aesthetics, the continuous convergence of historical and aesthetic evaluation. Thus Marxist aesthetics resolves the question with which men of stature have long been grappling (a question which eluded lesser men simply because they were lesser men): the integration of the enduring aesthetic value of a work of art into the historical process, the process from which the work in its very perfection and aesthetic value is inseparable.

The Ideal of the Harmonious Man in Bourgeois Aesthetics

I F we are to attempt a serious examination of the question indicated in our title, we cannot direct our attention to the theory and practice of those who make "an art of living" in the contemporary stage of imperialism. The aspiration towards harmony of man's accomplishments as against his potential is never quite extinguished. The bleaker and emptier life becomes under capitalism, the more intense is the yearning after beauty. But this yearning for harmony under imperialism too often takes the form of a craven retreat or a faint-hearted withdrawal before the contradictory problems thrown up by life. By seeking inner harmony men cut themselves off from society's struggles. Such "harmony" is illusory and superficial; it vanishes at any serious contact with reality.

The great thinkers and artists who have championed this aspiration for harmony have always recognized that harmony for the individual presupposes his harmonious integration into his environment, into his society. The philosophical advocates of the integrated man from the Renaissance through Winckelmann to Hegel not only admired the Greeks for realizing this ideal but also recognized that the basis for the harmonious development of the individual in Classical Greece lay in the social and political structure of ancient democracy. That they more or less ignored the fact that this democracy was based on slavery is another matter.

Hegel has this to say about Greek harmony: "The Greeks, as far as their immediate reality was concerned, lived happily in the midst of a self-conscious subjective freedom and a self-conscious moral order." And expatiating upon this thought, Hegel contrasted Greek democracy both with oriental

89

despotism, under which the individual had no rights, and with modern society with its fully fledged social division of labour. "In Greek moral life, the individual enjoyed independence and freedom without being isolated from the interests of the state. In accordance with the basic principle of Greek life, the universal morality existed in an undisturbed harmony with the abstract subjective and objective freedom of the individual, and . . . there never was a question of a dichotomy between political principles and personal morality. The rare sensitivity, intellectuality and spirituality in this felicitous harmony permeates all the works in which the Greeks expressed their freedom and in which the essence of their freedom is exposed."

It was left to Marx to disclose the economic and social basis of that unique flourishing of human culture, of the harmonious fulfilment of the individual personality among the free citizens of the Greek democracies. He also explained the rational core to the unappeasable longing of mankind's finest spirits for this harmony, which has never been regained. Because of Marx we understand why this period of the "normal childhood" in man's development can never return.

But the longing to recapture this harmony has persisted since the Renaissance among the most progressive intellectuals. The revival of Classical thought, poetry and art during the Renaissance has admittedly visible causes in the class struggles of the time. Unquestionably, too, the study of Classical constitutions and of the civil wars from the Renaissance to Robespierre provided all bourgeois and democratic revolutionaries with powerful weapons in their struggle against feudalism and absolute monarchy. Whatever illusions accompanied these struggles were heroic illusions which sought to restore Classical democracy on the basis of a capitalist economy. And there is no doubt that it was precisely these heroic illusions which were necessary to sweep away the rubble of the Middle Ages.

But beyond all this, the revival of antiquity both during and after the Renaissance is distinguished by a (self-contradictory) tendency which points, sometimes more and sometimes less, beyond the bourgeois horizon. With turbulent enthusiasm and brilliant versatility of talent, scarcely imaginable today, the great men of the Renaissance strove to develop all the productive forces of society. Their lofty aim was to shatter the narrow localized restrictions of medieval social life and to create a social order in which all human capacities and potentialities would be liberated for an understanding of nature for the benefit of mankind. And these great men recognized that the development of the productive forces meant simultaneously the development of man's own productive capacities. The mastery of nature by free men in a free society—such was the Renaissance ideal of the harmonious man. Engels said of this great progressive human revolution: "The men who established the modern hegemony of the bourgeoisie were anything but narrow bourgeois." Engels perceived, however, that such an impressive, many-sided development of individual capacities, of even the most outstanding men, was possible only while capitalism was still undeveloped: "The heroes of that time had not yet been enslaved in the specialized division of labour whose crippling one-sidedness we so often encounter in their successors."

With the development of the productive forces of capitalism, the subjugation inherent in the capitalist division of labour became more pronounced. By the manufacturing stage, the worker had already become a narrow specialist in a single operation, and the state appartus had already begun to transform its civil servants into mindless and soulless bureaucrats.

The leading thinkers of the Enlightenment fought against the vestiges of the Middle Ages with even greater passion than the men of the Renaissance; as honest thinkers who hid nothing from themselves they saw symptoms of the contradictions within the emerging forces of production, within the very progress for which they were vanguard fighters. Thus Ferguson "denounced" (as Marx noted) the capitalist division of labour which grew before his eyes: "Many occupations demand in fact no intellectual capacity. They succeed best when there is complete suppression of feeling and thought;

and ignorance is the mother of industry as well as of superstition." He predicted pessimistically that if the trend continued "we will create a nation of helots and have no free citizens any more".

With Ferguson as with all the important men of the Enlightenment, this harsh criticism of the capitalist division of labour accompanies (though is not directly related to) a keen championing of the development of productive forces and the elimination of all social obstacles to continued progress. Thus these men exhibit the dichotomy, basic to our discussion, that continues in modern bourgeois thought regarding society, a dichotomy in all significant modern aesthetics and in all serious thought about harmony in life and art. It is a road full of contradictions which the leading eighteenth and nineteenth century thinkers seek between two equally false yet socially necessary extremes.

The one extreme is the glorification of the capitalist mode of developing the means of production—for a long time, indeed, the only possible mode—and concomitantly an apologetic evasion of the enslavement and fragmentation of the individual and of the horrifying ugliness of life which inevitably and increasingly accompanies this development. The other false extreme is to ignore the progressive character of this development because of its shocking human consequences—to escape from the present into the past, from the present of meaningless work in which a man has become a mere appendage to the machine back to the Middle Ages, when the varied labour of the craftsman could "reach a certain limited artistic awareness" (Marx), when a man still enjoyed a "comfortable bondage relationship" (Marx) to his work. These extremes are apologetics, on the one hand, and romantic reaction, on the other.

The great poets and aestheticians of the Enlightenment and of the first half of the nineteenth century did not succumb to this dilemma. But neither were they capable of resolving the contradictions in capitalist society. Undaunted by the conditions that confined them, they exhibited greatness and brilliance in maintaining an unrelenting critique of bourgeois society without abandoning their affirmation of progress. As a result, these antithetical attitudes are to be found side-by-side in the works of the men of the Enlightenment.

The poets and thinkers of German Classicism, whose major activity followed the French Revolution, seek various utopian solutions. Their criticism of the capitalist division of labour is no less incisive than that of the men of the Enlightenment. They, too, stress ever more sharply the fragmentation of the individual. Goethe's Wilhelm Meister poses these questions: "What use is it to manufacture good iron when inside I am full of slag? What good is it to put an estate in order if I am never at one with myself?" And he perceives that this disharmony is a product of bourgeois society. He says: "A bourgeois can make profit and with some difficulty even develop his mind; but he will lose his individuality, do what he will. He may not ask: "What are you? but only what do you have? what ability, what understanding, what knowledge, how great a fortune? He has to exploit individual aptitudes in order to put them to use, and it is taken for granted that he may not enjoy an inner harmonious development, for he must neglect everything that cannot be put to use."

The great poets and thinkers of German Classicism sought in art for the harmonious integration of the individual and the beauty accompanying it. Active after the French Revolution, they had lost the heroic illusions of the Enlightenment. They did not, however, give up the struggle for harmony in the individual and for its artistic expression. As a result, they assigned to questions of aesthetic practice an excessive and often an exaggeratedly idealistic significance. They saw artistic harmony not only as a reflection and expression of the harmonious individual but also as the chief means of overcoming subjectively the fragmentation and distortion resulting from the capitalist division of labour. This approach resulted in their abandoning all practical attempts at overcoming in life itself the absence of harmony under capitalism. Their concepts of harmony in man and of beauty are divorced and alienated from life. Schiller sings of beauty with such a view:

Piercing even unto Beauty's sphere,
In the dust still lingers here
Gravitation, with the world it sways,
Not from out the mass, with labour wrung,
Light and graceful, as from nothing sprung,
Stands the image to the ravish'd gaze.
Mute is ev'ry struggle, ev'ry doubt,
In the uncertain glow of victory;
While each witness hence is driven out
Of frail man's necessity.[1]

Here the idealistic side of classical philosophy and poetry is clearly exemplified. There is idealism, too, in the rigid opposition which Schiller makes between aesthetic activity and ordinary work. With astute historical insight, he finds the origin of man's aesthetic activity in his surplus energy. His resultant "play" theory is directed toward the elimination of the division within man under the capitalist division of labour. With this theory he campaigns for the total, many-sided and developed human personality, yet only sees this development as happening outside the labour process of his time: "For . . . man plays only when he is human in the fullest sense of the word, and he is only fully human when he plays."

The idealism in such theories is clear. It is necessary, however, to recognize that the idealism of these great German classicists was the inevitable product of their social situation. It is precisely because they neither wish to disguise the inhumanity of capitalism nor make concessions to the reactionary and

[1] Aber dringt bis in der Schönheit Sphäre
Und im Staube bleibt die Schwere
Mit dem Stoff, den sie beherrscht, zurück.
Nicht der Masse qualvoll abgerungen,
Schlank und leicht, wie aus dem Nichts, gesprungen,
Steht das Bild vor dem entzückten Blick,
Alle Zweifel, all Kämpfe schweigen
In des Sieges hoher Sicherheit;
Ausgestossen hat es jeden Zeugen
Menschlicher Bedürftigkeit.

From "The Ideal and Life", translated by Edgar A. Bowring, *The Poems of Schiller*, London, 1910, p. 189.

romantic critique, being in no way able to foresee the displacement of capitalism by socialism, that they are forced to seek these solutions in order to preserve the ideal of the integrated man.

This aesthetic utopia does not merely avoid dealing with actual labour as it exists but also seeks utopian solutions in a general social sense. Goethe and Schiller believed that small groups could achieve the ideal of the integrated individual among themselves and provide nuclei for a general diffusion of this ideal—rather after the model of Fourier, who hoped that from the establishment of a phalanstery a gradual transformation of all society to socialism, as he understood it, might be achieved. The educational philosophy in *Wilhelm Meister* is based on a theory of this kind; similar utopianism is echoed in Schiller's "On the Aesthetic Education of Man".

Insofar as fragmentation and its cure were sought primarily within the individual, the problem of the fragmentation of sensibility and intellect was emphasized. Clearly, once again, the importance of this position is closely related to philosophic idealism. It is also clear, however, that there did exist, objectively, a fundamental problem in the fragmentation of the individual through the capitalist division of labour. The specialized, forced cultivation of certain individual capacities under this division of labour set the remaining qualities and passions "free" to atrophy or to run riot. In tackling this aspect of the question, Goethe and Schiller were raising the important question of whether it is possible to bring the human passions into harmony.

Some decades later this question was to become crucial to Fourier's utopian socialism. Fourier started with the premise that there is no human emotion that is intrinsically evil. An emotion becomes evil only as a consequence of the anarchy and inhumanity of the capitalist division of labour. Thus Fourier carries his criticism far beyond that of the Enlighteners or the German Classicists, making it a critique of the basic objective problems of the social division of labour; for example, the separation of town and country. The socialism of his utopian dream, with all its social constructs, aimed primarily at developing the abilities and sensibilities latent in every man and at promoting within the harmonious co-operative effort of varied personalities under socialism the integration of the capacities within each individual as well.

Fourier's great contemporaries, Hegel and Balzac, experienced the contradictions emerging from the capitalist division of labour at a more advanced stage than Goethe and Schiller during the period of their collaboration. The note of elegiac resignation which echoed through all the utopian dreams of Goethe and Schiller now predominates. Both the great thinker and the great realist see the inhumanity of capitalist society, that all the harmony within man, his every creative expression, is being ruthlessly crushed. For Hegel the aesthetic harmony in Greek life and after has been irretrievably lost: the "World Spirit" has moved beyond the sphere of the aesthetic and hastens to other goals. The dominion of prose has been established over mankind. And Balzac portrays with what cruel relentlessness capitalist society generates discord and ugliness in every manifestation of human existence, how all human aspirations toward a beautiful and harmonious existence are inexorably crushed by society. Balzac does include episodes in which "islands" of harmonious personalities appear; these are, however, no longer nuclei for a utopian renewal of the world but just exceptional instances of fortunate individuals rescued by chance from under the iron heel of capitalism.

Thus the heroic struggle for the integrated man of the bourgeois revolutionary period terminates in elegiac mourning; for the conditions for developing man's capacities into a harmonious integration have been irretrievably lost. Only where the critique of capitalism evolves into a prescience of socialism does this atmosphere of elegiac mourning, characteristic of the utopian dreamers who founded socialism, disappear.

With the destruction of the heroic illusions of the revolutionary period and the illusions of a possible revival of ancient democracy, there is an accompanying loss of appreciation of the classical experience in bourgeois art and aesthetics. The purely formal "harmony" that takes the place of the classical conception bears little relationship to life, whether of the past or the present; it is "academic", without content, an expression of a smug and complacent evasion of the ugliness of life.

The leading artists and thinkers of the period of bourgeois decline became increasingly dissatisfied with this banal academicism. There are fundamental social and artistic grounds for their renunciation of the ideals of classical harmony. The serious realists seek to depict the social life of their day with uncompromising verisimilitude and thus reject any pretence of harmony in life and of beauty in human personality.

But what lies behind this rejection and how does it manifest itself? Academicism can indeed reduce beauty and harmony to matters of no importance or treat them as mere questions of form, but by their very nature beauty and harmony cannot be matters of indifference to mankind. Concepts of beauty and harmony seem empty only because capitalist society denies them any realization in life. The dream of harmony can be realized and be effective in art only when occasioned by genuinely serious, progressive tendencies in actual life.

Such a dream of human harmony is diametrically opposed to that envisaged by the academician, who, though supposedly the perpetuator of the classics, actually proposes a fraudulent substitute, a false and empty pseudo-harmony. His flight from the ugliness and inhumanity of capitalist life is nothing but a capitulation without struggle.

This is not the only form of artistic capitulation before the fundamental hostility towards art and before the growing barbarism. Leading artists, dedicated fighters against their times, passionate defenders of progress also capitulate—without wishing to, indeed without knowing it—and do so as artists in the face of the philistinism of their time.

In this situation the social and humanist content of the "old-fashioned" concepts of beauty and harmony continue to exert a powerful influence extending far beyond literature and art. In their dedication to truth great realists of the period of mature capitalism like Balzac had to reject any representation of beauty in life or of the integrated personality. To be faithful realists they could only depict disharmonious, shattered lives, lives in which the beautiful and noble in man is inexorably crushed, worse, lives inwardly warped, corrupted and brutalized. The conclusion at which they must arrive is that capitalist society is a vast cemetery for integrity and human capacity, that under capitalism, as Balzac notes with pungent irony, men become either bank clerks or swindlers, that is, either exploited dupes or scoundrels.

This courageous condemnation is what distinguishes genuine realism from apologetic academicism, which seeks escape from life's discord. The creative artist may follow one of two courses in his denunciation of capitalist society. Either he can depict the mere result of this human disintegration or he can, in addition, portray the fine and noble human energies destroyed in the struggle to resist. Superficially, the distinction seems to be of a purely literary artistic kind. And indeed the analogy with the political and the social opposition to capitalist and imperialist barbarism does not hold mechanically. There is a whole group of seemingly left-wing writers who accept the degradation and destruction of the individual under capitalism as fact; they are indignant and express their indignation in their art; they expose the horror, but they do not depict the human nobility in the resistance to this horror. There are others who do not proclaim their political and social convictions so obviously in their own rebellion but who nevertheless describe with passionate vividness the daily, even hourly, resistance which mankind maintains against the crippling capitalist environment in defence of human integrity. In this uneven battle the individual is doomed if he relies solely on his own powers; he can maintain resistance only as a participant in the opposition movement destined to secure the final victory of humanism in society, economically, politically, socially and culturally.

In this regard Maxim Gorki is the foremost figure in contemporary world literature since his works depict with superb artistry this association of the individual and the popular movements. The horror of life under capitalism has probably never been so accurately exposed or painted in such bleak colours; yet the result is quite different from that in the works of most of his contemporaries, including leading writers of our time, for Gorki never presents the destruction under capitalism as an accomplished fact. He shows what is being destroyed and how, in what kind of struggle, the destruction is taking place. He reveals the beauty, the innate drive to harmony and to the unfolding of the varied but repressed, distorted and misdirected potentialities even in the worst of humanity. The fact that the vital aspiration toward beauty and harmony is crushed before our eyes is what makes his condemnation so resounding, what gives it an echo that can be heard everywhere.

Furthermore, Gorki points to a concrete solution in his work, that is, he shows how the revolutionary labour movement, the popular revolt, awakens an individual, matures him, encourages his inner life to bloom and imbues him with awareness, power and sensitivity. Gorki does not counterpose one social system to another or one ideology to another, but presents the emergent new kind of human being through whom the reader can experience directly and concretely the content of the new life.

Thus a principle of artistic representation turns into a political and social principle. None of Gorki's contemporaries reveals either the revulsion against the old or enthusiasm for the new with as much passion as Gorki. This revulsion and enthusiasm and certainty of victory—embodied in living people—exemplifies what has just been discussed : no artistic capitulation to capitalism! Gorki achieves a coincidence of the artistic and the political, a unity that is neither automatic nor mechanical. A writer only a trifle less consequent ideologically and artistically in his radicalism might attempt swifter, more direct effects and fall into lifeless propaganda and provide a dead, fetishized picture of life.

Capitalist antipathy to art is not one-dimensional; every dedicated artist must—consciously or not—end up as an enemy of capitalism in his attempt to create richly investigated characters. He may consider himself "uncommitted", he may seek refuge in scepticism, he may even claim to be conservative. But unless, profoundly confused about social and intellectual issues, he embraces a romantic reaction against progress, his revolt will emerge clearly in his work.

In the defence of repressed human values and of frustrated humanity, Anatole France is more radical and decisive than Emile Zola, the early Sinclair Lewis than Upton Sinclair, Thomas Mann than Dos Passos. It is no accident that the leading realists of our time have succeeded in obtaining a popular audience because their revolt is profound, for they really detest the destruction they see about them and do not merely dress up slogans in a formalist literature. Romain Rolland pursued this course most resolutely. Progressive writers must give careful consideration to the approaches followed by Heinrich and Thomas Mann and many others, too, in this regard. The revolt of the leading realists is the most significant development in the art of the bourgeois world today. This revolt has produced important art in a period most unfavourable to art, a period of a general decline in bourgeois culture. How aware each of the outstanding exponents of this genuine realism is in his association with the great humanist tradition is not decisive. With Romain Rolland or Thomas Mann the association is conscious and of importance. What is decisive is the objective relationship to, the objective continuation of, the fundamental humanist view, a continuation adapted, of course, to the special conditions of the day, in opposition to capitalist culture, a culture which every artist of integrity must reject.

There is another road, however, one which many writers, by no means insignificant in literature or in the general cultural life, have taken. They reject without compromise all ideals of beauty and harmony as "out-of-date"; they take people and society "as they are", or rather as they usually appear in ordinary life under capitalism. And in a depiction of such a given world, the categories of the old aesthetics do indeed lose meaning. Not because they are out-of-date! (We have seen how pertinent and valid they are when adapted to changed conditions by the leading realist of our time.) But they have lost all meaning since capitalism is destroying their social and individual base day by day; and these writers set out to represent a world destroyed and not the battle against the destruction, not a dynamic process but a lifeless result. The consequence is that they reject beauty and harmony and produce a mere chronicle of the "iron age".

Such has been the general course in this development. Writers have produced intellectual quintessences, local colour studies—presenting the primary material with which a dynamic re-creation of the world should start. They sketch characters and lives, arranged as in a chronicle, and expose the most obvious aspects of the destruction of the individual in capitalist society. The readers feel no impelling compassion for the characters or their experiences since the authors have presented only the consequences or nearly completed results of the destructive process. The readers cannot experience what was destroyed in this process nor appreciate at all the consequences of a continuation of such a process in the view of the author, for the author provides them with nothing but an abstract ideological programme.

Needless to add, this is not the only current in literature, nor is it ever to be found in absolute purity, for there is scarcely a true writer—no matter what his political philosophy—who rejects beauty altogether. Beauty, however, becomes something extraneous, something essentially alien to their subject matter and even antithetical to it. Flaubert turns beauty into a mere formal quality in rhetoric or picturesque diction; beauty is a quality to be imposed artificially on subject matter that is inherently unbeautiful. Baudelaire carries this alienation of beauty from life and the antipathy of life to beauty to the point of transforming beauty into a thing in itself—exotic, demonic, and vampire-like.

In the profound pessimism of their art and ideologies, leading writers reflect capitalism's hostility to art and the general ugliness of life under capitalism. Artists and thinkers become increasingly overwhelmed by the bleakness of life in the age of imperialism. Though they represent the inhumanity of capitalism with ever-greater intensity, they no longer manifest a rebellious fury but exhibit a conscious or unconscious respect for its "monumentality". The Greek ideal of beauty disappears and is replaced by a modern orientalism or a modernized glorification of the Gothic or the baroque. Nietzsche completes the ideological transformation by pronouncing the harmonious man of Greece a myth and by transfiguring Greece and the Renaissance "realistically" into civilizations of "monumental inhumanity and bestiality". Fascism inherits these decadent tendencies of bourgeois development and adapts them to its own demogogic purposes, using them to provide an ideological rationale for its prisons and torture chambers.

The power and vitality of anti-fascist literature lies in its reawakened humanism. The Hitlerites knew what they were doing when they set as the principle task for their "Professor for Political Pedagogy", Alfred Baeumler, the struggle against classical humanism. Imbued with a humanistic spirit and a humanistic revolt, the works of Anatole France, Romain Rolland, Thomas and Heinrich Mann and of all the outstanding anti-fascist writers represent a literature of which we can be proud, a literature which will in the future bear witness to artistic integrity in our time. This is a literature "against the stream", fighting the barbarous reactionary attitudes and deeds of our day, maintaining a courageous and effective resistance to the attempts to annihilate great art and defending the great realist tradition against the dominant current that is the inevitable reflection of contemporary capitalist society.

How far the individual anti-fascist writers consider themselves or profess to be the inheritors and perpetuators of the classical tradition is not decisive; what is important is that they are in fact carrying on the best traditions of mankind.

Healthy or Sick Art?

IN a lecture on Marxist aesthetics in Paris I touched on this topic in passing. Because of the brevity of the discussion, my remarks aroused certain misunderstandings. I will attempt now to correct these misunderstandings as cogently as I can.

First of all, sickness and health are being considered here primarily not from a biological but from a social and historical point of view. From such a standpoint, they prove to be factors in aesthetics.

On the historical relativism of what is to be considered normal Marx spoke very clearly in a letter cited by Engels. After quoting the line in Wagner's *Nibelungen*, "Were brothers ever permitted to lie with their sisters?" Engels continues: "Marx commented on Wagner's divine lechers who spice their love affairs in a very modern fashion through the addition of a little incest by saying: "In primitive times the sister *was* the wife and *that was moral.*""

Men's relationships are subject to historical change, and intellectual and emotional evaluations of these relationships change accordingly. Recognition of this fact, however, does not imply an acceptance of relativism. In a particular time, a certain human relationship is progressive, another is reactionary.

Thus we find that the conception of what is socially healthy is equally and simultaneously the basis for all really great art, for what is socially healthy becomes a component of man's historical self-awareness.

In this regard, a possible misunderstanding must be eliminated. The correspondence with social reality is dialectical, for in class societies the social reality implies movement, the struggle of antagonistic opposites and contradictions. Men's attitude in these struggles (always considered in historical

103

perspective) is decisive. Marx says regarding the position of the bourgeoisie and the proletariat : "The propertied class and the class of the proletariat both suffer from alienation. But the former class finds satisfaction and sanction in this alienation, recognizing the alienation as its particular power and possessing in it the illusion of a human existence; the latter class feels annihilated in the alienation and sees in it its own impotence and the reality of its inhuman existence."

But this observation still does not provide full clarification. If it is true that, broadly speaking, health stands on the side of progress and sickness on the side of reaction, the mere representation of sickness, even as the central theme in a work of art, does not by any means imply a morbidity in the creative approach. On the contrary, without this clash, especially in the art of class societies, the representation of what is healthy and positive is impossible.

Thus healthy art implies the knowledge of what is healthy and of what is sick. Such clear and mature insight in Shakespeare struck the young Schiller as coldness. The supposed cruelty of great humorists like Cervantes and Molière is similarly to be evaluated : except for various sentimental touches and a certain high-flown idealism, through their comedy they do establish the true historical and social balance.

In the same connection, one must not conceive of progress in a vulgar way. Because of the antagonistic contradictions in the development of class societies, in particular phases that which is declining may even appear as human greatness and purity (Antigone).

From these observations the general definition of the normal and the healthy should be emerging. Thus in this regard perfection in form in great works of art means the harmony of rational human and social content with a form which in itself provides a generalized reflection of the lasting truth of human relationships, of what is to be preserved in them, an expression of their fundamental essence.

Thus, inevitably, abnormality and morbidity in artistic content brings about dissolution of forms.

As for abnormality itself, it is in most cases a sterile opposition to the structure and direction in a specific stage of human progress, an opposition that does not point toward the future. The sterility of such opposition is the opposite pole to the servile adaptation to the degenerate. Contemporary literature offers numerous examples of how these antitheses actually coincide in practice : Knut Hamsun and Gide, Savinkov and Malraux, etc.

The objective basis for this coincidence lies in the fact that both poles represent extremes of philistinism. Gottfried Keller exposed this fact with the happy insight of a great humorist, noting "that the bohemian petit bourgeois is not a bit wittier than the solid citizen". Both represent the psychic and moral degeneration of men who have no normal relationship to the society in which they live. Goethe's Goetz von Belichingen, the defender of what is in decline, is as normal as Gorki's fighters for the future. But Anouilh's rebellious Antigone is as abnormal as Giono's "cosmic" hidebound peasant.

Such an abnormality in the artist's relationship to society is always the product of a decaying class society. (That accounts, for example, for the renewed interest in England in the lyrics of the seventeenth century.) This false attitude of the artist toward society fills him with hate and disgust for it and isolates him from the great social currents pregnant with the future. The isolation of the individual implies a personal psychic and moral degeneration. These artists vainly attempt a brief guest appearance in the progressive movements of their time but always end their adventure with embittered hostility (like Gide or Malraux). There follows a sterile opposition to society in general (not a revolutionary struggle against a particular society); it increases to an opposition to the idea of social order altogether and to any individual ties.

The stunting and consequent impoverishment of an inner life from which all social and especially all progressive inclinations (now adjudged unimportant) have been whittled away affect the inner structure of the intellectual life. Along with the social sense, the intellectual powers, understanding and reason, lose significance and yield to instinct; more and more the bowels dominate the head.

This process begins in literature with the substitution of pure psychologism for the representation of the real and complete, that is, social, human being and slowly transforms the individual into a shapeless bundle or uncontrolled torrent of free, undisciplined associations, finally eliminating all discipline, direction and stability from psychology and morality. Gide's nihilism springs from such soil, the morality of *Nourritures terrestres* : "To act *without making a judgment* whether your deed is good or bad; to love without being concerned whether you love good or evil." Thus love becomes mere eroticism; the erotic declines into mere sexuality; finally sexuality is reduced to mere phallicism. The ultimate in modern decadence we owe to D. H. Lawrence, who writes : "Anyone who calls my novel pornographic is a liar. It is not even a pornographic novel; it is a phallic novel. Sexuality is something that exists in the head, its reactions are cerebral, its process, mental. On the other hand, the phallic reality is warm and spontaneous."

These deformities arise with grim inevitability. The man of decadent bourgeois society who stunts himself spiritually and morally not only has to go on living and acting in his crippled state; in this inhuman self-deformity, he must even seek a psychological and moral "cosmic" justification for his condition. And he finds this justification, too, no longer basing his conception of the world on how the world is objectively constituted or how it affords a real object of mankind's revolutionary practical activity; instead he adapts his conception of the world to fit his own deformity and to provide an appropriate environment for his own crippled state. He undergoes the same adaptation, of course, inwardly. Friedrich Hebbel, who like Dostoyevsky stood on the threshold of bourgeois decadence but is still an important artist, yearned passionately for health and normality. He wrote about this inner state :

> For the eternal law which rules
> Seeks harmony even in destruction,
> And it unfolds in the same measure
> With which a creature, too, must fade and die.

All parts attune themselves to the one
On which Death has stolen,
And thus it can appear quite healthy
When Life has withdrawn from it.

This inner and outer correspondence, this "harmony" of ideology and expression, is in the first place simply formal. It is not grounded in the nature of objective reality but in certain peripheral, extravagant, parasitic and individualistic propensities and needs. Thus it can provide the basis only for a formal artistic unity that does not spring from the soul of the subject matter. What we today call formalism is the expression of this establishment of a peripheral point as the centre of objectivity, a subjectivist principle as the basis for objectivity.

In the second place this new structuring produces a complete overturning of values. Since Nietzsche's "revaluation of all values" this has become the general intellectual fashion. Not without social basis. The hypocrisy, superficiality and blatant injustice in all evaluations under capitalism understandably stimulate a rebellion among the clever. When not directed toward changing the fundamental weaknesses in capitalism, however, this rebellion is sterile; the social bases remain unimpugned even intellectually, while more or less superficial symptoms are vigorously attacked. Thus, as we have previously noted, the political career of these figures becomes understandable, even of those who dream up pseudo-socially and pseudo-politically a "third road" between the two great opposing camps of the era.

What is important in this overturning of values is that the paltry appears significant; the distorted, harmonious; the sick, normal; the dying and destructive, vital. And the intellectual and moral basis for art is thereby lost; the artistic insight into and the precise knowledge of the subject being depicted. Great artists like Goya or Daumier depicted the deformation of men under class society. They did so with artistry and harmony since the deformation appears for what it is and not as a standard for a supposedly new artistic synthesis.

To repeat, it is not the representation of the morbid even

when it provides the basic thematic material that is unhealthy and anti-artistic under decadence but this overturning of values alone.

It goes without saying that this deformity is not restricted to artistic practice; it extends to the entire conception of art and of the artist. The abnormal attitude toward life is canonized by decadent aesthetics. While the philosophy of art in healthier periods viewed the artist as a normal and even exemplary human being, today artistic creativity and artistic greatness are associated with disease in every respect. Schopenhauer first expressed this attitude by calling the genius a "monstrum per excessum", and this conception has continued till this day. Tolstoy protested against such a view in his essay on Maupassant, though certainly with some injustice to the latter. Essentially, however, his protest was aesthetically justified, for he attacked the modern artist's refusal to recognize any difference between the moral and immoral, the true and false. This neutrality, as we have seen with Gide, always turns into an aggressive rejection of such differences and culminates in the exaltation of crime and madness to be found in modern American fiction. Not without reason did Thomas Mann characterize modern decadence as sympathy with disease, decay and death.

The ultimate consequence is the inhumanity and anti-humanism of modern decadent art, sometimes explicit as in the theories of such writers as Ortega y Gasset, Lawrence and Malraux, and sometimes only implicit in artistic practice. The inhumanity is not accidental. Any sterile, impotent opposition to the dominant social system or, rather, to certain cultural symptoms of this system must inflate and distort the concrete problem of capitalist inhumanity into a hazy, universal, "cosmic" inhumanity. And since, as we have seen, there are strong elements of capitulation in every sterile opposition, this falsely universalized, desocialized inhumanity is itself transformed into a principle of art. Whether this development is accompanied by a tone of resignation, hate or enthusiasm is immaterial as far as the result is concerned.

Thus there arises in cultural life a revolt against the very nature of art often carried on with the most sophisticated, technical virtuosity. When we consider mankind's evolution through the ages, art is seen to be one of the most important vehicles for the production and reproduction and for the development and continuity of man's consciousness and sense of identity. Because great and healthy art fixes those moments of our development—otherwise transitory—that point ahead and enhance man's self-consciousness and are thus lasting and because perfected forms allow the re-experiencing of these moments, great and healthy works of art remain an ever-renewing treasure for mankind.

It is no accident that the decadent view of art, in love with decay, carps continually at healthy art, even at its outstanding productions. Between these two conceptions of art, as between the two class ideologies they represent, there is really irreconcilable enmity. Gide says: "Hold on only to what can't be found elsewhere than in you."

In such and similar tendencies (even when they may seem superficially in opposition) lies the reason why all sick art is ephemeral. At best it seeks its subject matter in what is secondary, peripheral, merely momentary and without future. The more honest the artist in his subjectivity, the more strongly the form represents a fixing of what has been doomed to destruction. And no one who follows the development of modern ideology carefully can miss the swift change and short life of its fads. What yesterday pretended to be smart avant-garde, today is dull *vieux jeu*. The older generation still distinctly remembers the impressive effect of the English fin de siècle religion of evil of Swinburne and his school, and, above all, of Oscar Wilde. Today's spokesman for decadence, T. S. Eliot, writes that these men understood nothing of evil or sin.

This swift transiency is not limited to the decadence of our times. Literary and art history is a mass graveyard where many artists of talent rest in deserved oblivion because they neither sought nor found any association to the problems of advancing humanity and did not set themselves on the right side in the vital struggle between health and decay.

Narrate or Describe?

A PRELIMINARY DISCUSSION OF NATURALISM AND FORMALISM

> To be radical is to grasp things by the roots. The
> root of humanity, however, is man himself.
> —*Marx*.

L E T ' S start *in medias res*! In two famous modern novels,
Zola's *Nana* and Tolstoy's *Anna Karenina*, horse races are
depicted. How do the two writers approach their task?

The description of the race is a brilliant example of Zola's
virtuosity. Every possible detail at a race is described precisely,
colourfully and with sensuous vitality. Zola provides a small
monograph on the modern turf; every phase from the saddling
of the horses to the finish is investigated meticulously. The
Parisian public is depicted in all the brilliance of a Second-
Empire fashion show. The manœuvring behind the scenes, too,
is presented in detail. The race ends in an upset, and Zola
describes not only the surprise outcome but also the betting
fraud responsible for it. However, for all its virtuosity the
description is mere filler in the novel. The events are loosely
related to the plot and could easily be eliminated; the sole
connection arises from the fact that one of Nana's many fleeting
lovers is ruined in the swindle.

Another link to the main plot is even more tenuous, hardly
an integral element in the action of the novel at all—and is
thus even more representative of Zola's creative method: the
victorious horse is named Nana. Surprisingly, Zola actually
underlines this tenuous chance association. The victory of the
coquette's namesake is symbolic of her own triumph in
Parisian high society and demi-monde.

In *Anna Karenina* the race represents the crisis in a great drama. Vronsky's fall means an overturning in Anna's life. Just before the race she had realized that she was pregnant and, after painful hesitation, had informed Vronsky of her condition. Her shock at Vronsky's fall impels the decisive conversation with her husband. The relationships of the protagonists enter a new critical phase because of the race. The race is thus no mere tableau but rather a series of intensely dramatic scenes which provide a turning point in the plot.

The absolute divergence of intentions in the scenes in the two novels is further reflected in the creative approaches. In Zola the race is *described* from the standpoint of an observer; in Tolstoy it is *narrated* from the standpoint of a participant.

Vronsky's ride is thoroughly integrated into the total action of the novel. Indeed, Tolstoy emphasizes that it is no mere incidental episode but an event of essential significance in Vronsky's life. The ambitious officer has been frustrated in advancing his military career by a set of circumstances, not the least of which is his relationship with Anna. For him a victory in the race in the presence of the court and of the aristocracy offers one of the few remaining opportunities for furthering his career. All the preparations for the race and all the events of the race itself are therefore integral to an important action, and they are recounted in all their dramatic significance. Vronsky's fall is the culmination of a phase in his personal drama. With it Tolstoy breaks off the description of the race. The fact that Vronsky's rival subsequently overtook him can be noted in passing later.

But the analysis of the epic concentration in this scene is not yet exhausted by any means. Tolstoy is not describing a "thing", a horse-race. He is recounting the vicissitudes of human beings. That is why the action is narrated twice, in true epic fashion, and not simply picturesquely described. In the first account, in which Vronsky was the central figure as a participant in the race, the author had to relate with precision and sophistication everything of significance in the preparations and in the race itself. But in the second account Anna and Karenin are the protagonists. Displaying his consummate epic artistry, Tolstoy does not introduce this account of the race immediately after the first. Instead he first recounts earlier events in Karenin's day and explores Karenin's attitude towards Anna. Thus he is able to present the race as the climax of the entire day. The race itself develops into an inner drama. Anna watches Vronsky alone, oblivious to all other events in the race and to the success and failure of all other participants. Karenin watches no one but Anna, following her reactions to what happens to Vronsky. This scene, almost devoid of dialogue, prepares for Anna's outburst on the way home, when she confesses her relations with Vronsky to Karenin.

Here the reader or writer educated in the "modern" school may protest: "Granted that these do represent two different fictional approaches, does not the very linking of the race with the destinies of the protagonists make the race itself a chance event, simply an opportunity for the dramatic catastrophe? And does not Zola's comprehensive, monographic, effective description provide an accurate picture of a social phenomenon?"

The key question is: what is meant by "chance" in fiction? Without chance all narration is dead and abstract. No writer can portray life if he eliminates the fortuitous. On the other hand, in his representation of life he must go beyond crass accident and elevate chance to the inevitable.

Is it thoroughness of description that renders something artistically "inevitable"? Or does inevitability arise out of the relationship of characters to objects and events, a dynamic interaction in which the characters act and suffer? Linking Vronsky's ambition to his participation in the race provides quite another mode of artistic necessity than is possible with Zola's exhaustive description. Objectively, attendance at or participation in a race is only an incident in life. Tolstoy integrated such an incident into a critical dramatic context as tightly as it was possible to do. The race is, on the one hand, merely an occasion for the explosion of a conflict, but, on the other hand, through its relationship to Vronsky's social ambitions—an important factor in the subsequent tragedy—it is far more than a mere incident.

There are examples in literature of more obvious contrasts

of the two approaches to inevitability and accident in the representation of fictional subject matter.

Compare the description of the theatre in the same Zola novel with that in Balzac's *Lost Illusions*. Superficially there is much similarity. The opening night, with which Zola's novel begins, decides Nana's career. The première in Balzac signifies a turning point in Lucien de Rubempré's life, his transition from unrecognized poet to successful but unscrupulous journalist.

In this chapter Zola, with characteristic and deliberate thoroughness, describes the theatre only from the point of view of the audience. Whatever happens in the auditorium, in the foyer or in the loges, as well as the appearance of the stage as seen from the hall, is described with impressive artistry. But Zola's obsession with monographic detail is not satisfied. He devotes another chapter to the description of the theatre as seen from the stage. With no less descriptive power he depicts the scene changes, the dressing-rooms, etc., both during the performance and the intermissions. And to complete this picture, he describes in yet a third chapter a rehearsal, again with equal conscientiousness and virtuosity.

This meticulous detail is lacking in Balzac. For him the theatre and the performance serve as the setting for an inner drama of his characters : Lucien's success, Coralie's theatrical career, the passionate love between Lucien and Coralie, Lucien's subsequent conflict with his former friends in the D'Arthèz circle and his current protector Lousteau, and the beginning of his campaign of revenge against Mme. de Bargeton, etc.

But what is represented in these battles and conflicts—all directly or indirectly related to the theatre? the state of the theatre under capitalism : the absolute dependence of the theatre upon capital and upon the press (itself dependent upon capital); the relationship of the theatre to literature and of journalism to literature; the capitalistic basis for the connection between the life of an actress and open and covert prostitution.

These social problems are posed by Zola, too. But they are simply described as social facts, as results, as *caput mortuum*

of a social process. Zola's theatre director continually repeats :
"Don't say theatre, say bordello." Balzac, however, depicts *how*
the theatre *becomes* prostituted under capitalism. The drama
of his protagonists is simultaneously the drama of the institution in which they work, of the things with which they live, of
the setting in which they fight their battles, of the objects
through which they express themselves and through which
their interrelationships are determined.

This is admittedly an extreme case. The objective factors in
a man's environment are not always and inevitably so intimately linked to his fate. They can provide instruments for his
activity and for his career and even, as in Balzac, turning
points in his fortunes. But they may also simply provide the
setting for his activity and for his career.

Does the contrast in approach we have just noted arise where
there is a simple literary representation of a setting?

In the introductory chapter to his novel *Old Mortality,*
Walter Scott depicts a marksmanship contest during some
national holiday in Scotland after the Restoration, organized
as part of a campaign to revive feudal institutions, as a review
of the military power of the Stuart supporters and as a provo-
cation for unmasking disaffection. The parade takes place on the
eve of the revolt of the oppressed Puritans. With extraordinary
epic artistry Walter Scott assembles on the parade ground all
the opposing elements about to explode in bloody conflict. In
a series of grotesque scenes during the military review, he
exposes the hopeless anachronism of the feudal institutions
and the stubborn resistance of the population to their revival.
In the subsequent contest he exposes the contradictions within
each of the two hostile parties; only the moderates on both
sides take part in the sport. In the inn we see the brutal out-
rages of the royal mercenaries and encounter Burley, later to
become the leader of the Puritan uprising, in all his gloomy
magnificence. In effect, in narrating the events of this military
review and describing the entire setting, Walter Scott introduces the factions and protagonists of a great historical drama.
In a single stroke he sets us in the midst of a decisive action.

The description of the agricultural fair and of the awarding of prizes to the farmers in Flaubert's *Madame Bovary* is among the most celebrated achievements of description in modern realism. But Flaubert presents only a "setting". For him the fair is merely background for the decisive love scene between Rudolf and Emma Bovary. The setting is incidental, merely "setting". Flaubert underscores its incidental character; by interweaving and counterposing official speeches with fragments of love dialogue, he offers an ironic juxtaposition of the public and private banality of the petty bourgeoisie, accomplishing this parallel with consistency and artistry.

But there remains an unresolved contradiction: this incidental setting, this accidental occasion for a love scene, is simultaneously an important event in the world of the novel; the minute description of this setting is absolutely essential to Flaubert's purpose, that is, to the comprehensive exposition of the social milieu. The ironic juxtaposition does not exhaust the significance of the description. The "setting" has an independent existence as an element in the representation of the environment. The characters, however, are nothing but observers of this setting. To the reader they seem undifferentiated, additional elements of the environment Flaubert is describing. They become dabs of colour in a painting which rises above a lifeless level only insofar as it is elevated to an ironic symbol of philistinism. The painting assumes an importance which does not arise out of the subjective importance of the events, to which it is scarcely related, but from the artifice in the formal stylization.

Flaubert achieves his symbolic content through irony and consequently on a considerable level of artistry and to some extent with genuine artistic means. But when, as in the case of Zola, the symbol is supposed to embody social monumentality and is supposed to imbue episodes otherwise meaningless, with great social significance, true art is abandoned. The metaphor is over-inflated in the attempt to encompass reality. An arbitrary detail, a chance similarity, a fortuitous attitude, an accidental meeting—all are supposed to provide direct expression of important social relationships. There are innumerable possible examples in Zola's work, like the comparison of

Nana with the golden fleece, which is supposed to symbolize her disastrous effect on the Paris of before 1870. Zola himself confessed to such intentions, declaring: "In my work there is a hypertrophy of real detail. From the springboard of exact observation it leaps to the stars. With a single beat of the wings, the truth is exalted to the symbol."

In Scott, Balzac or Tolstoy we experience events which are inherently significant because of the direct involvement of the characters in the events and because of the general social significance emerging in the unfolding of the characters' lives. We are the audience to events in which the characters take active part. We ourselves experience these events.

In Flaubert and Zola the characters are merely spectators, more or less interested in the events. As a result, the events themselves become only a tableau for the reader, or, at best, a series of tableaux. We are merely observers.

II

The opposition between experiencing and observing is not accidental. It arises out of divergent basic positions about life and about the major problems of society and not just out of divergent artistic methods of handling content or one specific aspect of content.

Only after making this assertion can we attempt a concrete investigation of our problem. As in other areas of life, in literature there are no "pure" phenomena. Engels once noted ironically that "pure" feudalism had existed only in the constitution of the ephemeral Kingdom of Jerusalem. Yet feudalism obviously was an historical reality and as such is a valid subject for scientific investigation. There are no writers who renounce description absolutely. Nor, on the other hand, can one claim that the outstanding representatives of realism after 1848, Flaubert and Zola, renounced narration absolutely. What is important here are philosophies of composition, not any illusory "pure" phenomenon of narration or description. What is important is knowing how and why description, originally one of the many modes of epic art (undoubtedly a subordinate mode), became the principal mode. In this development the character and function of description underwent a fundamental transformation from what it had been in the epic.

In his critique of Stendhal's *Charterhouse of Parma*, Balzac had emphasized the importance of description as a mode of modern fiction. In the novel of the eighteenth century (Le Sage, Voltaire, etc.) there had scarcely been any description, or at most it had played a minimal, scarcely even a subordinate, role. Only with romanticism did the situation change. Balzac pointed out that the literary direction he followed, of which he considered Walter Scott the founder, assigned great importance to description.

But after emphasizing the contrast with the "aridity" of the seventeenth and eighteenth centuries and associating himself with the modern method, he adduced a whole series of stylistic criteria for defining the new literary direction. According to Balzac, description was only one stylistic mode among several. He particularly emphasized the new significance of the dramatic element in fiction.

The new style developed out of the need to adapt fiction to provide an adequate representation of new social phenomena. The relationship of the individual to his class had become more complicated than it had been in the seventeenth and eighteenth centuries. Formerly a summary indication of the background, external appearance and personal habits of an individual (as in Le Sage) had sufficed for a clear and comprehensive social characterization. Individualization was accomplished almost exclusively through action, through the reactions of characters to events.

Balzac recognized that this method could no longer suffice. Rastignac is an adventurer of quite another sort to Gil Blas. The precise description of the filth, smells, meals and service in the Vauquier pension is essential to render Rastignac's particular kind of adventurism comprehensible and real. Similarly, Grandet's house and Gobseck's apartment must be described accurately and in precise detail in order to represent two contrasting usurers, differing as individuals and as social types.

But apart from the fact that the description of the environment is never "pure" description but is almost always transformed into action (as when old Grandet repairs his decayed staircase himself), description for Balzac provides nothing more than a base for the new, decisive element in the composition of the novel : the dramatic element. Balzac's extraordinarily multifaceted, complicated characterizations could not possibly emerge with such impressive dramatic effectiveness if the environmental conditions in their lives were not depicted in such breadth. In Flaubert and Zola description has an entirely different function.

Balzac, Stendhal, Dickens and Tolstoy depict a bourgeois society consolidating itself after severe crises, the complicated laws of development operating in its formation, and the tortuous transitions from the old society in decay to the new society in birth. They themselves actively experienced the crises in this development, though in different ways. Goethe, Stendahl and Tolstoy took part in the wars which were the midwives of the revolutions; Balzac was a participant in and victim of the feverish speculations of emerging French capitalism; Goethe and Stendhal served as government officials; and Tolstoy, as landowner and as participant in various social organizations (the census and famine commissions, for example) directly experienced important events of the transitional upheaval.

In their public activity as well as in their private lives, they followed the tradition of the writers, artists and scientists of the Renaissance and of the Enlightenment, men who participated variously and actively in the great social struggles of their times, men whose writing was the fruit of such rich, diverse activity. They were not "specialists" in the sense of the capitalist division of labour.

With Flaubert and Zola it was otherwise. They started their creative work after the June uprising in a firmly established bourgeois society. They did not participate actively in the life of this society; indeed they refused to do so. In this refusal lay the tragedy of the important generation of artists of the transitional period. This renunciation of social activity was above all a manifestation of their opposition, an expression of their hate, revulsion and contempt for the political and social order of their time. People who made peace with the order turned into soulless, lying apologists for capitalism. But Flaubert and Zola had too much integrity. For them the only solution to the tragic contradiction in their situation was to stand aloof as observers and critics of capitalist society. At the same time they became specialists in the craft of writing, writers in the sense of the capitalist division of labour. The book had become merchandise, the writer, a salesman of this merchandise—unless he had been born a coupon clipper. In Balzac we still see the gloomy magnificence of primary accumulation in the realm of culture. Goethe and Tolstoy can still exhibit the aristocratic disdain of those who do not live exclusively from writing. But Flaubert becomes a voluntary ascetic, and Zola is constrained by material pressures to be a writer in the sense of the capitalist division of labour.

New styles, new ways of representing reality, though always linked to old forms and styles, never arise from any immanent dialectic within artistic forms. Every new style is socially and historically determined and is the product of a social development. But to recognize the determining factors in the formation of artistic styles is not to assign equal artistic value or rank to these styles. Necessity can also be necessity for the artistically false, distorted and corrupt. The alternatives, experiencing and observing, correspond to what was socially determined for writers of two different periods of capitalism. Narration and description represent the principal modes of fiction appropriate to these periods.

To distinguish the two modes effectively, we can counterpose statements by Goethe and Zola regarding the relationship of observation to creation. "I have never," said Goethe, "contemplated nature with poetic purpose in mind. But my early landscape sketching and later investigations in natural science trained me to a constant, precise observation of nature. Little by little I became so well acquainted with nature in its smallest details that when I need something as a poet, I find it at hand and do not easily err against truth." Zola also expressed himself clearly about his method of approaching a subject: "A naturalistic novelist wants to write a novel about the world of the theatre. He starts out with this general idea *without possessing a single fact or character*. His first task will be to take notes on what he can learn about the world he wants to describe. He has known this actor, attended that performance. . . . Then he will speak with the people who are best informed about this material, he will collect opinions, anecdotes, character portraits. That is not all. He will then read documents. *Finally* he will visit the locale itself and spend *some days* in a theatre to become familiar with the minutest details; he will spend his evenings in the dressing room of an actress and will absorb the atmosphere as much as possible. And once this documentation is complete, the novel will write itself. The novelist must only arrange the facts logically. . . . *Interest is no longer concentrated on originality of plot; on the contrary, the more banal and general it is, the more typical it becomes.*" [Emphasis by G.L.]

These are two basically divergent styles. Two basically divergent approaches to reality.

III

Understanding the social necessity that has produced a given style is something quite different from evaluating the aesthetic results of the style. In aesthetics the precept does not apply "tout comprendre, c'est tout pardonner". Only vulgar sociology, which views its sole task as the discovery of so-called "social equivalents" for individual writers or styles, believes that with the identification of social origin every question is answered and resolved. (How it seeks to accomplish this is not in our province here.) In practice this method means reducing all art history to the level of the decadent bourgeoisie: Homer or Shakespeare are just as much "products" as Joyce or Dos Passos; the task of literary investigation consists only in discovering the "social equivalent" for Homer or Joyce. Marx put the question quite differently. After analysing the social origins of the Homeric epics, he declared: "But the difficulty is not in understanding that Greek art and epic are related to certain stages of social development. The difficulty is in understanding why they still provide us with artistic pleasure and still serve in certain measure as the norm and unattainable example."

Naturally Marx's observation applies equally in cases of negative aesthetic judgment. In neither case may aesthetic evaluation be mechanically separated from the question of historical origin. That the Homeric epics are true epics, while those of Camoens, Milton and Voltaire are not, is simultaneously a social, an historical *and* an aesthetic question. No "artistry" can exist independently of and in isolation from social, historical and subjective conditions which are unpropitious to a rich, comprehensive, many-sided and dynamic artistic reflection of objective reality. Social presuppositions and objective conditions adverse to artistic creation inevitably lead to a distortion in the fundamental forms of literary representation.

This fact is relevant to the problem in question.

In this regard Flaubert's criticism of his novel *L'education sentimentale* is illuminating. He wrote: "It is too true, and aesthetically speaking, it lacks the falsity of perspective. Because it was so well contrived, the plan disappeared. Every work of art must have a point, a climax, must form a pyramid, or else light must fall on some point of the sphere. But in life nothing like this exists. However, art is not nature. Never mind, I believe no one yet has gone further in honesty."

Like all Flaubert's declarations, this confession shows his unsparing truthfulness. Flaubert characterizes the composition of his novel correctly. He is right, too, in emphasizing the artistic necessity of the climax. But is he also right in saying there is "too much truth" in his novel? Do "climaxes" exist in art alone? Of course not. Flaubert's frank confession is important not only as a personal criticism of his significant novel but even more as a disclosure of his basically erroneous conception of reality, of the objective existence of society, and of the relationship between nature and art. His belief that "climaxes" exist only in art and that they are therefore created by artists at will is simply subjective prejudice. It is a prejudice arising from a superficial observation of the characteristics of bourgeois life and of the forms life takes in bourgeois society, an observation ignoring the motive forces of social development and their unremitting influence on even the superficial phenomena of life. In such an abstract view life appears as a constant, even-tenored stream or as a monotonous plain sprawling without contours. The monotony, admittedly, is interrupted at times by "sudden" catastrophes.

In reality, however—and naturally in capitalist reality as well—"sudden" catastrophes are actually long in preparation. They do not stand in exclusive contrast to an apparently peaceful flow but are the outcome of a complicated, uneven evolution. And this evolution shapes the supposedly unruffled surface of Flaubert's sphere. The artist must illuminate the important stages in this process. Flaubert is under a misconception in imagining that this process does not occur independently of him. The shaping of society conforms to laws of historical development and is determined by the action of social forces. In objective reality the false, subjective and abstract contrast between the "normal" and "abnormal" vanishes. Marx, for example, considered the economic crisis as the "most normal" characteristic of capitalist economy. "The autonomy assumed by interrelated and complementary factors," he wrote, "is violently destroyed. Hence the crisis reveals the unity of factors which had become independent of each other."

Reality is viewed quite differently by apologetic bourgeois science of the second half of the nineteenth century. A crisis appears as a "catastrophe" which "suddenly" interrupts the "normal" flow of the economy. By analogy, every revolution is considered catastrophic and abnormal.

Neither as individuals nor as writers were Flaubert and Zola defenders of capitalism, but they were children of their time and were profoundly influenced ideologically by the attitudes of their time—especially Zola, on whose works the shallow prejudices of bourgeois sociology had a decisive impact. That is why life for Zola develops almost without movement or change so long as it is, in his conception, socially normal. According to him, men's actions are normal products of their social environment. There are, however, other diverse and heterogeneous forces at work, like heredity, which affect men's thinking and emotions with a fatalistic inevitability and provoke catastrophes interrupting the normal course of life. Thus the congenital drunkenness of Etienne Lantier in *Germinal* causes explosions and calamities with no organic connection to Etienne's character; nor does Zola seek any such connection. A similar case is provided in the calamity caused by Saccard's son in *Gold*. In each instance the normal, undifferentiated action of the environment is contrasted with the sudden, unrelated catastrophe caused by an hereditary factor.

Here obviously there is no precise and profound reflection of objective reality but a trivial distortion of its principles, a distortion resulting from the influence of apologetic prejudices on the ideology of the writers of this period. An accurate appreciation of the motive forces of the social process and a precise, impartial, profound and comprehensive reflection of their effects on life are always manifested in movement which exposes the organic unity of the normal and the exceptional.

This fact of the social process is also a fact of the life of the individual. Where and how is this truth revealed? It is clear not only in science and in politics founded on a scientific basis but also in man's everyday practical common sense that truth is revealed only in practice, in deeds and actions. Men's words, subjective reactions and thoughts are shown to be true or false, genuine or deceptive, significant or fatuous, in practice—as they succeed or fail in deeds and action. Character, too, can be revealed concretely only through action. Who is brave? Who is good? Such questions can be answered solely in action.

And only in activity do men become interesting to each other; only in action have they significance for literature. The sole test for confirming character-traits (or exposing their absence) is action, deeds—practice. Primitive poetry—whether fairy tales, ballads or legends or the spontaneous anecdote which developed later—is always based on the primacy of action. This poetry has continued to have a profound meaning because it depicts the success or failure of human purpose in the test of practice. It remains vital and interesting despite any fantastic, naïve and outlandish presupposition because it focuses on this eternal, fundamental truth. And the interest in individual deeds and actions which are arranged within an organic framework is due solely to the fact that in diverse and variegated adventures the same typical character trait is constantly maintained. With an Odysseus or a Gil Blas, there is the same poetic basis for the eternal freshness of the adventures. Of course, the decisive element is the man himself and the revelation of essential human traits. We are interested in how Odysseus or Gil Blas, Moll Flanders or Don Quixote react to the decisive events of their lives, how they stand up to danger, overcome obstacles, how the character traits which make them interesting and important to us unfold in action in ever-greater breadth and depth.

Without the revelation of important traits and without an interaction of the characters with world events, objects, the forces of nature and social institutions, even the most extraordinary adventures would be empty and meaningless. Yet one must not overlook the fact that even when not revealing significant and typical human qualities, all action still offers the abstract pattern, no matter how distorted and tenuous, for exploring human practice. That is why the schematic narration of adventures of shadowy characters rouses a certain passing interest (tales of knights in the past and detective novels today). The effectiveness of these romances testifies to one of the most profound and impelling attractions of literature : man's interest in the richness and colour, the constant change and variety of human experience. When the artistic literature of a period does not provide actions in which typical characters with a richly developed inner life are tested in practice, the public seeks abstract, schematic substitutes.

Such was the case with literature in the second half of the nineteenth century. Literature based on observation and description excludes this interaction to an ever-increasing extent. There has probably never been a time like the present when so much empty literature of pure adventure has flourished alongside the official, serious literature. Nor can there be any illusion that this literature is read simply by the "uneducated" while the "élite" stick to the significant artistic literature. Rather the opposite is the case. Modern classics are read partly out of a sense of duty and partly out of an interest in the content—to the extent that they deal with the problems of the time even hesitantly and with distortion. For recreation and pleasure, however, the public turns to detective stories.

While working on *Madame Bovary*, Flaubert complained repeatedly that his novel failed to provide entertainment. We encounter similar complaints from many outstanding modern writers; they note that the great novels of the past combined the representation of significant human beings with entertainment and suspense, for which modern art has substituted monotony and tedium. This development is not entirely the result of the lack of talent, for there is a considerable number of uncommonly gifted writers today. Monotony and tedium result from the writers' creative approach and from their general philosophical views of the world.

Zola harshly condemned Stendhal's and Balzac's introduction of the exceptional into their works as "unnatural", complaining, for example, of the portrayal of love in *Scarlet and Black* : "Thus the truth we encounter every day is abandoned, and the psychologist Stendahl carries us into the realm of the extraordinary as much as the story-teller Alexandre Dumas. As far as exact truth is concerned, Julien provides me with as many surprises as d'Artagnan."

In his essay on the literary activity of the Goncourts, Paul Bourget formulates the new principle of composition very accurately : "Drama, as its etymology implies, is action, and action is never a good expression of manners. What characterizes a man is not what he does in a moment of acute and impassioned crisis but his daily habits, which do not mark a crisis but a state of being." In the light of this observation, Flaubert's criticism of his own technique of composition becomes comprehensible. Flaubert confused life with the everyday existence of the ordinary bourgeois. Naturally, such a preconception has social roots, but it does not thereby cease to be a preconception, a subjective distortion which inhibits an adequate and comprehensive artistic reflection of reality. Flaubert struggled throughout his life to escape the vicious circle of socially determined preconceptions. Because he did not battle against the preconceptions themselves and even accepted them as incontestable objective facts, his battle was tragic and hopeless. He complained unceasingly and passionately of the boredom, pettiness and repugnance of the bourgeois subject-matter he was forced to depict. During his work on each bourgeois novel he swore never again to occupy himself with such filth. The only escape he could find was in a flight to the exotic. His preconceptions barred him from discovering the inner poetry of life.

The inner poetry of life is the poetry of men in struggle, the poetry of the turbulent, active interaction of men. Without this inner poetry to intensify and maintain its vitality, no real epic is possible and no epic composition can be elaborated that will rouse and hold people's interest. Epic art—and, of course, the art of the novel—consists in discovering the significant and vital aspects of social practice. From epic poetry men expect a clearer, sharper mirror of themselves and of their social activity. The art of the epic poet consists in a proper distribution of emphasis and in a just accentuation of what is essential. A work becomes impressive and universal according to how much it presents the essential element—man and his social practice—not as an artificial product of the artist's virtuosity but as something that emerges and grows naturally, as something not invented, but simply discovered.

Thus the German novelist and dramatist Otto Ludwig, whose own literary practice is very dubious indeed, arrived at a very correct insight from studying Walter Scott and Dickens. He declared : ". . . the characters seem the decisive elements, and the wheel of events serves only to impel the characters into a game in which they are naturally involved; hence they are not included to help turn the wheel. The fact is that the author makes interesting what requires interest and simply gives free play to that which is interesting in itself. . . . The characters are what is important. And actually an event, no matter how amazing it may be, will in the long run not have as much effect on us as men who have won our affection through our association with them."

Description, as we have discussed it, becomes the dominant mode in composition in a period in which, for social reasons, the sense of what is primary in epic construction has been lost. Description is the writer's substitute for the epic significance that has been lost.

But in the genesis of new ideological forms, an interaction always takes place. The predominance of description is not only a result but also and simultaneously a cause, the cause of a further divorce of literature from epic significance. The domination of capitalist prose over the inner poetry of human experience, the continuous dehumanization of social life, the general debasement of humanity—all these are objective facts of the development of capitalism. The descriptive method is the inevitable product of this development. Once established this method is taken up by leading writers dedicated in their own way, and then it in turn affects the literary representation of reality. The poetic level of life decays—and literature intensifies the decay.

IV

Narration establishes proportions, description merely levels.

Goethe demands that epic poetry treat all events as past in contrast to the drama, which contemporizes all action. Thus Goethe perceptively defines the stylistic distinction between epic and drama. Drama in principle stands on a much higher level of abstraction than the epic. A drama is concentrated about a single conflict; whatever does not pertain directly or indirectly to the conflict must be excluded as a disturbing, superfluous element. The opulence of a dramatist like Shakespeare results from a varied and rich conception of the conflict itself. In the exclusion of all details not pertaining to the conflict, there is no fundamental difference between Shakespeare and the Greeks.

Goethe insisted that the action of the epic be set in the past because he understood that only thus could there be an effective poetic selection of the essential elements within the varied richness of life and only thus could there be a representation of the essential elements that would promote the illusion of life in its full breadth. The criteria for determining whether a detail is pertinent, whether it is essential, must be more generous in thè epic than in the drama and must encompass more complex and indirect relationships. Within this broader and fuller conception of the essential, however, selection is still as rigorous as for the drama. What does not pertain to the subject here too is ballast, no less an impediment than in the drama.

The involved complexity of patterns of life is clarified only at the conclusion. Only in activity are particular personal qualities in the totality of a character revealed as important and decisive. Only in practical activity, only in the complicated intercatenation of varied acts and passions is it possible to determine what objects, what institutions, etc., significantly influence men's lives and how and when this influence is effected. Only at the conclusion can these questions be resolved and reviewed. Life itself sorts out the essential elements in the subjective as well as in the objective world. The epic poet who narrates a single life or an assemblage of lives retrospectively makes the essential aspects selected by life clear and understandable. But the observer, necessarily a contemporary to what he observes, loses himself in a whirlwind of details of apparently equal significance, for life has not done its selecting through the test of practice. The use of the past tense in the epic is thus a basic technique prescribed by reality for achieving artistic order and organization.

Of course, the reader does not know the conclusion in advance. He possesses an abundance of details of which he cannot always and immediately determine the importance. Certain expectations are awakened which the later course of the narrative will confirm or refute. But the reader is involved in a rich web of variegated motivations; the author in his omniscience knows the special significance of each petty detail for the final solution and for the final revelation of character since he introduces only details that contribute to his goals. The reader takes confidence from the author's omniscience and feels at home in the fictional world. If he cannot foretell the events, he feels confident about the direction which the events will take because of their inner logic and because of the inner necessity in the characters. Perhaps he does not know everything about the future progress of the action and the future evolution of the characters, but in general he knows more than the characters themselves.

Indeed, with the gradual exposition of their significance, the details are seen in a new light. When, for example, in his short story "After the Ball", Tolstoy describes with subtle touches the self-sacrifice of the father of the hero's fiancée for his daughter, the reader accepts the information without grasping its significance. Only after the account of the running of the gauntlet, where the same tender father acts as the brutal commander at an execution, is the suspense resolved. Tolstoy demonstrates his epic artistry in maintaining the unity within this suspense by avoiding depicting the old officer as a dehumanized "product" of czarism and by showing instead how the czarist régime transforms people, decent and self-sacrificing in their private lives, into passive and even eager instruments of its brutality. It is clear that all the nuances of the events at the ball could be revealed only in retrospect from the gauntlet scene. The "contemporary" observer, who could not view the ball from this perspective or retrospectively at all, would have had to see and describe other, insignificant and superficial details.

The necessary distance in narration, which permits the selection of the essential after the action, is not lost when true epic poets use the first-person point of view, where a character is himself the narrator, as in this Tolstoy short story. Even in a novel in diary form like Goethe's *Werther*, individual passages are set back in time, if only a short period of time, to provide the perspective necessary for the selection of details essential for revealing the effect of events and people upon Werther.

Only in this perspective can characters assume definite outline without at the same time losing their capacity to change. As a matter of fact, with this approach their transformation can proceed as an enrichment, as a fulfilment of the outline with ever more intense vitality. Tension in the novel results from this evolution; it is a suspense regarding the success or failure of characters with whom we have become acquainted.

That is why in masterworks of epic art the conclusion can be anticipated from the very beginning. In the opening lines of the Homeric epics the content and conclusion are even summarized.

How then does suspense arise? Indubitably it does not arise out of an aesthetic interest in how the *poet* goes about arriving at his goal. It arises rather from the natural human curiosity regarding the capacities *Odysseus* will yet disclose and the obstacles he has still to overcome to achieve his goal. In the Tolstoy story we know from the outset that the love of the hero-narrator will not result in marriage. The suspense therefore is not in what will happen to his love but in how the hero developed his present maturity and sense of irony. The tension in genuine epic always develops out of concern for the destinies of the characters.

Description contemporizes everything. Narration recounts the past. One describes what one sees, and the spatial "present" confers a temporal "present" on men and objects. But it is an illusory present, not the present of immediate action of the drama. The best modern narrative has been able to infuse the dramatic element into the novel by transferring events into the past. But the contemporaneity of the observer making a description is the antithesis of the contemporaneity of the drama. Static situations are described, states or attitudes of mind of human beings or conditions of things—still lives.

Representation declines into genre, and the natural principle of epic selection is lost. One state of mind at any moment and of itself without relation to men's activity is as important or as irrelevant as another. And this equivalence is even more blatant when it comes to objects. In a narrative it is reasonable to mention only those aspects of a thing which are important to its function in a specific action. In and of itself everything has innumerable qualities. When a writer attempts as an observer and describer to achieve a comprehensive description, he must either reject any principle of selection, undertake an inexhaustible labour of Sisyphus or simply emphasize the picturesque and superficial aspects best adapted to description.

In any case, the loss of the narrative interrelationship between objects and their function in concrete human experiences means a loss of artistic significance. Objects can then acquire significance only through direct association with some abstract concept which the author considers essential to his view of the world. But an object does not thereby achieve poetic significance; significance is assigned to it. The object is made a symbol. As this process demonstrates, the aesthetic approach of naturalism inevitably engenders formalist methods of fiction.

But the loss of inner significance and hence of any epic order and hierarchy among objects and events does not stop at mere levelling and transformation of an imitation of life into a still life. Bringing characters to life and representing objects on the basis of immediate, empirical observation is a process with its own logic and its own mode of accentuation. Something much worse than mere levelling results—a reversed order of significance, a consequence implicit in the descriptive method since both the important and the unimportant are described with equal attention. For many writers this process leads to genre description deprived of all human significance.

With devastating irony Friedrich Hebbel dissected a typical exponent of this genre-like description, Adalbert Stifter, who, thanks to Nietzsche, has been elevated to a classic of German reaction. Hebbel demonstrates how the pressing problems of mankind vanish in Stifter; all basic aspects of life are smothered under a blanket of delicately delineated minutiae. "Because moss shows up more impressively if the painter ignores the tree, and the tree stands out better if the forest disappears, there is a general cry of exultation, and artists whose powers scarcely suffice to render the pettiest aspects of nature and who instinctively do not attempt loftier tasks are exalted above others who do not depict the dance of the gnats because it is scarcely visible next to the dance of the planets. The 'peripheral' begins to bloom everywhere: the mud on

Napoleon's boot at the moment of the hero's abdication is as
painstakingly portrayed as the spiritual conflict in his face. . . .
In short, the comma puts on coat-tails and in its lofty complacency smiles haughtily at the sentence to which it owes its
existence."

Hebbel astutely defines the other basic danger latent in
description : the danger of details becoming important in themselves. With the loss of the art of narration, details cease to be
transmitters of concrete aspects of the action and attain
significance independent of the action and of the lives of the
characters. Any artistic relationship to the composition as a
whole is lost. The false contemporaneity in description brings
a disintegration of the composition into disconnected and autonomous details. Nietzsche, observing with an acute eye
symptoms of decadence in art and life, defined the stylistic
impact of this process on the individual sentence. "The individual word," he declared, "becomes sovereign and leaps out
of the sentence, the sentence bursts its bounds to obscure the
sense of the page; the page acquires life at the expense of the
whole—the whole is no longer a whole. But this is the picture
of every decadent style . . . the vitality, vibrance and exuber-
ance of life withdraws into the minute image; whatever is left
over lacks life. . . . The whole is no longer alive; it is a synthetic, contrived artifact."

The autonomy of the details has varied effects, all
deleterious, on the representation of men's lives. On the one
hand, writers strive to describe details as completely, plasticly
and picturesquely as possible; in this attempt they achieve an
extraordinary artistic competence. But the description of things
no longer has anything to do with the lives of characters. Not
only are things described out of any context with the lives of
the characters, attaining an independent significance that is
not their due within the totality of the novel, but the very
manner in which they are described sets them in an entirely
different sphere from that in which the characters move. The
more naturalistic writers become, the more they seek to portray
only common characters of the everyday world and to provide
them only with thoughts, emotions and speech of the everyday

world—the harsher the disharmony. The dialogue sinks into the arid, flat prose of everyday bourgeois life : the description declines into the strained artificiality of a synthetic art. The characters have no connection at all with the objects described.

But if the relationship is established on the basis of description, the situation becomes even worse. Then the author describes everything from the point of view of the psychology of his characters. Not only is a consequent representation of reality impossible in such an approach (except in an extremely subjective first-person novel), but, in addition, there is no possibility of artistic composition. The author's point of view jumps from here to there, and the novel reels from one perspective to another. The author loses the comprehensive vision and omniscience of the old epic narrators. He sinks consciously to the level of his characters and sometimes knows only as much about situations as they do. The false contemporaneity of description transforms the novel into a kaleidoscopic chaos.

Thus every epic relationship disappears in the descriptive style. Lifeless, fetishized objects are whisked about in an amorphous atmosphere. Epic relationships are not simply successive; and when in description individual pictures or sketches are arranged chronologically, epic relationship is not thereby established. In genuine narration an author can render a chronological series of events lifelike and meaningful only by utilizing approaches of considerable complexity. In narration the writer must move with the greatest deftness between past and present so that the reader may grasp the real causality of the epic events. And only the experience of this causality can communicate the sense of a real chronological, concrete, historical sequence, as in the double narration of the race in Tolstoy's *Anna Karenina*. Similarly, with what art does Tolstoy in *Resurrection* expose bit by bit the background to the relationship between Nechlyudov and Maslova, introducing an additional detail whenever the illumination of a moment in the past is needed to advance the action another step !

Description debases characters to the level of inanimate objects; as a result a basic principle of epic composition is abandoned. The writer using the descriptive method starts out with *things*. (We have seen how Zola conceives the writer's confrontation of a subject. The actual core of his novels is a complex of facts: money, the mine, etc.) The consequence of this approach is that the varied manifestations of a complex of objects determine the organization of the novel, as in *Nana*, where the theatre is described in one chapter from the viewpoint of the audience and in another from backstage. The characters' lives, the careers of the protagonists, merely constitute a loose thread for attaching and grouping a series of pictures of objects, pictures which are ends in themselves.

Matching this spurious objectivity is an equally spurious subjectivity. For from the standpoint of epic interrelationships not much is gained when a simple succession of events provides the motive principle of the composition or when a novel is based on the lyrical, self-orientated subjectivity of an isolated individual; a succession of subjective impressions no more suffices to establish an epic interrelationship than a succession of fetishized objects, even when these are inflated into symbols. From an artistic point of view, the individual pictures in both cases are as isolated and unrelated to each other as pictures in a museum.

Without the interaction of struggle among people, without testing in action, everything in composition becomes arbitrary and incidental. No psychology, no matter how refined, and no sociology, no matter how pseudo-scientific, can establish epic relationships within this chaos.

The levelling inherent in the descriptive method makes everything episodic. Many modern writers look contemptuously at the old-fashioned, complicated methods by which the old novelists set their plots into motion and elaborated an epic composition with all its involved interaction and conflict. Thus Sinclair Lewis contrasts Dickens' method of composition with Dos Passos' to the latter's advantage: "And the classical method—oh yes, was painstakingly spun out. Through an ill-fated coincidence Mr. Jones and Mr. Smith are sent out in the same coach so that something pathetic and entertaining may occur. In *Manhattan Transfer* people do not run into each other on the road but meet in the most natural fashion." "The most natural fashion" implies that the characters either fall into no relationships at all or at best into transient and superficial relationships, that they appear suddenly and just as suddenly disappear, and that their personal lives—since we scarcely know them—do not interest us in the least, and that they take no active part in a plot but merely promenade with varying attitudes through the externalized objective world described in the novel. That is certainly "natural" enough. The question is: what is the result for the art of narration?

Dos Passos is no common talent and Sinclair Lewis is an outstanding writer. Thus what Sinclair Lewis says in the same essay about Dickens' and Dos Passos' characterization is significant: "Of course Dos Passos created no such enduring characters as Pickwick, Micawber, Oliver, Nancy, David and his aunt, Nicholas, Smike, and at least forty others, and he will never succeed in doing so." An invaluable admission and quite honest. But if Sinclair Lewis is right, and undoubtedly he is, what then is the artistic value of the "most natural fashion" of relating characters to the action?

V

But what about the intensive existence of objects? The poetry of things? The poetic truth of description? These are the objections of the admirers of the naturalistic method.

In reply one must return to the basic principles of epic art. How are things rendered poetic in epic poetry? Is it true that a description accomplished with virtuosity and perfection of technical detail of a setting like a theatre, a market or a stock exchange will really transmit the poetry in the theatre or the stockmarket? It is certainly doubtful. Boxes and orchestra, stage and parterre, backstage and dressing-room are in themselves inanimate, absolutely unpoetic and void of interest. And they remain so even when thronged with characters in whose lives we have been involved. Only when a theatre or a stock exchange provide the arena for human ambitions, a stage or a battlefield for men's struggles with each other, do they become poetic. And only when they furnish the indispensable vehicle for transmitting human relationships do they acquire poetic value or become poetic in themselves.

A "poetry of things" independent of people and of people's lives does not exist in literature. It is more than questionable whether totality of description, so highly praised, and accuracy of technical detail even result in an effective representation of the objects being described. Anything which plays a meaningful role in the activity of a man about whom we are concerned becomes poetically significant (given a certain literary competence) precisely because of its relationship to the character's activity. One has only to recall the profound poetic effect of the tools rescued from the shipwreck in *Robinson Crusoe*.

On the other hand, consider any description at all in Zola. Take, for example, backstage in *Nana*. "A painted curtain was lowered, the set for the third act : the grotto on Mt. Aetna. Stagehands planted poles in slots in the floor, others fetched the flats, pierced them and tied them with strong rope to the poles. In the background a lightman set a spot with flames behind red panes to simulate the blaze of Vulcan's forge. The entire stage was a mad rush, a hustle and bustle in which, however, the tiniest movement was purposeful and calculated. In the midst of this hurly-burly the prompter strolled with tiny steps, stretching his legs."

What purpose does such a description serve? Anyone ignorant of the theatre obtains no real insight; for the sophisticated such a description presents nothing new. Artistically it is superfluous. And this striving after maximum objective "accuracy" harbours a serious danger for the novel. One does not need to understand anything about horses to appreciate the drama in Vronsky's race. But the naturalists aspire to ever greater technical "precision" in terminology; in increasing measure they employ the jargon of the field with which they are dealing. Thus just as he speaks professionally of "flats", Zola would, whenever possible, describe a studio in the terms of the painter and a metal shop in the terms of the metalworker. What results is a literature for specialists, for literateurs who have a connoisseur's appreciation of the painstaking assimilation of such technical knowledge and jargon. The Goncourts expressed this tendency most clearly and paradoxically, writing: ". . . every artistic production comes to grief when only artists can appreciate its beauty. . . . This is one of the greatest stupidities ever expressed. It is d'Alembert's." To combat the profound truths of the Enlightenment, the forerunners of naturalism embraced without reservation the theory of art for art's sake.

Objects come to life poetically only to the extent they are related to men's life, that is why the real epic poet does not describe objects but exposes their function in the mesh of human destinies, introducing things only as they play a part in the destinies, actions and passions of men. Lessing understood this principle of poetic composition. "I find that Homer depicts nothing but action," he wrote, "that he depicts all individual objects and people only through their participation in action". In the *Laocoon* Lessing provides an example of this observation so striking that it is worth quoting in entirety.

He is discussing the description of the two sceptres, Agamemnon's and Achilles': ". . . if, I say, we needed a more complete, a more precise image of this important sceptre, what would Homer do? Would he picture the wood and the carved head in addition to the gold nails? Yes, if the description were to serve later as an heraldic emblem[1] that someone might subsequently reproduce in every detail. And yet I am certain that many modern poets would give a description of such an heraldic emblem in the sincere conviction that they had achieved a true picture if a painter would be able to reproduce it. What does Homer care about how much he leaves for the painter to do? Instead of a detailed picture he gives us the history of the sceptre. First its carving by Vulcan, then how it shines in Jupiter's hands; now as a symbol of Mercury's dignity, then as the staff of command of the warlike Pelops, next as the shepherd's crook of the peaceful Atreus. . . . When Achilles swears by his sceptre to avenge himself for the contempt shown him by Agamemnon, Homer relates the history

[1] Here, in effect, Lessing is criticizing the "precision" of the Goncourts and of Zola.—*G.L.*

of this sceptre. We see it green on the hill, the axe sheers it from the branch, strips it of leaves and bark and shapes it to serve the people's judge as symbol of his divine office. . . . It did not seem important to Homer to represent two staffs of different materials and appearance in order to give a convincing picture of the varied powers of which these staffs had been the symbols. This one was a work of Vulcan. The other had been cut by an unknown hand in the mountains. The former was the ancient possession of a noble house; the latter was destined to fill the first and best fist that grasped it; the former's authority extended from the hand that wielded it over many islands and over all Argos; the latter was borne by a Greek king to whom had been entrusted, among other things, the guardianship of the laws. In them was embodied the disparity between Agamemnon and Achilles, a disparity which Achilles himself had to grant for all his blind rage."

Here we have a precise exposition of what really brings objects to life in epic poetry and makes them truly poetic. And when we think of the examples we have cited from Scott, Balzac and Tolstoy, we recognize that these writers also—*mutatis mutandis*—followed the principle Lessing discovered in Homer. We say *mutatis mutandis* having already noted that greater complexity in social relations necessitates the introduction of new methods.

It is quite otherwise when description is the dominant technique, and writers attempt a vain competition with the visual arts. When men are portrayed through the descriptive method, they become mere still lives. Only painting has the capacity for making a man's physical qualities the direct expression of his most profound character qualities. And it is no accident that at the time descriptive naturalism in literature was degrading human beings to components of still lives, painting was losing its capacity for intensified perceptual expression. Cézanne's portraits are mere still lives compared to Titian's or Rembrandt's with their sense of individual and spiritual totality; even as the characters of the Goncourts or of Zola are still lives compared to those of Balzac or Tolstoy.

A character's physical appearance possesses poetic vitality

only when a factor in his rapport with other men, only in its effect on other men. This fact, too, Lessing recognized and analysed in Homer's depiction of Helen's beauty. In dealing with this problem, the classics of realism again fulfilled the requirements of epic art. Tolstoy portrayed Anna Karenina's beauty exclusively as it influenced the action, through the tragedies it caused in the lives of other people and in her own life.

Description provides no true poetry of things but transforms people into conditions, into components of still lives. In description men's qualities exist side by side and are so represented; they do not interpenetrate or reciprocally effect each other so as to reveal the vital unity of personality within varied manifestations and amidst contradictory actions. Corresponding to the false breadth assigned the external world is a schematic narrowness in characterization. A character appears as a finished "product" perhaps composed of varied social and natural elements. The profound social truth emerging from the interaction of social factors with psychological and physiological qualities is lost. Taine and Zola admire the representation of sexual passion in Balzac's Hulot, but they see only a pathological diagnosis of "monomania". They do not appreciate at all the profound analysis of the connection between Hulot's particular kind of sexuality and his career as a Napoleonic general, a connection Balzac emphasizes through the contrast with Crevel, the typical representative of the July monarchy.

Description based on *ad hoc* observation must perforce be superficial. Among naturalist writers, Zola is certainly the one who worked most conscientiously and investigated his subject matter most thoroughly. Yet many of his characterizations are superficial and even faulty in essential respects. We need examine only one single example, one analysed by Lafargue. Zola diagnoses the alcoholism of the bricklayer Coupeau as the effect of his being unemployed, but Lafargue demonstrates that alcoholism is endemic to several categories of French workers, including construction workers, and shows that it is to be explained by the fact that they work only intermittently and spend their free time in the taverns. Lafargue also shows how Zola in *Gold* explains the contrast between Gundermann and Saccard as the difference between a Jew and a Christian, whereas the conflict Zola is trying to represent is actually between old-style capitalism and the newer investment capitalism.

The descriptive method lacks humanity. Its transformation of men into still lives is only the artistic manifestation of its inhumanity. Its inhumanity is more decisively exposed in the ideological and aesthetic intentions of its principal exponents. In her biography of her father, Zola's daughter quotes his comments about his novel *Germinal* : "Zola accepts Lemaître's description, 'a pessimistic epic of the animal in man,' on condition that one defines the term 'animal'; 'in your opinion the mind is what makes people what they are,' he wrote to the critic, 'I find that the other organs also play an important role' ".

We know that Zola's emphasis on man's bestiality was in protest against the bestiality of capitalism, a bestiality which he did not understand. But his irrational protest became transformed into an obsession with the bestial, with the animal-like.

The method of observation and description developed as part of an attempt to make literature scientific, to transform it into an applied natural science, into sociology. But investigation of social phenomena through observation and their representation in description bring such paltry and schematic results that these modes of composition easily slip into their polar opposite—complete subjectivism. Such is the legacy the various naturalistic and formalistic movements of the imperialist period inherited from the founder of naturalism.

VI

Compositional principles of a poetic work are a manifestation of an author's view of life.

Let us take as simple an example as possible. In the centre of the action of most of his novels, like *Waverley* or *Old*

Mortality, Walter Scott places a character of moderate importance who has not taken a clear stand on the great political questions at issue. What does Scott achieve by this device? The indecisive hero stands between both camps—in *Waverley* between the Scots rebelling in favour of the Stuarts and the English government, in *Old Mortality* between the Puritan revolutionaries and the supporters of the Stuart restoration. Thus the hero can become involved alternately with the leaders of each of the opposing parties, and in this interaction these leaders can be portrayed not merely as social and historical forces but as men in human relationships. If Walter Scott had set one of these decisive personalities in the centre of his narrative, he would not have been able to bring him into adequate personal interaction with his opponents. The novel would have been a mere stage for a description of important historical events and not a moving human drama in which we get to know the typical agents of a great historical conflict as human beings.

In his method of composition Walter Scott exhibits his mastery of epic narration. This achievement is not, however, purely a matter of artistry. Walter Scott himself assumes a "centre" position on issues of English history. He is as much against radical Puritanism, especially its plebeian wing, as he is against the Catholic reaction of the Stuarts. The artistry in his composition is thus a reflection of his own political position, a formal expression of his own ideology. The hero's vacillation is not only an effective device within the general composition for a dynamic and personalized depiction of the two parties but also simultaneously an expression of Walter Scott's own ideology. Scott further demonstrates his artistry in convincingly portraying the energetic exponents of the political extremes as superior human beings despite his personal ideological preference for his own hero.

This example is effective because of its simplicity. In Scott there is always an uncomplicated and direct interrelationship between ideology and composition. In the other great realists this connection is generally more indirect and complicated. The intermediate position of the hero so suitable for the composition of a novel provides a formal and compositional principle which can take varied forms in literary practice. The "centre" figure need not represent an "average man" but is rather the product of a particular social and personal environment. The problem is to find a central figure in whose life all the important extremes in the world of the novel converge and around whom a complete world with all its vital contradictions can be organized. Rastignac is such a figure—a propertyless aristocrat who can mediate between the world of the Vauquier pension and the world of the aristocracy; another is Lucien de Rubempré, with his vacillation between the world of the aristocratic, opportunistic journalist and the world of serious art of the d'Arthez circle.

But the writer himself must possess a firmly established and vital ideology; he must see the world in its contradictory dynamics to be able to choose a hero in whose life the major opposing forces converge. The ideologies of the great writers are certainly various; the ways in which their ideologies are manifested in epic composition, still more various. The deeper, the more differentiated, and the more steeped in vital experience the ideology, the more variegated and multifaceted its compositional expression.

And without ideology there is no composition. Flaubert felt this truth acutely. He constantly quoted Buffon's profound and impelling statement: "To write well means to feel well, to think well and to express well." With Flaubert the process was reversed. He wrote to George Sand: "I try hard to think correctly in order to write correctly. But writing correctly is my goal, I do not conceal it." Flaubert never forged an ideology out of his life experiences to express in his work; he did struggle honourably and with artistic integrity for an ideology, understanding that without ideology there can be no great literature.

His inverted approach could lead to no result. With impressive sincerity Flaubert admitted his failure in the same letter to George Sand. "I lack a firm, comprehensive outlook on life. You are a thousand times right, but where does one find the way to change? I ask you. You will not illuminate my ignorance with metaphysics, neither mine nor others. The words religion or Catholicism, on the one hand, and progress, fraternity and democracy, on the other, no longer meet the intellectual demands of the present. The new dogma of equality, which radicalism preaches, is refuted by physiology and history in practice. I see no possibility today either of finding a new principle or of respecting old principles. Thus I seek in vain for the ideal on which everything else depends."

Flaubert's confession is an uncommonly honest expression of the general ideological crisis of the bourgeois intelligentsia after 1848. Objectively, all his contemporaries experienced this very crisis. In Zola it expresses itself in agnostic positivism; he says that one can only recognize and describe the "how" of an event, not its "why". In the Goncourts the result is a spiritless, sceptical, superficial indifference to ideological questions. And this crisis intensified as time went on. Nor, as many writers pretend, did the transformation of agnosticism into mysticism during the imperialist period provide a solution to the ideological crisis; it just rendered it more acute.

A writer's ideology is merely a synthesis of the totality of his experience on a certain level of abstraction. The significance of ideology, as Flaubert recognized, is that it provides the possibility of viewing the contradictions of life in a fruitful, ordered context—the basis for feeling and thinking well and thus for writing well. When a writer is isolated from the vital struggles of life and from varied experiences generally, all ideological questions in his work become abstractions, no matter whether abstractions of pseudo-scientism, mysticism or of an indifference to vital issues; such abstraction results in the loss of the creative productiveness provided by questions of ideology in the earlier literature.

Without an ideology a writer can neither narrate nor construct a comprehensive, well-organized and multifaceted epic composition. Observation and description are mere substitutes for a conception of order in life.

How can epic compositions develop in the event of such a lack? And what kind of compositions would they be? Spurious objectivism and subjectivism in modern writers lead to schematism and monotony in composition. In objectivism like Zola's, the unity of the objects chosen as the thematic material provides the principle of composition. The composition consists of the assemblage of all the important details as seen from various points of view. The result is a series of static pictures, of still lives connected only through the relations of objects arrayed one beside the other according to their own inner logic, never following one from the other, certainly never one out of the other. The so-called action is only a thread on which the still lives are disposed in a superficial, ineffective fortuitous sequence of isolated, static pictures. The possibility of artistic variety in such a mode of composition is meagre. The writer must strive to counteract the intrinsic monotony through the novelty of the objects depicted and the originality of the description.

Nor is the capacity for variation enhanced in novels of pseudo-subjectivism. Here the pattern is derived from an immediate reflection of the basic experience of modern writers : disillusionment. They describe subjective aspirations psychologically, and in the description of different stages of life they depict the shattering of these hopes under the brutality of capitalist life. At least there is a temporal sequence in the theme. But it is always the self-same sequence, and the opposition between the individual and the objective world is so stark and crude that no dynamic interaction is possible. The most evolved subjectivism in the modern novel (Joyce and Dos Passos) actually transforms the entire inner life of characters into something static and reified. Paradoxically, extreme subjectivism approximates the inert reification of pseudo-objectivism.

Thus the descriptive method results in compositional monotony, while narration not only permits but even promotes infinite variety in composition.

"But was not this development inevitable? Indeed, it does destroy the older epic composition; indeed, the newer composition is not of equal artistic merit. Grant all this! Still, does not the new mode of composition provide an adequate picture of fully developed capitalism? Yes, it is inhuman, it does transform men into appurtenances of things, static beings, components of a still life. But is that not what capitalism does to people?"

The rationale is provocative but none-the-less erroneous. In the first place, the proletariat also has an existence in bourgeois society. Marx emphasized the divergence in the reactions of the bourgeoisie and the proletariat to the inhumanity of capitalism. "The proprietary class and the class of the proletariat experience the same alienation. But the former class feels at ease and justified in this alienation, recognizing in it its source of power and the basis for a sham existence. Contrarily, the latter class feels destroyed in this alienation, recognizing in it its helplessness and the inhumanity of its existence." And Marx goes on to demonstrate the significance of the *revolt* of the proletariat against the inhumanity of this alienation.

When this revolt is represented in literature, the still lives of descriptive mannerism vanish, and the necessity for plot and narration arises of its own, as in such novels as Gorki's masterpiece *The Mother* and Martin Andersen Nexo's *Pelle the Conqueror*, novels which break with descriptive mannerism. (Naturally this new use of the narrative method is an outgrowth of the authors' commitment to the class struggle.)

But does the revolt described by Marx against the alienation in capitalism involve only the workers? Of course not. The repression of the workers under capitalism is carried on in struggles and inspires the most varied forms of rebellion. And after embittered struggles a not inconsiderable portion of the bourgeoisie becomes "educated" to the dehumanization of bourgeois society. Modern bourgeois literature bears witness against bourgeois society. Its predilection for certain themes —disappointment and disillusionment—is evidence of such rebellion. Every novel of disillusion is the history of the failure of such a rebellion. But such rebellions are conceived superficially and thus lack impact.

That capitalism is now perfected does not mean, of course, that everything henceforth is fixed and finished or that there is no more struggle or development in the life of the individual. The "perfection" of the capitalist system merely means that it reproduces itself on ever higher levels of "perfected" inhumanity. But the system reproduces itself continuously, and this process is in reality a series of bitter and implacable struggles—a process evolving simultaneously in the life of the individual, who is transformed into a soulless appurtenance of the capitalist system though he had not come into the world "naturally" as such.

The decisive ideological weakness of the writers of the descriptive method is in their passive capitulation to these consequences, to these phenomena of fully-developed capitalism, and in their seeing the result but not the struggles of the opposing forces. And even when they apparently do describe a process—in the novel of disillusion—the final victory of capitalist inhumanity is always anticipated. In the course of the novel they do not recount how a stunted individual had been gradually adjusted to the capitalist order; instead they present a character who at the very outset reveals traits that should have emerged only as a result of the entire process. That is why the disillusionment developed in the course of the novel appears so feeble and purely subjective. We do not watch a man whom we have come to know and love being spiritually murdered by capitalism in the course of the novel, but follow a corpse in passage through still lives becoming increasingly aware of being dead. The writers' fatalism, their capitulation (even with gnashing teeth) before capitalist inhumanity, is responsible for the absence of development in these 'novels' of development."

Thus it is incorrect to claim that this method adequately mirrors capitalism in all its inhumanity. On the contrary! The writers dilute this inhumanity despite themselves. A dreary existence without a rich inner life, without the vitality of continuous development is far less revolting and shocking than the daily and hourly unremitting transformation of thousands of human beings with infinite capacities into "living corpses".

When one compares the novels of Maxim Gorki on the life

of the bourgeoisie with the works of modern realism, one sees the contrast. For all its close observation and description, modern realism has lost its capacity to depict the dynamics of life, and thus its representation of capitalist reality is inadequate, diluted and constrained. The degradation and crippling under capitalism is far more tragic, its bestiality viler, more ferocious and terrible than that pictured even in the best of these novels. It would be an impermissible simplification, of course, to affirm that all modern literature has capitulated without struggle to the fetishizing and dehumanizing of capitalism. We have already noted that French naturalism after 1848 represents a subjective protest against this process. Important exponents of later literary currents also attempt to protest. The most notable humanistic artists of the various formalist movements have sought to combat the emptiness of capitalistic life. The symbolism of the later Ibsen, for example, represents a revolt against the monotony of bourgeois existence. These revolts, however, are without artistic consequence when they do not probe the *root* of the emptiness of life under *capitalism*, when they do not afford direct experience with the struggles to restore meaning to life, and when they do not investigate and seek to depict artistically such struggles with ideological understanding.

Therein lies the literary and theoretical significance of the humanist revolt of the outstanding intellectuals of the capitalist world. Because of the extraordinary variety of the currents and personalities in this humanist revolt, not even a cursory analysis of this development can be attempted here. It is sufficient to note that the open humanist revolt of Romain Rolland is a serious effort at breaking through the limitations of the literary traditions of bourgeois literature since 1848. And the reinforcement of humanism through the victory of socialism in the Soviet Union and the definition of its goals and intensification of its struggle against fascist bestiality, the most ferocious form of capitalist inhumanity, have raised these efforts to a higher theoretical level. Theoretical essays of the last years like Ernst Bloch's offer the perspective of a basic critique of the art of the second half of the nineteenth century and of the twentieth century. Of course this critical battle has not yet reached a decisive stage, it has not everywhere achieved clarity of principles, but the very existence of such a battle, of such a basic re-valuation of the decadence of the period, is a symptom of not inconsiderable significance.[1] 1936

[1] The final section of this essay, dealing primarily with problems of Soviet literature in the thirties, has been omitted.—*Trans.*

The Intellectual Physiognomy
in Characterization

*Awake, men have a common world, but each sleeper
reverts to his own private world.*

—Heraclitus.

I

THE continuing effectiveness of Plato's "Symposium" after
more than two thousand years is hardly due to its intellectual
content alone. The perennial vitality which distinguishes it
from other dialogues in which Plato developed equally
important aspects of his philosophic system, results from the
dynamic characterization of a group of outstanding personalities—Socrates, Alcibiades, Aristophanes, and many others; the
dialogue not merely transmits ideas but also brings characters
to life.

What generates the vitality in these characters? Plato is a
great artist. He can depict the appearance and environment
of his characters with true Greek plasticity. But this artistry
in depicting the outer man and his surroundings is matched in
other Platonic dialogues which do not attain the same anima-
tion. And many of Plato's imitators have used this very
dialogue as a model without attaining a modicum of its liveli-
ness.

It seems to me that the source of the vitality of the
characters in the "Symposium" is to be sought elsewhere. The
realism with which the characters and environment are depicted is an indispensable but not decisive factor. What is decisive
is that Plato reveals the thinking processes of his characters
and develops their varied intellectual positions regarding the
same problem—the nature of love—as the vital factor in their
characters and as the most distinctive manifestation of their

personalities. The ideas of the individuals are not abstract, generalized and unmotivated. Instead the total personality of each character is synthesized and exemplified through his mode of thinking, in his mode of self-expression, and in his conclusions regarding the subject at hand. Through the specific style and process of thinking, Plato is able to expose the characteristic approach of each individual : how he confronts a problem, what he accepts as axiomatic, what he seeks to prove and how he proves it, the level of intellectual abstraction he attains, the sources of his examples, what he underplays and evades and how he does so. A group of living people emerges before us, unforgettably etched in their individuality. And all these people have been individualized exclusively through their intellectual physiognomy, distinguished one from the other and developed into individuals who are simultaneously types.

This work, of course, is an extraordinary phenomenon in world literature. But it is not unique. In Diderot's *Rameau's Nephew* and Balzac's *Unknown Masterpiece*, too, the characters are individualized through their dynamic personal, vital positions on abstract questions; the intellectual physiognomy again is the chief factor in creating living personality.

These extreme cases illuminate an otherwise neglected problem of characterization which is of contemporary significance. In the great masterpieces of world literature, the intellectual physiognomy of the characters is always carefully delineated. Literary decadence, on the other hand, is always evidenced—perhaps in modern times more sharply than ever before—by vagueness in the intellectual physiognomy and by conscious neglect of the problem or the incapacity of writers to deal with the problem imaginatively.

In every great creative work characters are represented in a pervasive, many-faceted interaction with each other, with society, and with the great issues of their society. The more profoundly this interconnection is grasped and the denser the mesh of the interconnections, the greater the potential significance of the work and the closer its approximation to the actual richness of life and that "deceptive subtlety" in the process of social evolution of which Lenin speaks so often.

Anyone free of decadent bourgeois prejudices or of the misconceptions of vulgar sociology will recognize that the capacity of characters to give expression to their conscious ideology is an essential factor in a creative representation of reality.

Characterization that does not encompass ideology cannot be complete. Ideology is the highest form of consciousness; ignoring it, a writer eliminates what is most important in his delineation of a character. A character's conception of the world represents a profound personal experience and the most distinctive expression of his inner life; at the same time it provides a significant reflection of the general problems of his time.

Before proceeding in this investigation, we must eliminate some immediate misconceptions regarding the intellectual physiognomy. In the first place, the term does not presuppose a correct view of the world. Personal ideologies do not always mirror objective reality accurately.

Tolstoy is certainly one of the outstanding masters in the creation of intellectual physiognomy. But take a character with as clearly delineated an intellectual physiognomy as Constantine Levin—when is he right? Strictly speaking : never. Tolstoy portrays his favourite's invariable errors of judgment with merciless incisiveness. In Levin's discussions with his brother or with Oblonsky, for example, Tolstoy skilfully depicts Levin's constant shifting of opinion, his erratic thinking, his restless veering from one extreme to another. But this continuous and abrupt vacillation, this ready assumption of opposing viewpoints, is just what provides unity to Levin's intellectual physiognomy. This specific quality in Levin's modes of thinking and experiencing is just what is constant and consistent. And yet this kind of response is not restricted to him as a particular personality; in its very personalization and error, there is a certain universal validity.

A second possible misunderstanding may arise from the belief that abstract ideas are an essential factor in the representation of an intellectual physiognomy. In polemics against the shallowness of naturalism critics often fall into this opposite error. In such an attack against naturalism, for example, André Gide proposed Racine's *Mithridates* as a peerless example of proper literary practice, singling out the scene in which the king and his sons debate whether to wage war against Rome or to capitulate. Gide says: "Of course no fathers or sons would ever have spoken to each other in such a manner, and yet (or just for this reason) all fathers and all sons will recognize themselves in this scene." According to this judgment, the abstract ratiocination in Racine or Schiller provides the most appropriate means for delineating the intellectual physiognomy. But this judgment is not justified. Compare Racine's king and his sons with any pair of Shakespearean heroes with opposing ideologies like Brutus and Cassius. Compare the ideological conflicts among Schiller's Wallenstein, Octavio and Max Piccolomini with those between Goethe's Egmont and Oranien. Without question Goethe's and Shakespeare's characters possess not only more vitality but also more clearly delineated intellectual physiognomies.

The reason is obvious. The interplay between ideology and personal decision of Schiller's and Racine's characters is simpler, more direct, more obtuse and superficial than of Shakespeare's or Goethe's. In his attack on banal, flat "naturalism" and defence of the poetry of the universal, Gide overlooks the fact that in Racine (or Schiller) the universality is too pat; Schiller's characters are, as Marx said, mere "mouthpieces of the spirit of the age" (*Sprachrohre des Zeitgeists*).

Let us examine the scene lauded by Gide—the debate between the king and his sons. The pros and cons of a war with Rome are carefully weighed in three great speeches on a lofty intellectual and stylistic level, with wonderfully modulated, elegant, epigrammatic rhetoric. But how the different positions arise out of the lives of the characters or how their personal experiences and sufferings determine their particular arguments remains obscure. The single personal complication in the tragedy, the love of the king and of his two sons for the same woman, is linked to the debate loosely and superficially. The exquisite intellectual debate hovers in the air unrooted in the passions of the characters; Racine thus fails to provide the well-defined intellectual physiognomy that would have been provided in Shakespeare.

It is easy to find a contrasting example among Shakespeare's numerous masterpieces of characterization. Brutus is a stoic, Cassius an epicurean. These facts are noted merely in passing. But how profoundly Brutus's stoicism permeates his entire life : his wife, Portia, is Cato's daughter, and their entire relationship is implicit with Roman stoic feeling and thought. How typical of his special kind of stoicism is his idealistic, naïve confidence and his unadorned speech, devoid of all rhetorical ostentation. And Cassius's epicureanism is equally significant. I will merely draw attention to one extraordinarily subtle detail : as soon as the tragic collapse of the revolt is apparent and all signs point to a debacle for the last republican insurrection, Cassius, ever firm and unyielding in his epicureanism, abandons his atheism and begins to believe in the omens and prophecies which epicureans always derided.

But we are investigating only an aspect of Shakespeare's creation of intellectual physiognomy and not the full richness of characterization in Brutus and Cassius. And what a wealth of detail there is, what a complicated intermeshing of private life and great social events ! What a contrast to the artificial, blunt, direct connections between the personal and the abstract in Racine.

The richness and vitality of Shakespearean characterization as compared to the relative abstractness of Racine's has generally been recognized, but the artistic and philosophic consequences in the contrast have not always been clearly understood. Once again it is really a question of the quality of the artistic representation of objective reality. Richness and depth in life arise out of the turbulent and protean interplay of human passions. In reality people do not act alongside each other but for and against each other, and their individuality develops and evolves only in and through their struggles with each other.

Plot as the synthesis of the interaction expressed in practical activity; conflict as the fundamental manifestation of this contradictory action and reaction; parallelism and contrast as expressions of the course in which human passions operate for and against each other—all these basic modes of composition mirror in artistic synthesis the general and fundamental modes of human existence. But we are not concerned here simply with a formal question. Universal, typical phenomena should emerge out of the particular actions and passions of specific individuals. The artist invents situations and develops modes of expression through which he can invest private passions with a significance extending beyond the life of the individual.

In this creative approach lies the secret for exalting the individual to the typical—not with loss of individuality in a character but with the intensification of his individuality. An individual's awareness—like an emotion intensified to the extreme—provides the potential for disclosing capacities which remain embryonic or exist only as intentions or potentialities in real life. For a true representation of objective reality, an author may reveal in his fiction only that which really exists as potentiality within his characters. Artistic excellence is the result of an exhaustive disclosure of these latent potentialities.

And contrarily—a character's awareness will appear abstract and bloodless (as is sometimes the case in Racine or Schiller) to the extent that it is divorced from his concrete potentialities—unless it is founded on a rich, concrete interplay of human passions and unless through this intensification it produces a human quality. An artist achieves significance and typicality in his characterization only when he successfully exposes the multifarious interrelationships between the character traits of his heroes and the objective general problems of the age and when he shows his characters directly grappling with the most abstract issues of the time as their own personal and vital problems.

Clearly in this connection a character's own capacity for intellectual generalization plays an enormous role. Generalization degenerates into empty abstraction if the relationship between abstract thinking and personal experience escapes the reader, if we do not experience this relationship along with the character. If the artist can depict this interrelationship in all its vitality, then in saturating his work with ideas he does not weaken it but renders it more intense.

Consider Goethe's *Wilhelm Meister's Apprenticeship*. A decisive stage of this important novel is reached in the preparation of a performance of *Hamlet*. Goethe puts little emphasis on the description of the technical details (on which Zola would have concentrated) but emphasizes the psychological and intellectual implications by including wide-ranging, profound discussions of the characterizations in *Hamlet*, of Shakespeare's method of composition and of epic and dramatic poetry. But these discussions are never abstract since each statement, each argument, each exchange is important not only for the theme but also simultaneously and integrally for further insight into the characters—insight we would not otherwise obtain. Wilhelm Meister, Serlo and Aurelie reveal their personalities through their diverse intellectual approaches to the problems of performing Shakespeare—as theoretician, actor and director respectively. The consequent delineation of the intellectual physiognomy consummates and concretizes Goethe's characterization.

But the intellectual physiognomy has further significance in composition. Every important writer establishes a specific hierarchy among his characters which serves not only to expose the social content of the work and the author's ideology but also to provide the means for defining the place of each character within the entire compositional scheme—from the centre to the periphery and back again. Such an hierarchic order is vital to composition. Every work of true artistic composition contains an hierarchy through which the author ranks his characters as main or subsidiary. So essential is this formal arrangement that the reader instinctively seeks the hierarchy even in jejune works and becomes unsatisfied if the protagonist, for example, does not command the "rank" due him in relationship to the other characters and to the general compositional plan.

The protagonist's rank depends essentially on the level of his self-awareness, his capacity consciously to raise what is individual and incidental in his existence to a specific level of universality. Shakespeare, who employs the technique of parallelism in many of his mature dramas, always establishes the rank of his characters according to their ability for conscious generalization about their fate—an ability which enables them to act as protagonists. I point merely to the well-known parallels of Hamlet and Laertes and Lear and Gloucester. In both cases the protagonist is superior to the subordinate figure in that he does not suffer or accept what he experiences as mere fortuity and does not simply react instinctively to his destiny. Essential to his personality is his ability to reach beyond his immediate experience and environment, to strive with his entire subjective being to experience his existence in its universal implications and in its inter-relationship with the universal. The character with the richer, more many-sided, more sharply delineated and more profoundly explored intellectual physiognomy can maintain his central position in the composition with conviction.

Although a well-defined intellectual physiognomy is a prerequisite for the central role, the protagonist need not represent a correct philosophical outlook. In fact, Cassius is always right against Brutus, Kent against Lear, Oranien against Egmont. But Brutus, Lear or Egmont can serve as protagonists because of their clearly delineated intellectual physiognomies. Why? Because the compositional hierarchy is not established according to abstract intellectual criteria but within the concrete, complex problem in the work. It is not a question of an abstract opposition of the true and the false. Historical situations are much too complicated and contradictory for that. Tragic heroes of history neither commit fortuitous errors nor possess accidental flaws. Their errors are inevitably interrelated with the important problems of a critical transition. For Shakespeare, Brutus represented, as did Egmont for Goethe, significant qualities characteristic of a tragic conflict at a specific stage, in a specific kind of social conflict. When an author grasps this conflict profoundly and correctly, he must then seek protagonists with personal qualities (culminating in an intellectual physiognomy) through whom he can expose the conflict most palpably and appropriately.

The capacity for intellection and for abstract generalization is only one quality through which an author can relate the individual to the universal.

In any case we are dealing here with an important factor in artistic creation. The capacity of characters for self-consciousness plays a key role in literature. Admittedly, the methods by which a writer elevates the personal experience of his characters above mere individual significance vary according to his ability, the kind of problem he is treating and the kind of intellectual physiognomy best suited for the illumination of this problem. Shakespeare elevates Timon's experience to universality in the invective against gold, which destroys and degrades society. Othello demonstrates his consciousness of his own fate in his realization that the shattering of his faith in Desdemona means the shattering of the very foundations of his existence. As far as the representation of self-consciousness, of the intellectual physiognomy and of the generalization of individual experience is concerned, there is no fundamental difference between Othello and Timon.

Naturally, the establishment of a hierarchy among the characters within the composition is not a mere formal requirement; like every other genuine artistic problem it is related to the reflection of objective reality, even if indirectly so. The typical, purest and most extreme factors in a social situation and in historical and social types find proper expression through this compositional method.

Balzac demonstrates most clearly how an artist's view of objective reality is mirrored in his composition. He depicted an almost unlimited number of people of the various classes of bourgeois society. Never content to represent any stratum or group by a single character, he always employed an entire series of characters to this end. Within these agglomerations, Balzac's protoganist is always the most conscious individual, the most sharply delineated intellectual physiognomy : Vautrin the criminal, Gobseck the usurer.

The elaboration of an intellectual physiognomy presupposes exceptional breadth, profundity and universality in characterization. Although the level of intellection is far above the average encountered in daily life, the result is not a weakening but an intensification of individuality in characterization. This intensification arises out of the continuous dynamic relationship between a character's personal experiences and his intellectual generalization about them; thoughts are depicted as a process of living and not as a result. Such an intensification can be achieved only when an author considers the capacity for abstract ideation an essential aspect of characterization.

Thus the elaboration of the intellectual physiognomy depends on a profound conception of the typical. The more acutely a writer grasps his epoch and its major issues, the less he will create on the level of the commonplace. In day-by-day existence, major contradictions are obscured in a whir of petty, disparate accidental events; they are exposed only when purified and intensified to such an extreme that their potential consequences are exposed and are readily perceived. The success of great writers in creating typical characters and typical situations requires far more than accurate observation of everyday reality. Profound understanding of life is never restricted to the observation of everyday existence. The writer first defines the basic issues and movements of his time and then invents characters and situations not to be found in ordinary life, possessing capacities and propensities which when intensified illuminate the complex dialectic of the major contradictions, motive forces and tendencies of an era.

In this sense, Don Quixote is one of the most typical characters in world literature. There is no question that scenes like the battle with the windmills are among the most successful and typical ever created, though scarcely imaginable in ordinary life. As a matter of fact, typicality in character and situation implies departure from everyday reality. If we contrast Don Quixote with the most significant attempt at transposing the problems treated by Cervantes to the level of everyday life—Sterne's *Tristram Shandy*—we can see how much less incisive and typical such contradictions become on the everyday level. (Sterne's very choice of commonplace subject matter is evidence of how much less profoundly and more subjectively he posed problems.)

Only through the extreme intensification of typical situations can an author evoke from his characters the expression of the major contradictions of the time and exact the ultimate capacity for such expression latent in them.

The great writers were not the only ones with a predilection for the extreme in character and situation. In their opposition to the prosaic bleakness of capitalist life, the romantics, too, employed exaggeration. With the pure romantics, however, exaggeration in character and situation was an end in itself, a lyrical and exotic rebellion. The classical realist employed extreme intensification in characters and situations as the most effective means for achieving typicality on the highest level.

This distinction leads us back to a discussion of composition, for clearly we cannot discuss the creation of types in isolation from the general composition. The typical does not exist in isolation. Extreme situations and characters become typical only within a context. Typicality is disclosed only in the interaction of characters and situations. Through intensified, extreme action in an intensified, extreme situation, an author can evoke the fundamental contradictions within a particular complex of social problems. A character becomes typical only in comparison with and contrast to other characters who, with more or less intensification, evoke other phases and aspects of the same contradictions, contradictions decisive to their lives and careers also. Only through a complicated dialectic rich in intensified contradictions can a character be elevated to typicality.

Take a character generally recognized as typical, Hamlet. Without the contrast with Laertes, Horatio and Fortinbras, Hamlet's typicality could not be revealed. In a plot replete with extreme situations, Shakespeare has a group of the most diverse characters manifest the most diverse intellectual and emotional reflections of the same vital objective contradictions. Within this context, Hamlet's typicality emerges.

The elaboration of a distinct, dynamic intellectual physiognomy is decisive to the representation of a type. A protagonist's consciousness of his own destiny on a high intellectual level is a prerequisite for eliminating the extremeness in situations depicted and for exposing the universality underlying these situations, that is, for representing contradictions on their highest and purest level. In itself the extreme situation contains the contradictions in the intense and pure form essential for art, but a character's reflections about his own actions are absolutely necessary for transforming this "thing in itself" into a "thing for us".

Normal, everyday reflection hardly suffices. The reflection must be raised to the superior level about which we have spoken—objectively (as regards the level of the intellection itself) and subjectively (as regards the linking of the reflection to the situation, character and experience of the protagonist).

When, for example, Vautrin suggests that Rastignac marry the disinherited daughter of the millionaire Taillefer while he himself sees to it that the millionaire's son falls in a duel and the daughter thus becomes the sole heir in order that the two of them can share in the inheritance, we have nothing more than the plot for an ordinary detective story. But Rastignac's inner conflicts are those of the entire younger generation in the post-Napoleonic period, a fact that is made clear in his contrasting discussions with Bianchon. The social contradictions which give rise to these conflicts are exposed on a high intellectual plane in the analysis of the experiences of such polar opposites of French society as Vautrin and the Viscountess de Beauséant. Goriot's fate provides a further contrasting example for Rastignac's reflection. Thus what had seemed a mere plot for a detective novel develops into a great social tragedy. Similar observations might be made regarding the poetic significance of the mad King Lear's trial of his daughters in the storm on the heath and of the play scene and subsequent Hecuba monologue in *Hamlet*.

But there is more to be investigated besides the direct function of the intellectual physiognomy in elevating extreme situations into artistic universality and to meaningful and perceptible particularity. There is the additional indirect function of establishing and exposing the interrelationship of extreme situations within a work. Only by this means were the classical writers able to create an impression within the abundance of extreme situations they presented of a total world in motion and of some kind of order within this world. Classical literature develops this indirect function of the intellectual physiognomy in the most varied forms imaginable. Contrast can be implied, for example, without conscious reflection as in the contrast between Hamlet's abstruse speculation and Laertes' instinctive spontaneity. It can be expressed directly as in Hamlet's reflections after his first encounter with Fortinbras. It can appear in conscious recognition of parallelism and of the consequences of such parallelism as in Rastignac's amazement that both Vautrin and Mme. de Beauséant hold the same opinions about how to deal with society. It can provide a kind of continuous musical accompaniment, an atmosphere behind the general movement, as in Goethe's *Elective Affinities*.

It is not simply a formal similarity that is common to these various modes. Parallelism and contrast, for example, are only generalized poetic modes of representing the turbulent relations among men. Only because they are modes for reflecting objective reality can they effect the poetic intensification for the expression of a type; and only because they are such can the character's intellectual physiognomy, intensified through them, react upon form and situation and make the unity of the individual and the typical, and the intensification of the particular to typicality more distinct.

The basis of great literature is Heraclitus's common world of men "awake", the world of men struggling in society, struggling with each other, acting for and against each other and reacting actively, not passively, to each other. If there is no "awake" consciousness of reality, there can be no intellectual physiognomy. Left to revolve about itself in an isolated subjectivity, the intellectual physiognomy becomes blind and amorphous. Without an intellectual physiognomy, no character can achieve the elevation at which it can lift itself to the full vitality of individuality above everyday reality with its spiritless fortuity, the elevation at which it can lift itself to the "rank" of true typicality.

II

In *Les Misérables* Victor Hugo seeks to make clear to the reader Jean Valjean's social and psychological situation. With extraordinary lyrical intensity he describes a man who has fallen overboard from a ship at sea. The ship continues on its way and gradually disappears over the horizon. In deathly loneliness the man struggles against the implacable waves until he sinks in despair. According to Victor Hugo, this scene exemplifies the fate society reserves for a man who has once made a false step. The implacability of the waves symbolizes the inhumanity of society.

This scene is a poetic and precise expression of a general feeling among broad masses in capitalist society. The simplicity, ease and directness of men's relationships in primitive societies disappear more and more. Man feels ever more isolated in face of a society which grows increasingly inhuman. As men become more and more isolated with the evolution of economic life, the inhumanity in society begins to loom as a second nature, vicious and implacable. In his effective evocation of the emotional reaction to this development, Victor Hugo expresses something real and of general import and shows himself to be a great lyric poet.

But that this phenomenon of capitalist society is an objective reality does not mean that capitalist society is then to be identified objectively by this phenomenon. The inhumanity in the society is no second nature divorced from men but the special expression of the new relations among men created by capitalism in full maturity.

Marx provides a provocative description of the basic difference in the economic life of embryonic and of mature capitalism. Contrasting the later stage with that of primary accumulation, he says : "A mute coercion inherent in the very economic relations characterizes the capitalist domination of labour. . . . In the ordinary course of events labour can simply be left to the 'natural laws of production'."

But the history of the period of primary accumulation is not merely a tale of innumerable atrocities against workers. This period was simultaneously the period of the bursting of the feudal fetters on production and thus a period of human progress. It was the period of the wars for freedom against the feudal yoke, which began with the Renaissance and culminated in the French Revolution. It was also the classical period of bourgeois culture, of its philosophy and science, its literature and art.

The advent of the advanced stage of capitalism described by Marx brought new social relationships and thus new subject matter, forms and problems of composition in literature. But recognizing the historical necessity and progress in the development of capitalism does not mean that one closes one's eyes to the dubious consequences for art and aesthetics. The classical period of bourgeois ideology yielded to a period of vulgar apologetics. The centre of gravity of the class struggles shifted from the destruction of feudalism to the battle between the bourgeoisie and the proletariat. Thus the period between the French Revolution and the June uprising is the last great period of bourgeois literature.

The emergence of the apologetic phase of ideological development did not mean that all writers automatically became apologists, certainly not conscious apologists; nor all aestheticians, though because of the very nature of their discipline, they are more prone to apologetic tendencies.

But no writer or literary theoretician remained unaffected. The liquidation of the traditions of the heroic, revolutionary period of the bourgeoisie is often exemplified in the very opposition to the dominant apologetic. Flaubert's and Zola's realism represented opposition (though of different kinds) to the cant and betrayal into which the old ideals had been transformed. Objectively, however, and despite themselves, their opposition developed affinities to the apologetics they were seeking to combat. For what is the essence of apologetics? Limitation of investigation to superficial aspects of social phenomena, evasion of decisive issues. Whereas Ricardo discussed the capitalist exploitation of the workers frankly and "cynically", vulgar economists took refuge in a superficial investigation of a factitious problem of money circulation in order to dismiss from their science the very concept of the accumulation of surplus value in the productive process. Concomitantly, the concept of class structure in society disappeared from sociology, class struggle from historical science, and the dialectical method from science.

Everyday existence, according to the subjective view of Flaubert and Zola, when the exclusive or at least the predominant subject matter of literature, can expose bourgeois hypocrisy. But what does the adoption of commonplace subject matter signify for the depiction and illumination of basic social contradictions? The use of everyday life as subject matter is nothing new. Great writers from Fielding to Balzac sought to capture the daily life of the bourgeoisie. What was new after 1848 was not merely that writers used commonplace reality as thematic material but that writers limited themselves exclusively to the aspects and phenomena of everyday existence.

We have already noted that basic social contradictions are submerged in day-by-day existence; only in exceptional cases can these contradictions emerge in everyday experience in full complexity, never in maturity and purity. Proclaiming everyday reality as the norm for realism implied renouncing the representation of social contradictions in full evolution and intensification. This new canon of realism inevitably resulted also in contracting everyday reality, for a logical consequence is that even those rare events of daily life in which basic contradictions might appear meaningfully and typically are rejected as inappropriate and that only the banality of daily reality, the commonplace and mediocre aspects, are allowed as subject matter.

This emphasis on the commonplace represents the culmination of the effort to evade the depiction of decisive social problems. The "average" is a dead synthesis of the process of social development. The emphasis on the "mean" transforms literature from a representation of life in motion into a description of more or less static conditions. Plot dissolves, being replaced by a mere sequence of static scenes. With the orientation on the average, the previous function of plot in evoking the basic objective and subjective social factors latent in characters and events becomes superfluous. Whatever social factors are evoked through the representation of the "average" are necessarily superficial and can easily be depicted through direct description or exposition.

One must distinguish between this slice-of-life approach and the approach of great works of literature, where everyday detail provides the aesthetic semblance of commonplace banality within the overall representation of significant types in broad social relationships. In modern literature the contrast between the two methods can be exemplified through Goncharov's *Oblomov* and any of the novels of everyday existence of the Goncourt brothers. Goncharov sustains a general impression of bleakness far more successfully than the Goncourts even though at first glance he seems to pursue the technique of plotlessness as consistently as they. But this impression of bleakness in Goncharov is the result of a classical characterization based on intense, varied interaction of characters with each other and with the society in which they live. Oblomov's inactivity is no accidental, superficial character trait. He is without question an extreme and consistent character developed in the classical manner through the intensification of a particular character trait. He does nothing but lie abed in sloth; but his very inaction provides the drama of the novel. He is a social type, not in the sense of an "average" man, but in the more significant social and aesthetic sense. Only because of his typicality could Goncharov's character achieve such significance for Russia—and not only for Russia.

Lessing exposed the error of those who recognize action only "when the lover falls to his knees, the princess faints and the heroes duel". The impact of turns in plot depends on the extent of the involvement of characters. Thus through the extreme exaggeration of typical traits of the Russian intelligentsia, Goncharov created in Oblomov a character who in his very indolence and inertia reflected the decisive and universal qualities that summed up an entire era, and he accomplished this dynamically and with profound individualization; on the other hand, the external, more variegated vicissitudes in *Madame Gervaisais*, for example, represents merely a series of multi-coloured stills in which an exotic Roman atmosphere exerts a mysterious, inexplicable, overwhelming power; the social forces remain invisible, and the characters pass each other without ever really encountering.

Oblomov has a well-defined intellectual physiognomy. His every statement, every conversation is on a high level of consciousness and is set in a context of complicated social forces with the result that he himself exemplifies, as a type, the tragedy of the intelligentsia of the time—and not just the intelligentsia under the yoke of Russian czarism. The shifts in attitude of the Gervaisais, on the other hand, are abstracted from the drama of social developments; as a result, the heroine cannot possess an intellectual physiognomy of her own.

The new realism of Flaubert, Zola and the Goncourts advanced under the banner of a revolutionary renovation of literature, of an art that truly corresponded to reality. The new movement pretended to offer a more exacting objectivity than the previous literature. Flaubert's struggle against subjectivity in literature is well known; and in his critique of Balzac and Stendahl, Zola set out to demonstrate how in their subjectivity and romantic propensity for the exceptional these writers had veered away from an objective rendering of reality (that is, everyday reality). Zola concludes his critique of Stendahl with the words: "Life is simpler." Of course, by "life" he meant day-by-day existence, which, in fact, is simpler than the "life" in Stendhal or Balzac.

The illusion of greater objectivity emerges naturally with the slice-of-life technique and approach. The artistic representation of the average, the mediocre, requires no extraordinary application of the imagination or the invention of unusual situations and characters. The commonplace can be depicted in isolation. It is right at hand, given *a priori*, and needs only to be described; in the description no new, surprising aspects of life need be revealed. It does not require any integration into a complicated compositional framework nor illumination through contrast. Thus it is easy for the illusion to arise that the everyday "average" is as much an objective "element" in social reality as the elements in chemistry.

This pseudo-objectivity in the theory and practice of the newer bourgeois literature complements its pseudo-scientism. Naturalism departs further and further from representing the dialectics of conflicting social forces and increasingly substitutes empty sociological abstractions for these dialectics. And this pseudo-scientism becomes more and more agnostic. The crisis of bourgeois ideals is represented in Flaubert as the collapse of all human aspirations, as the bankruptcy of any attempt at a scientific understanding of the world.

Zola formulates this pseudo-scientific agnosticism without equivocation: literature, he declares, can present only the "how" of an event, not the "why". And when the outstanding theoretician of the new realism, Taine, attempts to define the fundamental principle in society and history, he seizes on race as the ultimate factor in life.

Thus the mysticism inherent in this pseudo-objectivity emerges in the open. The rigid structures of Taine's literary sociology, like the static social conditions and static characters in the Goncourts, dissolve, upon closer investigation, into "états d'âme". It is no accident that psychology provides the scientific basis for the pseudo-objectivity in this literature and literary theory. Taine alludes to the environment as a mechanical, objective force operating according to natural law on the thinking and emotions of men. But when he begins to discuss the "elements" of this environment, he goes so far, for example, as to define the nature of the state as "a feeling of obedience as a result of which a mass of men assemble about the authority of a 'leader'". Here unconscious apology for capitalism, a consequence of the sociological method, is transformed into clear and conscious apology.

Though in the course of the development of bourgeois society, irrational tendencies that had been unconscious, latent and repressed with the founders of the new realism emerge more clearly and more consciously, the search for pseudo-objectivity persists. (The photo-montage movement of post-war imperialism is an example.) This opposition of abstract pseudo-objectivism and irrational subjectivism fully reflects the bourgeois feeling about life under capitalism in the nineteenth and twentieth centuries. In the period of the decline of the bourgeoisie this opposition appears in innumerable variants and evokes countless discussions about the "nature" of art and countless aesthetic manifestoes and doctrines.

Such conflicts are never invented by individual writers but are always socially-determined, distorted reflections of objective reality. Nor do these conflicts emerge from books into reality, but pass from reality into books. Hence the tenacious vitality of these traditions in the decadence of the bourgeoisie and the stubborn resistance to eliminating them.

The extreme subjectivism of the new bourgeois literature is only apparently in opposition to the trend toward the commonplace. Even the apparently fierce attempts to oppose naturalism by depicting the "exceptional" man, the "eccentric" and even the "superman" are locked in the stylistic vicious circle of the naturalism in which they originate. In literature and life the eccentric individual, alienated from daily reality, and the "average" man are complementary, interdependent polar opposites.

An eccentric hero, like one in a novel by Huysmans, is no more engaged in struggle with his social environment or with other men for the achievement of significant goals than any "average" man in a novel of everyday life. He expresses his "protest" against the prosaic banality of capitalist reality in mechanically doing the opposite to what others do, in formally transforming their clichés into shadowy paradoxes almost solely by changing the order of their words. In practice his relations with men are as impoverished as the "average" man's; that is why his "personality" is mere pretentiousness, as abstracted and static as that of the "average" man; like the "average" man he lacks a clear-cut personality, which can only evolve and achieve definition in practical, dynamic relations with other men. And such an impoverished base offers no foundation for the creation of an intellectual physiognomy. Even as formal paradoxes are nothing more than inverted commonplaces, so the eccentric is nothing but a masked philistine, a "common man" seeking to demonstrate his originality by standing on his head.

Both types—the superman and the philistine—are equally fatuous, equally divorced from significant social conflicts, equally devoid of historical content. They are pallid, single-dimensional phantoms, not living beings. In order to invest them with some meaning authors must represent such types as instruments of some mystical force. Otherwise, nothing at all can happen in a work in which the hero is supposed to be a superman. Naturalism and its opposing movements rest on the same philosophic base and offer essentially similar approaches to composition. Both rest on a solipsistic conception of man hopelessly isolated in an inhuman society.

The lyricism in Victor Hugo's man drowning in the sea is typical of the lyricism of all modern bourgeois realism. An isolated individual (man as a self-contained "psychic system") confronts a pseudo-objective, fetishized world ruled by mysterious forces. This dubious antithesis of pseudo-objective fatalism and the solipsism of all the human "elements" in the world is characteristic of the entire literature of the imperialist period. It constitutes, whether consciously or unconsciously, the basis for the varied theories of culture and sociology. Taine's "races", vulgar sociology's static "strata" (into which classes are transformed), and Spengler's "cultural cycles" have the same solipsist structure as d'Annunzio's or Maeterlinck's characters. Just as each of the characters of these writers has a particularized, isolated and unique existence from which there can be no bridge of communication to other men, so the "social groupings" of vulgar sociology or the "cultural cycles" of Spengler are always self-contained and unverifiable in experience; there is no bridge from them to objective reality.

Thus the individual living only in himself is abruptly cut off from the fatalistic universality within the literary composition. The individual is opposed directly to the abstract universal. The individual comes to be treated as a "case", as an "example", and as such is subordinated to the abstract and the universal through some arbitrary distinction; the universal, on the other hand, is presented either as an abstract scientific datum or its arbitrariness is emphasized as "poetic". It is symptomatic that both approaches can be applied in regard to the same characters. One thinks of Zola's pretension to a scientific attitude and of his subsequent influence in the creation of a fantastic, mystical romanticism.

What are the consequences for the creation of the intellectual physiognomy? Clearly, its formal basis disappears more and more. Lafargue criticized Zola because the dialogue of his characters was commonplace and flat in contrast to the spirited and suggestive dialogue of Balzac's characters. And this tendency in Zola was intensified by his successors. Gerhart Hauptmann exceeds Zola in the banality of his dialogue as much as he himself was later to be exceeded in the dialogue of the photo-montage.

The vapidity and lack of meaningful content in naturalistic literature has often been criticized, and there has been a constant demand for superior intellectuality in the characters and greater vitality in dialogue. But the solution is not simply to insert profound thoughts into the mouths of the heroes. Lively dialogue is no substitute for an intellectual physiognomy. Diderot showed that he recognized the hopelessness of a mechanical approach to this question when he had one of the characters in his *Les bijoux indiscrets* say: "Gentlemen, instead of supplying your characters with wit at every opportunity, simply put them in situations which will naturally evoke it." But in current literature that is an impossible proposal. Although the techniques of fiction are constantly being refined, the refinement is directed exclusively to the effective expression of what is unique, momentary and sensational. As contemporary philosophy and literary theory demonstrate, it is a question of a general trend of the times and not of an ephemeral literary fashion. In his book in celebration of the centenary of Kant's death, Simmel formulated the difference between Kant's time and his own (the period of imperialism) by noting that in both eras individualism was the key issue. Kant's individualism, however, was an individualism of freedom, whereas that of his day was an individualism of uniqueness.

The refinement of fictional technique in the last decades has permitted the capturing of the uniqueness in the individual. Artistic imagination strives to catch the evanescent aspects of the "here and now"—to use Hegel's terminology. In the modern bourgeois conception, reality is identical with the "here and now". Everything beyond is considered empty abstraction and distortion of reality. The exclusive orientation on the commonplace details of daily existence of the early days of the new realism, on the one hand, has resulted in more and more technical refinement and, on the other hand, has led to the conscious restriction of investigation to the empirical and fortuitous on the surface of life and to the acceptance of the random and incidental in life as the pattern and model in which nothing may be modified without falsification of reality. Thus the refinement in artistic technique leads to sterility and contributes to a mock "profundity" in decadent bourgeois literature.

Of course, the old writers began with fragments of life they had experienced or observed. But by extracting these events out of the immediate context and re-ordering and modifying them according to their needs, they were able so to represent the subtle dependence of their characters on each other and their interaction with each other as to permit their characters to live out their lives in full creative richness. Such a transformation is essential for elaborating character traits that are simultaneously intensely personal as well as typical, and especially for elaborating the intellectual physiognomy. If Shakespeare had not modified the plot of Cinthio's novella, or Stendhal the Besançon police report, neither would have been able to confer on an Othello or a Julien Sorel that typifying self-consciousness, that intellectual physiognomy, as a result of which they have become major figures of world literature.

Because it is the ultimate in uniqueness, as Hegel recognized, the "here and now" is absolutely abstract. And it is clear that the craze for the fleeting moment and for a factitious concreteness of twentieth-century Western European literature results in abstraction. In Maeterlinck, for example, the naturalist techniques arrive at complete abstraction. In more recent literature this development is clearest in writers like Joyce, who have expressly chosen as their fictional purpose the literary depiction of the unique, of the pure "here and now". Joyce creates his characters by assembling ephemeral thoughts and feelings and evanescent associations in their contact with the external world, describing all with minute and meticulous detail. It is this extreme particularization that eliminates individuality.

Joyce's is an extreme case. But he illustrates in his extreme intensification the idealogical aspects in the creation of characters. The extreme subjectivism in modern ideology, the increasing refinement in the depiction of the unique, and the increasingly exclusive emphasis on the psychological lead to the dissolution of character. Modern bourgeois thought dissolves objective reality into a complex of immediate perceptions and dissolves character by making the "I" a simple assembly point for such perceptions. Hoffmannsthal accurately expressed this concept in a poem in which he called such an "I"—"a dovecote".

Ibsen had already given this philosophical attitude poetic expression. He has the ageing Peer Gynt meditate on his past and on his personality and its evolution while peeling an onion. He compares each skin with a phase in his life until he recognizes with despair that his life consists of skins without a core, that he has lived through a series of incidents without having achieved a character.

As a consequence of the retarded development of capitalism in Norway, Ibsen, still relating ideologically to certain traditions of the revolutionary period of the bourgeoisie, expressed despair at this dissolution of character. Nietzsche already expresses no concern at such literary characterization. He derives any character in literature from a superficial and incomplete understanding of man; for him character in literature is a superficial abstraction.

Strindberg goes still further in his theoretical statements. With telling mockery he characterizes the superficiality of characterization in the run-of-the-mill bourgeois drama, the stereotyped repetition of certain characteristic expressions and the exaggerated underlining of certain superficial traits.

Though Strindberg's criticism is scarcely original (Balzac had jeered at such characterization earlier), it does apply to the persistent preference in modern literature for an abstract, mechanical and schematic "unity" of character. Strindberg, on the other hand, emphasizes complexity and dynamism in character. As a result, he dissolves character, as Joyce was later to do, into a Machian "complex of perceptions". He exposes his own philosophy of characterization by including Molière's characters, developed as types, among what he considers false and abstract characterizations.

Hoffmannsthal has Balzac declare in an imaginary dialogue that he does not believe in his characters. Hoffmannsthal's Balzac says: "My people are nothing more than litmus paper that turns red or blue; what is alive, great and real are the acids: the moving forces, the events."

Significantly, the theory of the disintegration of character has a complementary antithesis in the theory of the abstract unity of character. In the same dialogue Hoffmannsthal has his Balzac say that "the characters in a drama are nothing more than elements necessary to the counterpoint". The dynamic unity of characters dissolves, on the one hand, into a disordered whirl of perceptual dots and, on the other hand, into a factitious unity without inner movement. The influence of idealistic epistemology is obvious.

This is a question of approaches and of principles, not of "more" or "less" talent. Richness and depth in characterization depend upon richness and depth in the grasp of the social process. Man in reality—not as he appears in a lyrical reflection of the surface aspects of capitalist society—is not an isolated being but a social being. His every expression is enmeshed through innumerable strands with the lives of other men and with the social process. In the general current of modern bourgeois art, however, even the talented artist is diverted from the significant problems of our era, the era of great social transformations. In literature the technical capacity for expressing the insignificant, the fleeting phenomena of the purely personal has advanced, but the investigation of major social issues has deteriorated to banality.

Take a modern writer like Dos Passos. If he describes a discussion of capitalism and socialism, he depicts the locale vividly. We see the steaming Italian restaurant, the spots of tomato sauce on the tablecloth and the melted spumoni on the plate in front of us. The timbre of the voices is captured. But what they say is utter banality, the commonplace pro and con of any philistine conversation of any place or time.

Demonstrating the failure of modern writers in the delineation of the intellectual physiognomy does not mean denying their craftsmanship, their sophisticated technique. The question is: what is the basis of this technique and what is its goal? What is to be expressed with this technique? The chief subject this literature seeks to represent, for the sake of which it has developed this technique to such virtuosity, is the unknown and unknowable man. When the aim is to represent such a subject adequately and effectively, all the modes of representation of earlier literary periods will be rejected and replaced. Invention in plot, description, characterization and dialogue obtain a new function altogether; now modes of literary representation are directed toward exposing as superficial illusion our belief that we know men and things when they are actually enigmatic. All is in a fog presaging misfortune:

> ... all these things
> are otherwise, and the words we use
> are further otherwise.

declares one of Hoffmannsthal's characters.

Consequently, the chief purpose of dialogue now, for example, is to demonstrate how men talk past each other without actually communicating, to expose their absolute solitude and their incapacity to establish contact with each other. Dialogue is no longer what it had been: the expression of men in struggle or in a give-and-take, in encounters with each other; now it is instead the empty sounds men make as they slip past each other. Speech is specially stylized to this end. It is no longer the speech of daily life intensified to provide the maximum expression of the thoughts and emotions implicit in human aspirations and to expose the point of contact in the complex dialectic between a man's personality and the major social developments of his time. Now the emphasis is on what is transient and commonplace in speech, an exaggeration and stylization of the superficial and incidental; and dialogue becomes ever more commonplace, more ephemeral and more irrelevent. The reader is not expected to pay attention to the words or the content of the dialogue but to the implication, the suggestion behind the words: the lonely soul and the hopeless effort at overcoming solitude.

Among modern dramatists, Strindberg probably exhibits the greatest virtuosity with dialogue. He diverts the audience from the content to the underlying isolation to an extreme extent. In *Miss Julie*, for example, in the scene in which the seduced daughter of the count vainly seeks to persuade the cook, her seducer's former mistress, to flee with her and the butler, Strindberg accomplishes his purpose in a masterly manner. He exposes the hope, the tension and the shattering of the hope through the tempo of the heroine's speech; the cook raises no objections; her silence affects the tempo of the heroine's speech and thus accomplishes Strindberg's purpose. The author consciously treats the content of the dialogue as subsidiary; what he considers important cannot be expressed in words. Verlaine provides a provocative description of this approach in his "Art poétique" when he urges the poet never to choose words that do not offer a possibility of misunderstanding ("sans quelque méprise"). The basic rationale is so to stylize speech that it is stripped of significant conceptual content.

Despite continuous counter-attacks on the part of "abstract art", this basic line of development has not been modified. Abstract universality rests inevitably on a crass empiricism, on the commonplace and fortuitous. One is justified in asserting that all the varied techniques developed by the various modern bourgeois literary movements—some with techniques demonstrating no insignificant skill—serve only to depict the superficial phenomena of daily life in capitalist society and represent even this narrow aspect of reality as more commonplace, more fortuitous and arbitrary than it actually is.

The exclusive concern with singularity is, of course, to be found also in reflections on literary practice. Especially revealing, for example, is the following quotation from Verlaine's "Art poétique":

> Car nous voulons la nuance encore,
> Pas la couleur, rien que la nuance!
> (For we still want the nuance,
> Not the colour, nothing but the nuance!)

The blunt antithesis of shading and colour, the exclusion of colour, that is of the factors in reality with implications beyond the momentary—this decline of poetry to a mere kaleidoscope of nuances is characteristic of modern literature. The result is an uninterrupted whir, a disquieting *perpetuum mobile* without real movement, for reality is actually represented as immobile and fixed.

This contradiction demonstrates the extent to which the overemphasis on personal experience, the exclusiveness of personal experience, result in the elimination of communication of significant experience from fiction. Exaggerated fidelity to the superficial phenomena in life and the equation of direct superficial experience with reality preclude any communication of real experience in literature.

In life when we hear a person speak, we are affected first by the content. We evaluate it according to our previous experience with and our knowledge of the speaker. In addition, a listener is rarely entirely passive. Listening usually provides only part of the act of communication. Factors like tone of voice, gesture and facial expression help considerably to convey impressions of genuineness or sincerity.

The "newer" writers are concerned almost exclusively with such impressions. They ignore the fact that even the most meticulous description of qualities like sincerity provides the result of a process unknown to the reader, but not the process itself. In life, where we are directly involved in a process of communication, such symptoms can have a direct and convincing effect. But in literature the naked results of an unknown process can never provide a substitute for the process itself. The "old" writers ignored the superficial aspects of everyday reality, seeking instead to expose the dynamics in the process of communication. By depicting experiences undynamically, by presenting the dead outcome of a process, modern writers fail to involve the reader in a real communication.

In modern literature situation and plot are treated comparably. The great scenes in classical literature clarified situations that were previously confused and obscure. The purpose of Aristotle's recognition scene was to illuminate such obscurity. In major literary works of the past there were always crises in the composition at which the past and future were illuminated. As we have seen, the goal of the writer was to explore the significance, variety and universality of events.

Dramatic crises in which quantity is transformed into quality are not possible in modern literature. Composition is no longer a reflection of the movement of basic contradictions of objective reality; in everyday reality contradictions are never conclusively resolved, for in life false situations, even "unbearable" situations, can persist for an extraordinary length of time. The explosions and catastrophes favoured in modern composition do not counteract this basic weakness but intensify it. Such catastrophes and explosions are always somewhat irrational; and after they are concluded, life merely returns to its accustomed course.

The older writers included such explosions at most as episodes, never as substitutes for a dramatic development in the plot. They provided turning points in the relationships of characters—for or against each other. But in works where characters have nothing in common, such crises are superfluous and even impossible. The connection between the immediate superficial phenomena of life and the major social processes can be established only abstractly. Thus the introduction of symbol and allegory into naturalistic literature was no accident but a stylistic necessity related to a view of society. Zola can relate Nana's life to the developments of the Second Empire only by a crude symbolic contrast. Thus while Nana lies sick and abandoned in her hospital room, the drunken, raving mob on the streets bellow "To Berlin!"

Contrast through symbols and sequences of contrasting static individual "pictures" more and more replace the old methods of composition. Increasingly the compositional scheme dissolves into the representation of a single step into the dark. When individuals are isolated from each other and thus incapable of communication and every man is imprisoned within his own solipsistic and egotistical world, it is impossible to illuminate even a comparatively uncomplicated situation. The result is the schematic plots of Gerhart Hauptmann's typical dramas, *Coachman Henschel* and *Rose Bernd*. This schematism is the antithesis to the old plot. In the old plot what was obscure is clarified; in the new pattern, the veil of obscurity becomes denser; what seemed clear is shown to be impenetrable; apparent clarity is exposed as superficial insight; and irrational insistence on the incomprehensibility of life is exalted as profundity. Wassermann's novel about Caspar Hauser is perhaps the grossest example of such an approach to composition, of such obscurantism; but this tendency is present in even greater definition in the last novels of Hamsun.

This ideology obtains a paradoxical intellectual formulation in various modern philosophies, as in Scheler's "impotence of mind" and Klages' defence of the "soul" against the "mind". In any event in literature the result is that here the incapacity for conscious expression, the inarticulateness of expression, not only provides the means for copying the triviality on the surface of daily life but also has the further function of expressing poetically the "profundity" of the ignorance of causes and effects in man's actions and of the passive resignation to the "eternal" loneliness of the individual.

In keeping with the increasingly blatant irrationality inevitable in the course of the development of imperialism, all these tendencies result in a depreciation of the intellect and in the disappearance and distortion of the intellectual physiognomy in characterization. When objective reality is reduced to a "complex of sensations" and a chaos of immediate impressions and the ideological and artistic base for the creation of character is eliminated, the principle of the well-defined intellectual physiognomy disappears from literature. Such an outcome is inescapable. . . .

III

We have analysed the disintegration of classical realism in the course of the nineteenth century. The new realism which succeeded it was no transient literary fashion but the exemplification in literature of the decay of bourgeois culture and of the failure of will of the bourgeoisie to look reality in the face. Despite all refinements in technique, the *art of realism* had to decline; the cultivation of realism as practised by the classical writers sank with the decline in the general cultivation of literature. . . .

The true cultivation of realism must ever be rediscovered and reclarified within the concrete historical situation. We must investigate how classical realism has been transformed today into its opposite, into the so-called "virtuosity" which impresses some of our writers so much.

Something must be said of the contrast between the true cultivation of realism and this superficial virtuosity as regards composition, characterization, etc. Realism which aimed at giving expression to the nobility of life and to man's potential nobility was the realism cultivated by the classical realists.

How much our literary direction and consequently our modes of literary representation diverge from theirs and must diverge from theirs in the cultivation of realism becomes apparent *only* after a study of their work. The new realism arose as a reflection of the destruction of the capacities of the individual under fully developed capitalism. It depicted this destruction and developed specific techniques for this purpose. Reflecting this historical change, realism declined, the cultivation of literature declined.

The insistence upon commonplace subject matter arising in this period reflects the disbelief in the exceptional as a manifestation of man's potential capacity for greatness. Capitalist society represses and cripples human potentialities. That is why a richly developed individual like Napoleon roused such enthusiasm among great writers. Goethe called him "the compendium of the world". But to portray such a richly evolved personality, a writer must be able to comprehend the exceptional *as typical social reality*; he must cultivate a literary approach to composition and to invention (of incidents, etc.) with which he can expose the exceptional aspects in a character truthfully, personally and typically. If Joyce had set Napoleon on the toilet of the petit bourgeois Bloom, he would merely have emphasized what was common to both Napoleon and Bloom.

This propensity for the superficial aspects of life often conceals a desire to unmask the factitious grandeur of today's so-called heroism. The result, however, is again absolute capitulation to the lifelessness of the commonplace.

The insistence upon a faithful representation of a "slice of life" (Zola's "coin de la nature") is historically determined; it is the result of an incapacity to conceive reality as a unity in motion. The more true to life the "slice of life", the more fortuitous, barren, static and single-dimensional compared to reality will this "reality" be.

No subjective flavour, no Zolaesque "tempérament" can overcome this impoverishment. And when Soviet writers voluntarily assume such fetters, they cannot break out of their bonds by infusing a bolshevik "tempérament" into their work (if they even possess such a "tempérament"). Only a writer whose own life is a dynamic entity and not a rubble heap can represent a segment of life so that all that is essential to the subject matter appears in a many-sided and dynamic unity. For such a writer only reality in its dynamic unity and no "slice" of reality in isolation, no matter how accurately depicted, offers a model for a literary illumination of life.

Maxim Gorki exemplifies a true cultivation of realism in our time. The revolutionary labour movement imbued him with a belief in the potential greatness of man and with an uncompromising hatred for the degradation and crippling of capitalist society. This confidence and hatred provide the spirit of audacity in his work : the discovery of the typical in the exceptional.

Let us examine the simplest example possible. In *Mother*, a novel composed with puritanical simplicity, the heroine Nilovna is expressly depicted as an exceptional character. Gorki eliminates all details of her development that do not serve his purpose : her husband dies comparatively early; her son devotes his life to the revolutionary labour movement. In these favourable conditions, Nilovna can awaken from the semi-consciousness, the insensibility into which she has been beaten, and can advance from an instinctive sympathy for the individual revolutionaries to an ever more conscious sympathy for the revolutionary movement, to a personal revolutionary consciousness. The road she follows is certainly unusual for an old, illiterate working woman of peasant background. And Gorki underlines its exceptionality. He shows how the youth are the standard bearers of the revolution in the factory and the industrial suburb. The old people hesitate even though they are attracted to the socialists. As Rybin says, Nilovna is "perhaps the first to follow the path of her son". But—and this is the significant aspect of Gorki's approach to composition— this very exceptionalism makes Nilovna's development so profoundly typical in the general revolutionary development in Russia. The glorious road which millions of workers and peasants were to follow later, the typical revolutionary course in the liberation of the workers, is represented in a single life with intense personal vitality and individualization. This life is anything but commonplace.

This lofty cultivation of realism is manifest throughout the composition. The parallelism and simultaneous contrast in Nilovna's and Rybin's development is extraordinarily rich and artistically disciplined. So are the friendship of her son with Andrei, their common influence on Nilovna's development and the difference in their intellectual physiognomies manifested in their attitudes toward every problem within their common dedication to the revolutionary movement. Gorki has his revolutionaries absorbed in party work and through this activity he defines their personalities, exploring every aspect of their lives from their spontaneous emotional reactions to their intellectual physiognomies. Through the labour movement they must take a stand on all important issues from the style of their agitation to their love affairs, and all in profound relationship to the revolution. Even their personalities are differentiated through their capacity to experience and deal with objective social problems as personal problems.

Because Gorki is faithful to reality, he refuses to restrict himself to the representation of the petty aspects of daily life. He creates situations in which motive forces can readily emerge; he creates men who evolve as individuals and as social beings in their unremitting struggles over basic issues. He enables his characters so to express themselves that they can expose this basic issue as adequately as possible.

Consequently all Gorki's characterizations culminate in the delineation of a significant intellectual physiognomy. Gorki reveals his especial artistry in depicting the unconscious, slow maturation of individuals and in isolating the crises in this development. With creative mastery he intensifies these crises to the level of consciousness and of conscious expression. When Nilovna stays with her son's comrades after his arrest, she discusses her life with them and declares finally : "Now I can say something about myself, about people, because I have begun to understand, I have learned to compare. Before I simply existed and had no terms for comparison. Basically, we all live alike. Now I see, however, how others live, remember how I lived, and that is bitter and hard!"

In both situation and expression Gorki attains poetic truth. The literary significance of works like *Mother* lies in the fact that both in content and in form they go beyond the restricted bourgeois view of life. Only people whose personalities emerge through their social relationships, people who do not merely pass each other by but communicate with each other, can be placed in situations in which they can express what Gorki's heroine says and in as effective language as Gorki's heroine uses.

Such a cultivation of realism is perforce absent in late bourgeois realism and is still absent with some of our writers.

Such cultivation of realism presupposes the elaboration of the intellectual physiognomy of characters. With our writers the traditional insistence upon verisimilitude in details of daily life hampers the elaboration of intellectual physiognomies in two respects. In the first place, the characters they introduce into their works simply are not capable of articulate intellectual interpretations of significant situations. Secondly, the superficial situations they present are so arranged that there is no possibility of such intellectual investigations. Life itself contains points of crisis, but these writers do not know how to intensify such crises in their compositions; as a rule, they even attenuate them.

It is characteristic in much of our literature for writers to break off dialogue just at the decisive moment. Either the author or his characters declare that there is "no time" for such talk, and what is of greatest import in the personal, social or ideological context is left unsaid. Thus these writers implicitly carry on the tradition dominant in recent Western literature which considers discussions of principles and fundamental issues as "superfluous intellectualism". In the view of the modern bourgeois writer such "clever" discussions are appropriate for naïve do-gooders, anarchists or old-fashioned writers. Modern heroes, writers and readers have no time for such speechifying. This attitude is understandable in decadent bourgeois literature. Where no nodal points in social development are depicted, there is no need for elevating subject matter to conscious awareness through an intellectual interpretation. For us, however, such crises are of fundamental significance.

Thus the fact that characters have "no time" for such important matters is simply evidence of the lack of sophistication in our literary composition. It makes no difference how impressively the writer accounts for his characters' having "no time" for such discussion. In the composition of sophisticated realism like Gorki's, characters always have sufficient time for what is essential to their characterization and for the elaboration of issues and problems in all their complexity and variety. Such is the case even when the writer maintains a swift tempo in his action.

Unfortunately, such evasion of decisive discussion in which problems and characters are intensified to a level appropriate to our reality is not uncommon with our writers.

Consider such an interesting work as Panfyorov's *Those Who Have Nothing*. The theme of the second part concerns the important and widespread conflict in two different phases in the building of communism in the villages. Panfyorov accurately sketches two typical representatives of these phases, Ogniev and Shdarkin. At the crisis between the two views regarding the transformation of the commune that had been organized under the abstract idealism of war communism, Panfyorov so arranges the action that a discussion between the two protagonists is made impossible. Ogniev accidentally overhears Shdarkin talking about him : "These people did their part at the front. Out there, this . . . what shall I call it . . . this enthusiasm was necessary, but now something ·else is needed." In his despair Ogniev almost drives himself to suicide in the defence of the dam against the ice pack. With Ogniev crippled, Shdarkin takes over the commune. Shdarkin realizes that it is time for a reckoning with the errors of the Ogniev period. "If Stepan were in good health, Cyril would have told him right to his face what he thought about the commune. But Stepan was sick, and Cyril respected Stepan, and so he could not find the courage to call the members of the commune together to tell them outright that they had not done things as they should have."

Panfyorov himself senses that he had evaded an important opportunity. It is certainly possible that events could have developed as he portrays them and that such a discussion might never have taken place. But when an aspect of reality is not suited to a literary purpose, it must be modified even as Shakespeare adapted the chronicles and Italian novelle and as Balzac and Stendahl transformed events of real life to suit their purposes. They transformed their basic material so that they would be able to portray reality in its essence.

Ogniev's accident and sickness are typical examples of experiences that have not been artistically transformed and even run counter to the basic movement in the composition.

Certainly, literature cannot exclude the fortuitous. But accident in literature is not the same as that in daily life. In life the totality of the millions upon millions of accidents produces necessity. In literature the infinity of accidents is represented through a few specific instances in which the significance of the dialectic between accident and necessity is revealed. In literature *only* accidents which underline and intensify the significant aspects of the plot, theme and characters are acceptable. If they fulfil this function, accidents may even be of the most arbitrary kind. Consider the handkerchief in Othello—the very arbitrariness of the events about it and the very crudeness of Iago's intrigues with it serve to illuminate Othello's and Desdemona's nobility and lack of mistrust. Tolstoy skilfully uses such fortuity in bringing Nechludov as a juryman face to face with Maslova as the defendant at a court trial.

The accident in Panfyorov's novel has a contrary effect within the composition and contrary consequences for the delineation of Ogniev and Shdarkin as characters, especially as regards the development of typicality through elaboration of distinctive intellectual physiognomies. The chance event has no artistic or logical justification and reduces the level of the novel to limited individual significance and to a pathological diagnosis. Sickness is, after all, nothing more than sickness.

In Panfyorov's novel, Cyril Shdarkin's development as a man is sensitively and effectively illuminated through his love relationships with three different women. One feels that these three women represent three different stages in his personal and social development and that the development and dissolution of each of the relationships is not accidental, in the highest literary sense. In his actual narration, however, Panfyorov fails to overcome the impression of mere accident.

In dealing with this problem, one can recognize clearly the particular importance of the intellectual physiognomy. What is there so intense and impelling about the love relationships in classical literature? Through them we experience the involvement of an entire personality at a specific level of development. The love between Goethe's Werther and Lotte would not have been so moving if Goethe had not demonstrated the typical necessity in just such a love. His artistic development follows a very circuitous route. First we must learn of Werther's special enthusiasm for Greece and his feeling about Klopstock and Ossian; thus we see him not only as a type of the rebellious intelligentsia of the period before the French Revolution but also understand why Lotte's character and *milieu* were *exactly* what the young Werther would seek in love, considering his psychology, his social situation and his rebellion against society. The love of Werther and Lotte is no mere outburst of passion of two young people; it is an intellectual tragedy. In this case the love can illuminate wonderful, obscure qualities of the life of the society. Few writers are capable of introducing this kind of intellectualization into the private lives of their characters. With most writers therefore the events in the characters' lives remain private, accidental, unsuggestive and lacking relevance.

We believe that these weaknesses are to be traced to the traditions of late bourgeois literature. After we analyse these traditions critically, we can no longer reconcile ourselves to the limitations of gross naturalism which we have adopted and which hamper the development of socialist literature.

It is not just a question of raising the spiritual level of our literature. Much has been said about this question, and appropriately. We want to emphasize the spiritual and intellectual aspect of *form itself*, and its importance in perfecting composition and characterization. For a true cultivation of realism, writers must apply a more profound, more dynamic and less schematic investigation of the relationship of the individual to society as well as of individuals to each other. Only when they attain such literary sophistication will writers be able to exhibit audacity in writing, will they be able to free themselves from the restrictions of the subject matter of everyday existence and, undistracted by commonplace detail, grapple with the *exceptional* that is so abundant in our socialist reality.

It is a favourable sign that many of our writers and even more of our readers sense the lack in our literature. But it is not sufficient that a writer sense the lack; he must be clear about the ideological and literary bases of the lack. Ehrenburg, for example, believes that none of his positive characters adequately represents the greatness exhibited in socialist construction. But how does he seek to eliminate this weakness? By introducing, as in his *Second Day*, a parade of representative characters—by seeking to substitute quantity for quality. Such an attempt must fail. Ten or twelve characters involved in a work of construction who are loosely and abstractly related to the general social movement cannot replace a single relationship concretely and richly investigated. Indeed with Ehrenburg the "intellectual" is important in characterization. But the genuine dramatic development in the intellection is missing; he presents his readers merely with a series of cinematic "stills".

Emerson once said that "the entire man must be set into motion simultaneously". This is the secret of characterization. The characterization of the great realists, Shakespeare, Goethe and Balzac, rests on a dynamic and integral unity encompassing both the simply physical and the most abstrusely intellectual all in an integrated movement and even in contradictory motion. This integration, impossible without the elaboration of the intellectual physiognomy, is the basis of the inexhaustible richness of the characters of the great writers. They appear as rich and as many-sided as reality itself; there is an inexhaustible richness and subtlety to them. The flashy pointillism of characterization in recent literature conceals a poverty of characterization : we can easily exhaust the characters, we can embrace them in a glance, in a thought. For a true artistic representation of our social reality, we cannot employ this pointillism either in small or large doses. Only realism cultivated in the classical sense and conforming to the new reality, with new content and forms, with new characters and a new art of character portrayal, with new plots and new composition, can adequately express our great reality.

In our reality millions have awakened for the first time in human history, awakened to consciousness and to conscious social effort. With its new economic relations and its new ideology, our reality has left behind the nightmare of the isolated solipsistic pseudo-personality. It is time for our entire literature to direct itself energetically and boldly to men "awake", to portray what men have in common emotionally and intellectually in general experience and in their personal lives and finally to awaken from the sleep of decadence in which each man revolves in his "private" world, in his own narrow, impoverished subjectivity.

1936

The Writer and the Critic

THOUGH it may sound obvious and even trite, this observation must be made before we begin our discussion : the predominant type of writer and critic has changed during the decline of capitalism; accordingly, the typical relationship between the writer and the critic must also have changed.

Equally obvious but still requiring reiteration is the observation that the decisive factor in this changed relationship is the specialization arising out of the capitalist division of labour. Both writers and critics have become narrow specialists and have lost the universality and concreteness of human, social, political and artistic interests which distinguished the literary figures of the Renaissance, the Enlightenment and of all periods preceding democratic revolutions. For both, the dynamic unity within the varied phenomena of life has been disintegrated into strictly circumscribed, disconnected "fields" (art, politics, economics, etc.) which have become frozen in their isolation in the consciousness of the individual or are related only through abstract, subjective (rationalistic or mystical) pseudo-syntheses.

Finally, it is obvious that these remarks apply particularly to the main direction of the last decades. The struggle of leading humanists, a struggle without prospect of success under reactionary capitalism but of uncommon ideological significance, against the entire complex of these phenomena merely underscores the historical necessity in the general development.

Like the critics, the writers have become specialists in a "field" of work. The writer makes a business out of his inner life. Even if he does not make a complete vocational adjustment to the day-by-day demands of the capitalist book market like most other writers, even if he offers stubborn personal resistance to the market and its demands, his relationship to life and thus to art is restricted and distorted as compared to that of writers of former times.

When the writer in opposition makes literature an end in itself and boldly argues for its autonomy, then the fundamental issues of artistic method and form become secondary, and problems which arise out of the social need for great art and for a comprehensive and profound artistic representation of the universal and enduring aspects of man's evolution disappear. These basic questions are replaced by shop talk about craft and technique.

The further this development advances, the more discussion is restricted specifically to craft, technique and self-expression and the greater the departure, in both the social and artistic sense, from the objective, general problems of literature. Capitalist hostility to art results in the obliteration of any clear distinction among literary genres, a consequence especially of the introduction of new subject matter so unsuitable for creative expression that only writers most sophisticated about the fundamental questions of art can master it; the pressures for corrupting artists, too, are so powerful and insidious that only staunch spirits can withstand them. The newspaper, theatre, cinema and mass-circulation magazines—all contribute consciously or unconsciously to the confusion and destruction of the concepts of real art. Writers who utilize a single inspiration for serial novels, film scenarios, dramas and opera librettos lose all sense of genuine artistic expression and all concept of appropriate creative method; writers who leave the final elaboration of their inspirations to theatrical producers or film directors; writers who become accustomed to delivering half-fabricated products to these outlets and even develop a theory to rationalize a practice so artistically immoral cannot possibly maintain a serious, vital involvement with the basic questions of art.

The historic irony in the development of art under capitalism is that many clear-sighted writers honestly opposing its destructive philistinism actually promote the dissolution of form through their own theory and practice. By expressing their own subjectivity, their own personal impressions and purely individual problems of creative expression with profound conviction and paradoxical bravado, they seek to stem the brutal levelling and depoeticization in bourgeois literature. What they achieve actually in theory and practice is a further undermining of poetic forms, a "prophetic" anticipation of literary fashions that supposedly will be dominant decades (sometimes only years) later, fashions of another kind of levelling and impoverishment of literature.

I will adduce only one example. The lyric poet Edgar Allan Poe not only founded the modern detective story, which generates suspense solely through novelty and surprise, but also hastened the dissolution of the epic and drama into lyric impressionism through his theoretical work. In his informative essay, "The Poetic Principle", Poe denies the viability of a long poem : "I hold that a long poem does not exist. I maintain that the phrase 'a long poem' is simply a flat contradiction in terms." And in his "Philosophy of Composition", Poe illustrates his contention that a literary work that cannot be read in "one sitting" has no unity and integrity in the poetic sense : "What we term a long poem is, in fact, merely a succession of brief ones—that is to say, of brief poetical effects."

Everyone recognizes that Poe, an artist of integrity, was seeking to promote lofty art and was completely justified in his rejection of banal, academic pseudo-epics and of mass-produced novels. But since his protest is restricted to a subjective investigation of problems of effects and of modes of expression, since he does not reach beyond "shop talk" about techniques to questions of the relationship of the public to art as well as of the relationship of art to society, Poe becomes merely the theoretical precursor of lyrical impressionism. After a brief, surprising success due to the novelty of its effects, this school degenerated into as empty a routine as the very literature against which Poe had directed his confused but spirited attack.

This example is only of symptomatic importance. In the subsequent course of the development we are tracing, many lesser writers advocated even more barren theories, attracting attention briefly before disappearing into deserved oblivion.

What is symptomatic in our example, to which we would direct the reader's attention, is the "workshop" viewpoint : expression and impression unrelated to content, to the problems which root literature in life, to whatever has been the basis of the effectiveness and popularity of great works of art over centuries and even over millenia. Significantly, Poe uses Homer and Milton as illustrations of the impossibility of "long poems". No one denies that important writers, including Poe, often make sensitive and astute observations regarding basic questions in art, despite their craft outlook. In such cases the talented writer instinctively and unconsciously, and counter to his own general philosophy, reaches beyond the intellectual limitations of the mere artisan. But his basic conception of art is not changed thereby. On the contrary. The more telling such individual observations, the worse young writers, critics and intelligent readers are misled into accepting the entire craft approach as the proper approach to a valid concept of art. The modern misconception that only artists understand any-thing about art, that only an investigation of the psychology of individual creation and an analysis of personal techniques of individual writers lead to a proper understanding of art has its theoretical roots in this restricted conception of art, a concep-tion which emerges among honest, dedicated writers in justified rebellion.

It should not be thought that my criticism is directed ex-clusively at the outright "l'art pour l'art" school. If such were the case, its application would still be broad. It is charac-teristic of this period of decadence that few opponents of the art-for-art's-sake school reach beyond its restrictive concepts in theory or practice.

Roughly speaking, the opposition is divided into two extremes. The one extreme rejects along with art-for-art's-sake all theories specifically referring to art itself. These writers place literature directly in the service of political and social propa-ganda. The other extreme seeks to preserve and extend all "achievements" of the new literary movements and to combine ingeniously but inorganically (in the strictest artistic sense) particular, often correct, social and political contact, with the modern dissolution of literary forms. Although these writers achieve respect and influence among the avant-garde, they are as incapable, despite their honourable intentions, of achieving any effective response among the broad public as is the apolitical literature to which their work is artistically related. Upton Sinclair epitomizes the first extreme as conspicuously as Dos Passos epitomizes the second.

The dubious division of modern literature, on the one hand, into inartistic thesis novels which attract attention solely by their unadorned content or through artificially imposed suspense and, on the other hand, snobbish experiments in craft cannot be overcome through any artificial politicalization. The abstract impersonality of effects based solely on content provides no more of a way out than the equally abstract subjectivity of formalist art inorganically associated with content that has not been artistically disciplined.

We have been discussing a small segment of contemporary literature, a segment far above the average socially and morally and thus also in purity of artistic conception. When artists abandon discussions of problems of artistic objectivity, discussions which, as we shall see, are directed toward establishing the point of intersection of aesthetic intensification, refinement and social content, then a spirit of personal pettiness invades the literary world.

Everyone knows that the literary coolies and the hucksters who gain from capitalist philistinism are concerned only with petty personal aggrandizement and with saving their own skins in the capitalist "free-for-all". More paradoxical and more difficult to understand is the personal pettiness among dedicated and talented writers. But they too suffer from the exaggerated emphasis on personal, technical and creative originality and on novelty in expression and subject matter. They too assign an exaggerated importance to "artistic" personality, idiosyncrasies in behaviour, subjectivism in their personal achievements and difficulties in creative method, and individuality in petty stylistic refinements—granting them a value they do not really possess either for society or for art, a value they never did possess for writers in times more propitious for art.

The petty hypersensitivity of talented, dedicated writers is the result. The writers' isolation in capitalistic society, which they can overcome only under favourable conditions as spokesmen for specific views but never as artists, provides the general social basis for the pettiness in modern literary life (the exaggerated subjectivity, the frantic striving after "discoveries", envy of "competition", inability to accept criticism—not to speak of intrigue and vicious gossip). Social isolation, hothouse cultivation of personal mannerisms, confusion regarding fundamental ideological questions intensified through a conscious and exaggerated subjectivity in posing these questions and through an overstrained rationalism and foggy mysticism, which are the inevitable concomitants; restriction of problems of art itself to those of the work desk—such are the chief factors making for the "abnormal" relationship of the writer to the critic (from the former's point of view) under present-day capitalism.

II

To organize our argument we have had to limit ourselves so far to just one side of our investigation. The relationship between the writer and the critic can be investigated fully only when we also examine the changes undergone by the critic during the same period of time and under the same social influences. Only then will it be clear that the "abnormality" we have been studying is the product of the transformations in both types.

Literary criticism became a paid profession very early, with the introduction of newspaper reviews; from the start the staff book reviewer was accorded little respect. He was contrasted with the true critic, for whom this activity represented a genuine calling and not just a livelihood (poorly remunerated at best).

The general introduction of conformity that accompanies the development of capitalism affected criticism, too. The facts are known: the subordination of almost all the press to the great capitalist firms and the consequent transformation of a large portion of criticism into an adjunct of the advertising apparatus of the finance groups. Only a few, generally small reviews with minimal circulations and limited backing attempt to defend the critic's right to free expression. And even their independence becomes increasingly problematical. Once capitalists discover that opposition in the art world provides a field for profitable speculation, these movements find their Maecenases and suffer the dubious financial and moral consequences of capitalist underwriting.

Thus the great mass of critics undergo a prostitution of opinion similar to that undergone by writers in regard to representation of experience. The danger in this doubly equivocal situation is intensified by a carefully nurtured semblance of freedom and independence accorded this "select" group.

This semblance of freedom arises out of a combination of circumstances. On the one hand, even under capitalism there are always gifted, cultured and incorruptible critics. On the other hand, capitalist influence on newspapers and periodicals appears in varied disguises, and there is rarely any direct and blatant pressure exerted on individual critics. Many newspapers cater to the intelligentsia, who demand critics of rank and stature who will express themselves freely about literature and art and even conduct vehement discussions about the arts —thus such critics "pay" from the standpoint of the backers. Then, too, as we have already noted, since some capitalists are interested in particular movements in modern literature and art, periodicals seek critics who will support these movements out of personal conviction. The more dedicated, talented and cultivated the critic, the more effectively he can serve these interests.

As a result, even during the period of monopoly capitalism, there is, at least intermittently, a certain leeway for the free expression of opinion about aesthetic questions. To investigate concretely the actual situation of the critic and the transformation he undergoes during this period, we must examine the nature and extent of the leeway granted to him.

We will exclude from our investigation the conscious or unconscious hucksters of criticism and study and consider, as we did with the creative writers, only the dedicated and talented representatives of the new type of critic. However, with the critics as with the writers, the mass of mediocre and corrupt scribblers furnish an environment that cannot be eliminated from our considerations. For this environment must affect the professional critic when he judges contemporary literature and the writer when he evaluates contemporary criticism; it establishes the atmosphere which helps to determine—whether they are aware of it or not—their evaluation of each other, especially since, as has been demonstrated, the contrast between the two extremes within each group, though obvious, is not clearly demarcated; the two extremes shade into each other.

Decisive to the leeway of freedom in opinion is that it is restricted solely to aesthetic questions. The social and political outlooks of bourgeois publications are strictly defined. Literary and artistic judgments are free so long as they keep within these bounds and so long as they are divorced from social considerations or from issues of the class struggle.

Generally this tacitly accepted precondition for the publication of criticism meets less resistance from the critic than might be expected. The general trend in criticism, literary theory and literary history precludes such resistance. The "purification" of criticism of all social and political implications obviates the need for any direct capitalist pressure.

The aesthetic protest against capitalist hostility to art, a protest we have already mentioned, is expressed with even more vehemence and consequence in literary theory than in literature itself. This is understandable. The writer confronts life directly and, under favourable conditions, is impelled to a realistic representation of life even against his own ideological intentions, but the literary theoretician does not deal with reality so directly and is not so readily compelled to a realistic position. Leading writers of this period, as we have noted, often express more support for "l'art pour l'art" in their theoretical statements than they exhibit in their literary practice. Theoreticians and critics are more consequent in their defence of art for art's sake since they do not directly experience the counterpressure from a creative representation of reality.

As a matter of fact, we are concerned with a far broader current than that which openly subscribes to art for art's sake. How far literary theoreticians and historians have abandoned all pretence at investigating the relationship between literature and society is evidenced by their attempts at interpreting literary developments in terms of literature itself, in terms of the influence exercised by individual writers, works or movements on other writers, works and movements, by their consequent attempt to demonstrate how literary themes, motifs and techniques emerge and develop autonomously, and by their analyses of biographical data, of the idiosyncrasies in a writer's creative process and of the direct "models" that supposedly provide the source material for the investigation of literary problems. Such and similar tendencies (for we have mentioned only a few) evidence how, for literary theoreticians and historians, literature has lost all real relationship to the life of society. They treat literature as a circumscribed, autonomous discipline, and literature becomes, to use an over-simplification, a mere caricature and distorted reflection of certain superficial phenomena of the capitalist division of labour. The only passage to life from literature is through the gates, all too narrow, of psychological biographies of individual writers.

Of course, even in the period of decadence some critics attempt to relate literature to society and to explain it on a social basis. But once again we encounter what we have already noted in regard to the question of social content in literature of this period: falsification and distortion in criticism is less restrained than in creative writing.

It is important to recall what kind of social science predominates in this period: vulgar sociology. The popular interpretation of vulgar sociology is too limited, for vulgar sociology represents more than an attempt at diluting and distorting Marxism. In fact, it is the dominant current in social science in the period of the decline of the bourgeoisie. In his own day Marx had pointed out that after the disappearance of the Ricardo school, vulgar economy took the place of Classical economy. Modern bourgeois sociology emerged at the same time and as a direct consequence of the same development.

Vulgar sociology represents an autonomous "specialization" within social science in the narrower sense, "freed" of all relationship to history and economics and transformed into a lifeless, abstract discipline divorced from reality. The basic direction of bourgeois sociology from Comte to Pareto exemplifies the abstract and direct application of schematic generalizations to social phenomena, generalizations which are nothing but commonplaces inflated into pedantic categories.

And the social insights of "sociological" literary criticism are on an even lower level and thus even more abstract and schematic than those of general sociology; this approach treats aspects of literature it sets out to illuminate as abstractly and formalistically and as much in aesthetic isolation as the non-sociological approaches to literature. The affinity of vulgar sociology to aesthetic formalism, often remarked upon, is not a speciality of those who distort Marxism. On the contrary, it is from bourgeois literary criticism that this tendency toward aesthetic formalism passes into the labour movement. One can discover this direct, inorganic mixing of abstract, schematic sociological generalizations with the aesthete's subjective approach to literary works in full bloom in such "classics" of sociology as Taine, Guyau or Nietzsche.

Thus the sociological approach to literature offers no escape from the narrow subjectivism of aestheticism. On the contrary, it draws criticism deeper into the morass. The constant vacillation between examining the content in literature from an abstract social or political point of view and examining form from a subjectivist point of view represents no real progress or constructive evolution. The absence of a principled basis for criticism is merely intensified, for both extremes open the doors to indirect and subtle domination by the capitalists who own the press.

In the first place, because their political opinions are superficial and abstract, honest and dedicated critics can easily arrive at a political accommodation with their capitalist employers and at readily serving the purposes of the entrepreneurs. In the second place, in social crises, their detached social and political attitudes provide no basis for meaningful resistance. (The Dreyfus Affaire and the First World War are examples.) Thirdly, and most important for our present discussion, their concepts of society do not afford critics an objective framework within which to judge the aesthetic value of literary works. A critic may evaluate literature simply on the basis of its political content and ignore its artistic quality. (Such criticism, blindly identifying an author's political attitude with his literary significance, has seriously hampered the artistic development of radical democratic literature and of revolutionary proletarian literature during the imperialist period, diverting it from all aesthetic and ideological enrichment and encouraging a sectarian complacency about its generally low artistic and intellectual level.) Or he may employ a dualistic approach (one that is to be found in a variety of manifestations), completely divorcing political content from aesthetic value. The consequence then is such schematic judgments as: "quite unpolitical, even politically backward, but what artistry!" . . . "artistically deficient—but the content, the attitudes make it a work of the greatest significance." The result is thus a judgment without any artistic standard, representing mere political expedience and resulting in a blind overvaluation or under-valuation of aspects of contemporary literature. Aspects of reactionary ideology dressed up in an aesthetic disciplining are neither recognized nor criticized (despite any correct political evaluation of the general content) and may even infect otherwise progressive ideology and art without being perceived by the critic. On the other hand, there is an aesthetic capitulation to the current fashions of decadence and, as an inevitable counterpart, a depreciation of significant works simply because they do not exhibit this "interesting", "avant-garde" dualism between political content and literary form.

Individual contemporary critics striving for consistency attempt to eliminate this dualism abstractly and fall into eclecticism. With a superficial ingenuity, they associate the techniques of specific literary fashions to some tenets of a philosophy popular at the moment and exalt ephemeral technical experiments into principles of art.

And so we arrive at a fundamental weakness in modern bourgeois criticism : it is unhistoric. It makes no difference whether this weakness appears as conscious anti-historicism or as pseudo-historicism.

So far we have been examining how these tendencies arise in "avant-garde" criticism. Now we must demonstrate the underlying similarity in the social, ideological and aesthetic principles of the bitterly antagonistic aesthetic schools. (We are speaking, of course, of the dedicated and talented critics.)

We refer to the abstract, isolated, one-sided over-valuation of novelty in art. Granted that the struggle of the new against the old is decisive in the dialectics of life and that investigating this struggle and orienting science on an accurate identification of what is new and emergent are decisive for literary history and criticism. But the determination of what is new and progressive is possible only when there is an understanding of the total historical process, only with the definition of the really significant movements. In life the most diverse tendencies and phenomena intersect and overlap; what at first sight appears striking or surprising must not be mistaken for what is really new.

Pre-1914 Social Democratic revisionists took as their slogan the championing of a "new" in counter-distinction to an "outmoded" Marxism. In fact, however, retention of "orthodox" Marxism as against the neo-Kantian, Machian "innovations" (Bergsonian pragmatism in the trade union movement) was really progressive. Lenin did introduce something genuinely new when on the basis of the "outmoded" Marxism he analysed the new economic, political and cultural phenomena emerging in the imperialist stage of capitalism and thereby developed new approaches to the revolutionary labour movement and to the preparation of the democratic and proletarian revolution.

In literary questions, too, a concrete understanding of history is a prerequisite for determining what is really new and progressive. But both academic literary history and "avant-garde" criticism lack a concrete historical base. Aestheticism and vulgar sociology (in the broad sense with which we are using the term) contribute equally to the elimination of historicism. Academicism fails to appreciate the popular roots and progressive quality of classical literature and the relationship of the aesthetic problems of this literature to critical social issues and to national history, past, present and future. Hence it transforms the classics into empty cocoons, isolating superficial stylistic elements (like "correctness") and abstract peripheral aspects of content ("pure art", "elevation" above social reality, "conservatism"). It sets up the classics as scarecrows against any real progress in art.

Although justified in their protest against such a caricature of the classics and against the attempt to block anything new, the "avant-garde" critics fail to go beyond the distortion of the abstract anti-historicism of the academics. They introduce an equally abstract distortion of history, one that inverts the academic error: academic literary history turns the classics into sacred cows; "avant-garde" literary theory uses the slogan of the "new" for the same purpose. The former extreme knows no present or future of art; the latter knows no past. The "avant-garde" critics speak of a "revolution in literature" at every supposed new achievement in writing technique and announce that everything "outmoded" must be thrown in the wastepaper basket.

The unhistoricism of both extremes becomes obvious when they provide an "historical" basis for their concepts. It is illuminating to discover that the two bitter antagonists concur in their basic methodology.

In the first place, they always divorce literature from social developments or at best relate it to social developments through abstract and anti-historical concepts (extending from environment and climate to the conceptions of class and nation of vulgar sociology).

In the second place, the continuity in the general development (admittedly full of contradictions and often advancing by "leaps") is disrupted; methodologically there is no difference whether one says: "With Goethe's death true art came to an end"; or, "With naturalism (or impressionism, expressionism or surrealism) an entirely new kind of art begins." The one-sided, abstract emphasis of difference alone, the characterizing of a new phase of development with the words, "it is something entirely different from what preceded it", without taking into account the dynamic dialectic in the struggle of the old and the new in the manifold variation of the forms of the elimination of the old, always means missing the really new and historically decisive and exalting superficial (technical, psychological) features to central categories.

In the third place, both extremes reveal their unhistorical and non-social view by deriving their basic critical terminology from biology and psychology, extending and inflating and generalizing these terms into formal abstractions and applying them uncritically to the superficial phenomena of declining capitalism. The academics employ naïve anthropological concepts like "ageing" or "weariness" or "exhaustion", while the "avant-garde" critics generally use terms like "the rights of youth" and the necessity for "new stimuli". Although this is the general pattern, many theoreticians of the "radically new" base their arguments on the biological, psychological or mystical "ageing" of contemporary civilization. One need only point to the "cosmic fear" that provides the rationale for abstract art in contrast to the "empathy" in Worringer, the ideologist of expressionism, or to the theories of Spengler, which continue to be influential.

If one investigates this mystical psychologism not to expose its inherent fallacy but to discover the motivation that generates it, the common methodology in both opposing movements emerges even more clearly. The obtuseness and overstimulation, the bored apathy and restlessness for new sensations, the dull accceptance of daily routine and the panic in the face of uncontrollable and unpredictable economic forces: these and similar reactions arise out of the common base of life under monopoly capitalism. They develop, simultaneously or alternatively, in the same individuals. The apparently limitless variety of these typical phenomena, essentially similar and uniform, is a manifestation of complicated class differentiation and of rapid transformations in the class struggle, which evoke diverse reactions from different individuals.

From this discussion it is clear that even with the best will and conviction, most critics and literary specialists today can mount only a weak and hesitant resistance to the general policies of their class. The inevitable result of the intensifying pressures and of their own refusal to apply objective evaluations to literature even in mere aesthetic judgments is anarchy —an anarchy of opinions, a war in which each man is on his own, an ideological chaos : the consequence, we must reiterate, of the general capitalist corruption of the great mass of creative writers and critics.

Under such social and ideological conditions how can the relationship between the writer and critic be normal? With few fortunate exceptions, each must consider the mass in the other camp as enemies of little account. For the writer a "good" critic is one who praises him and attacks his neighbour; a "bad" critic is one who scolds him or promotes his neighbour. For the critic the great body of literature represents a dreary livelihood that demands much effort and pain. In this atmosphere where no real criteria exist, where there are political and economic pressures from the capitalist employer, mounting routinism and sensationalism and inexorable competition constantly threatening financial and moral destruction, unprincipled cliques emerge for whose aesthetic and moral level no outsider can have any respect. (The few exceptions among writers and critics do not change the general situation.)

What does the relationship between the writer and the critic look like in the capitalist world today? A long time ago, without thinking specifically about writers and critics, Heine declared prophetically :

> Rarely did you understand me,
> And rarely did I understand you,
> Only when we met within the filth
> Did we understand each other right away.
> (Selten habt ihr mich verstanden,
> Selten auch verstand ich euch,
> Nur wenn wir im Kot uns fanden,
> Da verstanden wir uns gleich.)

III

Let us now consider the predominant type of significant writer before writing became a specialization. What strikes one first is that the overwhelming majority of these writers also occupy an important place in the history of aesthetics and of criticism. We are not speaking now just of those figures who come first to mind like Lessing, Goethe, Schiller, Pushkin or Gorki.

Consider the great writers who did not produce critical works in the strict sense. What are Hamlet's speech to the players and his subsequent Hecuba monologue (apart from their dramatic and poetic significance) but extraordinarily profound theoretical disquisitions on the aesthetics of the drama and, even more, on the relationship of art to reality? And we can go back further in history to the dispute between Aeschylus and Euripides in Aristophanes' *Frogs*. Apart from its direct comic effect, does it not provide an acute analysis of the social, moral and aesthetic factors in the dissolution of Greek tragedy, in the demise of the tragic era?

Examples of such literary criticism within literary contexts are numberless. From the Hamlet discussions in Goethe's *Wilhelm Meister* through Balzac to Tolstoy and Gorki there is an unbroken chain of splendid examples of this organic unity of literary effectiveness and theoretical insight. Such achievements cannot be over-emphasized in evaluating and defining the "old" type of writer. The literary greatness of these epoch-making figures rests in great part on their philosophic stature. Only because they investigated all the great cultural questions of their day thoroughly and on their own were they able to become comprehensive mirrors of reality and to illuminate and depict their time in all its aspects.

When viewed from such a standpoint, their original and profound meditation about problems of literature and art is seen as one aspect of their intellectual mastery of reality, as a prerequisite for an accurate and adequate representation of reality. The impoverishment in life experience we encounter in later "specialist" writers, the limitation and pettiness of their original philosophic preparation and of the deep and comprehensive ideology they forge out of their personal experience on their own shows itself in the low artistic level of their characterization. Paul Lafargue called attention to this development in literature in a comparison of Balzac and Zola (and as a thinker and creative artist, Zola is a giant beside most of his successors in the period of imperialism). The great writers of the past investigated literature and art as social phenomena of importance in a dynamic interrelationship with man's social and moral existence. A thorough understanding of the relationship of art to life is basic to comprehensive and incisive characterization. Such investigations were never developed *ad hoc* in the literature of the past. For a writer to do research in a particular field of knowledge because he requires facts for a work in progress is an "achievement" of our time. The writer of the past created out of the great reservoir of a rich life; any preliminary research he might make was merely to obtain specific details to expand the work he was preparing.

The direction and consequently the content and scope of an author's investigation were fundamentally different. The writers of the past concentrated on a profound investigation of their subject matter and sought a breadth and depth of understanding. But writers who set out to master an area of experience for an immediate task at hand, interested only in those aspects of the area which are directly related to the thematic material they have defined in advance are easily satisfied with one-sided, incomplete and superficial observations.

So far in our discussion we have not studied how literature itself provided a favoured subject of investigation for writers of the past. We have established the generally high ideological level of their apperceptions, and this high level carries over into their treatment of literature. We had to begin our discussion with these observations in order to demonstrate how the serious, precise objective investigation of aesthetic problems by outstanding writers was necessarily and organically related to the great breadth in their creative work. Figures like Hamlet or Wilhelm Meister could attain multidimensionality and poetic depth only because their creators had themselves mastered the problems which move them as characters and because their creators were equipped to delineate not only their biological, psychological, social and moral qualities but also to define precisely and sensitively their intellectual physiognomies. Balzac demonstrates as much command of the basic issues of art in his representation of Frenhofer or Gambara as of finance in his representation of Gobseck or Nucingen.

As far as general content and plasticity of characterization are concerned, this union of great writer and great critic is only an aspect of the general question of the artist's ideological level.

The effects of this union become everywhere apparent when we examine critical activity in the narrow and strict sense with such men as Diderot or Lessing, Goethe or Schiller. Equally striking here, too, are the universality of interests and the passion for objectivity. About the former we need not speak at length. Diderot and Schiller were thinkers who play an important role in the history of philosophy; Goethe's significance as a forerunner to Darwin, and Lessing's as a founder of modern Bible criticism are well known. These great writer-critics were never for a moment mere specialists in literature. They always considered literature in its broadest relationship to the decisive issues of the social and cultural life of their time. They posed their special aesthetic questions within such frameworks. They sought to relate their investigation of the nature of art and of particular concrete artistic questions to the most pressing and fundamental issues of the social and cultural life of their time.

Their passion for objectivity is more difficult to understand today. To grasp this endeavour in all its dedication and scope, we might well examine representatives of the type of writer who did not write independent formal criticism but made observations on literature in defence of their own work and as part of their search for self-clarification about their own creative practice. From this standpoint we might consider the prefaces of Corneille, Racine or Alfieri or Manzoni's manifesto against the *tragédie classique*, the scattered comments in Fielding's novels, Pushkin's notes, and even, to include writers of the transitional period, Hebbel's notebooks, Gottfried Keller's letters and Otto Ludwig's essays on drama and the epic.

The point of departure in each case is their own work, understandably and fortunately, for the writers' intimate acquaintanceship with the subtlest problems of the creative process makes these observations uniquely valuable both as regards the concrete questions posed and the solutions arrived at. But the problem with their own work provides only the point of departure and the foundation for the artistic investigation. Despite their diversity and often bitter opposition to each other, all these attempts represent a search for objective truth. Though varied in content, ideology and method, they all pose this question: what is objectively valid in my creative efforts? How can that which I strive after most profoundly as a writer flow into the objective laws of the artistic forms? How can I discipline my subjectivity and my artistic individuality within the objective requirements of art, within the objective social currents unconsciously demanding expression in the people?

This striving for objectivity with the passion of lives of rich experience and artistic discipline is what distinguishes the critical activity of leading writers both before and after the craft specialization that set in under capitalism. Manzoni began his investigation with special problems of his own creative practice just as Flaubert did (to cite the most profound and significant writer of the new direction). Both writers seek to define what particular problems the particular time in which they lived and wrote posed for their own work, how they had to prepare themselves as artists intellectually and artistically to deal with these problems.

But Manzoni passes beyond this subjective investigation of particular problems in his own creative work to the decisive objective problem: the problem of representing history in literature, a problem arising out of the ideological needs after the French Revolution and Napoleon, when a new historical sense and a desire for the representation of history in literature had developed. The fervent yearning of the Italian people for national unification that arose in this period imposed the responsibility to depict the tragic turning points of the national past so dramatically that the nation might understand the social and individual factors leading to the political splintering of the nation into small independent states and that the Italian people might learn and gather strength for future struggles from the tragic lessons of the national past.

Manzoni realized that the dramatic form that had developed in the Romance literatures from Corneille to Alfieri was too limited and generalized to provide adequate artistic expression of the new historic sentiments through struggles of richly evolved characters. Thus he declared war on the *tragédie classique*. Although Manzoni's investigation arose out of his own particular creative struggles, it expanded to comprehend questions of broad social and aesthetic significance. Clearly in his critique of the characterization, plot and the representation of history in classical tragedy, Manzoni was actually evaluating the old drama in terms of the ideal drama he felt was needed in his time, a powerful, popular drama that would rouse national patriotic sentiments.

Flaubert's reflections on aesthetic problems take an entirely different course. They are the tragic, aesthetic, socially penetrating confessions of a gifted writer about struggles against the artistically unpropitious environment of capitalist society, about the ugliness of bourgeois life, aesthetically and morally, and about the enforced isolation of the artist of integrity under capitalism. We certainly do not seek to underestimate the importance of Flaubert's memoirs. To grasp the social, psychological, moral and aesthetic problems of the modern artist, one can turn to no more revealing documents than Flaubert's letters. They are, in addition, crammed with sensitive observations and insights regarding individual aspects of the creative process and of particular technical problems of creation—language, prose rhythm, imagery—and comments on the styles of individual authors. But the basic direction and approach are subjective, especially when Flaubert treats his own decisive creative problems. From a social point of view, his confessions remain at the level of bitterly ironic complaints about the writer's isolation under capitalism, complaints which at best rise to brilliant anarchistic paradoxes. What strikes the critical reader of his letters is that though rich in content and provocative, none of his aesthetic comments ever probes the fundamental questions of literature. What changes plot, characterization, composition and subject matter undergo in the modern novel in the confrontation with the new unadaptable life experience and the new possibilities for reaching the public, what new fundamental questions arise for narrative technique; how Flaubert's own attempts at dealing with the new problems result in modification of the principles of the earlier epic technique; to what extent his attempts are mere personal attempts at solutions or how far they offer new general directions for narrative—to all these questions we find no clear response in Flaubert's journals, not even an attempt at a clear posing of principled questions. It is illuminating and characteristic that when a debate developed between Sainte-Beuve and Flaubert after the publication of *Salammbo*, the critic, by no means so astute as Flaubert regarding basic aesthetic questions, posed far more significant questions about the historical novel than the great novelist, who replied with subjective, technical comments about craft.

Schiller's point of departure in his essay "Concerning Naïve and Sentimental Poetry" is also subjective and even autobiographical. It is a commonplace of German literary history that the theoretical disagreement between Goethe and Schiller is rooted in the difference in their personalities and that Schiller wrote this essay as a theoretical defence of his creative method as against Goethe's. Where does this investigation advance to, despite its deeply personal motivation? It develops into a theory regarding the essential difference between modern and ancient art, a theory providing an aesthetic explanation for the decisive differences in fundamental questions of style between ancient and modern art; further, it clarifies these aesthetic contrasts in terms of the differences between ancient and modern societies, differences which produce differences in attitude toward the problems of life. Schiller set out to examine a question of vital personal importance and found his answer in a summary history of the philosophy of art, a work that provided a new direction to aesthetics and became the precursor for the systematic historical and theoretical achievement of Hegel.

Characteristic of such critical achievements of outstanding writers, despite all their differences, is the integration of the social necessity of art with the subtlest problems of form as well as the integration of the artistic concreteness in all special questions of art with the general laws of literary form. Thus it is not surprising that most critical analyses by the writer-critics deal with problems of genre. The theory of genres more or less provides an intermediate sphere, a sphere of conceptual transmission between a general philosophic formulation of ultimate aesthetic problems and the writer's personal efforts at consummating his mode of representing reality in an individual work. The theory of genres provides the sphere of objectivity and of objective criteria for individual works and for the individual creative process of each writer.

Nothing, therefore, characterizes a writer who is conscious of his art so much as his attitude toward this complex. Ideological capitulation to capitalist philistinism is reflected in nihilism regarding genres; the anarchy in the surface manifestations of capitalist life, the fetishizing of human relationships, the disappearance of the determining influence of public reaction on the forms of literary production—against these conditions, the majority of modern writers no longer mount any resistance; they accept these conditions (even if with grinding of teeth) as they are. Further, many even welcome new manifestations of the intensified inhumanity of capitalist life as "brand-new stimuli" providing the basis for a "radically new" art. Thus, consciously or not, they hasten the dissolution of literary forms and the confusion of the genres.

The modern writer thereby demonstrates his alienation from his potential audience and his contempt for the ordinary reader. The two extreme positions approximate each other in their attitudes toward society. On the one hand, the writer gives no thought to the artistic expression of his content and relies simply on the direct impact of the content itself or perhaps plays with meretricious effects to provide suspense; on the other hand, the writer concerns himself exclusively with finesse in diction or mere technical innovations. In either case, underlying the apparent contrast is an artistic and social nihilism, a rejection of popular judgment. Such an attitude appears in varied forms and in varied degrees, from the fanatical ascetism of the literary missionary to the outright cynicism of the potboiler and the scepticism of the aesthete, who not only does not afford the public the possibility of understanding his esoteric literary contrivances but even denies such possibility to the so-called literary connoisseurs.

In contrast, the great writer-critics were intensely preoccupied with questions of genre because they were convinced of the enduring impact of great art on the public. Respecting the judgment of readers of the present and future, they earnestly sought the form suitable to their content.

Of course, we have merely introduced the ramifications of the philosophy and aesthetics of genres with these preliminary remarks. The search for the specially suitable forms of expression can get bogged down in semantics or can be elevated to an analysis of the fundamental questions of art and of the relationship of art to reality. The latter was the approach of the classical writer-critics. They recognized that the variety in forms of literary expression is not the result of chance or whim. On the contrary, forms embody particular, enduring modes of human relationship and conditions of life. Investigating the principles governing these relationships and conditions and evaluating their own subject matter in the light of these principles to determine how all the potentialities in their subject matter can achieve full exposition, the writer-critics strike out in the most varied directions, but they always end with an investigation of objective reality and the relationship of art to life.

First the life material to be represented is objectivized. The writer who ponders over his content does not simply take it as he finds it in his immediate experience or as it is presented in immediate reality. Instead he probes for the essential content in this experience, in this aspect of reality; next he seeks a plot through which the potentialities of this material can be fully explored and exposed. At this stage of his creative effort, he confronts the principles governing genres. In investigating the artistic problems of his material, the artist discovers the suitability or unsuitability of certain forms for particular content; the dramatic form, for example, is suitable for exposing certain content but restricts the movement of other content. Nor is this accidental. The exploration of the laws of the individual genre leads to objectivity not only aesthetically (revealing the principles governing the dialectic between content and form, a dialectic which determines the success or failure of a work of art independently of an artist's conscious effort) but also in the personal and social sense: the deeper the artist probes, the more clearly he exposes the social and human premises on which individual genres are based.

Such investigations only seem abstract (particularly with the current prejudices or the fads of subjectivist immediacy). Through such apparently abstract explorations, the artist exposes what is concretely relevant historically, what is "the order of the day" (Goethe) in the real historical sense—as was the case, for example, with the principal issue in the *Ham burgische Dramaturgie*. It is generally recognized that Lessing's goal in his aesthetic and theoretical struggles was the national unity of Germany on a democratic basis and the destruction of the ideology of the semi-feudal, splinter-state absolutism. His devastating critique of the *tragédie classique*, his correct interpretation of Aristotle in his polemic against the French distortion of the seventeenth and eighteenth centuries and his championing of the Greeks, Shakespeare and Diderot—all were directed toward his single goal.

In his grappling and investigating, he discovered the basic laws of the drama. Decisive to his investigations was his search for objective aesthetic truth. The writer-critic Lessing, who as a writer sought to develop a bourgeois drama that would express the tragedy and comedy of bourgeois life with the same dramatic power with which Sophocles and Shakespeare had depicted earlier societies, as a critic greeted Diderot's experiments with enthusiasm while recognizing the unresolved problems in Diderot's work. In seeking the point where all these theoretical and creative efforts intersect, Lessing, the writer-critic, arrived at an understanding of the essential integrity of tragedy as a genre, above and beyond all historically and socially conditioned variations.

His recognition of the essential similarity in the form used by Sophocles and Shakespeare is one of the decisive aesthetic insights we owe to the great writer and critic—an insight as profound and penetrating as Schiller's distinction between ancient and modern art. In each case, questions were posed and solutions arrived at in connection with immediate problems of personal literary practice; the resolution of the immediate problems required investigations reaching far beyond the personal and subjective to the objectivity of art as art and as an element of social existence. To elevate these investigations above mere personal problem-solving requires strength and an inner richness in the creative personality. The general exaggeration today of the importance of subjectivity in creative work arises primarily out of the flabbiness and poverty of the writers as individuals. The more writers are distinguished from each other simply on the basis of spontaneous idiosyncrasies (almost solely physiological and psychological) or on the basis of artificially cultivated personal mannerisms, the greater the danger in the low level of ideology that any extension beyond the immediately personal would eliminate their "personalities" altogether; and the greater weight is assigned to simple and direct subjectivity, which is even equated with a writer's talent.

The writer-critics took personality and talent for granted and wasted no words discussing them; the absence of either could only be the object of contemptuous mockery. To them what was worthy of investigation was what resulted from the serious application of personality and talent in grappling with the problems of the objective world. What today is called artistic personality, Goethe labelled "manner". By this term he understood recurrent, obvious personality traits, elements of native talent not yet disciplined enough to penetrate subject matter but merely adding certain superficial qualities to a work. The break-through of creative individuality into art, into real creation, Goethe called "style"; he meant divorcing the work of art from what is merely personal to its creator and the independent existence of the reality represented in the work and the absorption of mere natural subjectivity (even more of artificially cultivated subjectivity) into the normal objectivity of real art. And Goethe knew that the resultant paradox is a contradiction vital to art : only through the subjugation of the native or even of the artificially cultivated subjectivity can the artist's real personality—the personality of the man as well as of the artist—properly emerge.

IV

Besides the writer-critic, only one other type of critic has made significant contributions in the history of aesthetics : the philosophic critic.

To understand this type, we must leave the bourgeois world of the last decade and abandon all its prejudices, just as we had to do in investigating the writer-critic. Under declining capitalism, the philosopher, too, has become a "specialist", whether in a narrow field like epistemology or in logic, the history of philosophy, ethics, aesthetics or any other strictly defined area of bourgeois philosophy, whatever its title. With such philosophers our investigation is not concerned. No man of considered judgment would pretend that a Husserl or a Rickert (even when called Dessoir and considered a "specialist" in aesthetics) has anything significant to contribute to the theory of art. To discover what constitutes a true philosopher, one must go back to the time before culture came under the domination of the market, before capitalist specialization.

It is obvious that real philosophers were indeed far removed from the snide and cowardly indifference to current social and political problems that characterizes the professorial "specialists"; nor did they have anything to do with apologetic glorification of reaction in their times. (Under the apparent non-partisanship conditioned by class relations of the day, it is easy to recognize with such serious philosophers as Epicurus or Spinoza a universality of interest in the problems of their time.) The philosophic critic is always well-informed about current social problems, often even a pamphleteer or a political figure.

Belinsky, Chernyshevski and Dobrolyubov provide examples of this type, thinkers to whom literary criticism owes a significant debt. The two greatest pre-socialist thinkers, Aristotle and Hegel, were social theoreticians as well as aestheticians. The momentous significance of their contributions to art theory derives from their general universality—a universality which encompasses basic social problems, indeed has its origin in social problems and its direction in the investigation of social problems.

The very names we have adduced show that among the truly productive aestheticians, the pure types are extremely rare; and the universality we have mentioned in both types makes it impossible to distinguish decisively the one from the other. When we take Aristotle or Hegel, on the one hand, and Pushkin, on the other, the contrast seems clear enough. But if we group such figures as Plato, Shaftesbury, Herder, Chernyshevski, Diderot, Lessing, Schiller and Goethe, we are hard put to determine where one type begins and the other ends. Any attempt at distinguishing clearly and absolutely leads to hair-splitting.

Yet there are substantial differences between the two types, in method and approach. No matter how broad the horizon of his social and personal interests or how original and profound his intellect, the writer-critic generally approaches aesthetic problems from the point of view of the concrete questions arising in his own creative work, and he refers his conclusions, even when he arrives at these conclusions only after investigating broad contemporary philosophic and artistic questions, back to his own work—not, of course, as we have seen, without raising the investigation of his own creative problems to a level of generalization approaching historical, social as well as aesthetic objectivity. But for the philosophic

critic, the writer-critic's point of conclusion, objectivity, provides the point of departure. (Both agree in their partisan
approach.) For the philosophic critic the arts are always in a
systematic relationship (an historically systematic relationship
with the thinkers of the last flourishing period of philosophy)
with all the other phenomena of reality. And since art is a
product of man's social activity and since the leading thinkers
were always probers of social problems, they were principally
concerned with the social origins and effects of art. Plato's and
Aristotle's reflections on art clearly exemplify the approach of
great philosophers to the problems of art.

To define the basic difference (and essential correlation)
between the philosophic critic and the writer-critic, one must
forget the conventional abstract, metaphysical categories of
recent bourgeois philosophy. To use an example at hand, one
may not conceive of the difference we are discussing in terms
of the philosopher's approaching his subject deductively or
analytically and the writer's approaching his subject induc-
tively or synthetically. Actually, there can be no serious
examination of a subject that is not both analytic and
synthetic, for the writer as well as for the philosopher.

For both it is a question of exploring the objective relationship at hand between art and reality, especially social reality.
For both types of productive criticism this relationship is the
starting point as well as the goal—as it is in reality itself. For
the writer-critic, however, this relationship is given *a priori* :
life itself with its infinite and inexhaustible complexity of
phenomena and determinants. His effort, primarily creative,
is directed toward representing within the microcosm of a
single work of art the inexhaustibility in the social organism
and in its dialectical movement. His theoretical approach is
accordingly intensive and microcosmic : the general laws of
reality (of the entire historical development) set the bounds—
often indefinite and blurred—for the clearly recognized
"intermediate zone" of the genres. The proper appreciation of
these general laws, an appreciation determined by richness of
life experience and profound reflection on the basic issues in
life, is the precondition, basis and means, not the goal and

object of knowledge. The converse is true for the genuine philosophic critic. His impetus to knowledge is directed at the totality of phenomena, the universal principles governing phenomena. Since, however, correct general knowledge is always concrete and never abstract (no matter how abstract the terminology used to describe it, as in Hegel), his investigation leads to a concrete analysis of the "intermediate zones" and even to the analysis of individual phenomena. These are, however, never conceived as autonomous microcosms but as components or aspects of a total development.

Thus the question is of two philosophic modes that are ultimately complementary: for art the relative autonomy of the "intermediate zones" and of individual works is as much a fact of reality as their relationship to the whole. Human knowledge can only approximate to the objective infinite variety in life. As Hegel declared, every phenomenon is a unity of unity and of diversity. The two major representative types of criticism approach this inexhaustible richness from opposing sides: from that of unity and from that of diversity; the one seeks to establish unity in diversity and the other, diversity in unity. The consequence of their productive complementary activity is an illumination about art, a theory of art which impels and facilitates the further development of art. Such is the normal relationship between the writer and the critic.

Goethe and Hegel, two mighty representatives of the two complementary types, were clear about the necessity of their complementary roles. Goethe repeatedly expressed his debt in science and in his creative work to the great philosophers from Kant to Hegel. Hegel, for his part, had the greatest admiration for Goethe's theoretical achievements and warmly and astutely praised Goethe's particular methodology (itself an outgrowth of Goethe's creative activity). This interrelationship characterizes Goethe's entire theoretical activity and is exemplified most clearly in his use of the term "Urphaenomen" (archetype). Goethe understood by this term the perceptible unity of concrete universality within a phenomenon itself; a phenomenon conceived abstractly with all accidental qualities eliminated but never losing its basic particularity. In the language of the idealistic dialectic of the time : the conceptual prototype of the particularity in the phenomenon.

Goethe employs the term "Urphaenomen" primarily in his writings on natural science. In an autobiographical note about these studies, he does remark, however, that he had composed his *Roman Elegies* and his aesthetic essay, "Simple Imitation of Nature, Manner, Style", and his "Metamorphosis of Plants" simultaneously and as part of a single investigation. "Together they show what was going on inside me and what position I was assuming in regard to these three cosmic areas [art, aesthetics and natural science—*G.L.*]." Thus one is justified in viewing the "Urphaenomen" as a methodological analogue to Goethe's theory of genres.

How decisively this methodology dominates Goethe's entire work in aesthetic theory and how it inevitably culminates in his theory of genres is most apparent in his short but pithy essay, "On Epic and Dramatic Poetry". This essay summarized a long discussion with Schiller conducted in correspondence and direct conversation about their specific creative problems; as always happened with the great poets of the past, the discussion developed into an investigation of the general laws of the epic and the drama.

We are investigating here only Goethe's methodology. In order to distinguish epic from drama conceptually and concretely without overlooking in the distinction what was common to both modes of reflecting life and the total life process, Goethe starts with a discussion of the mime and the rhapsodist. By accurate and creative abstraction, he identifies the mime and the rhapsodist with the performing artist and the poet and is thus able to define the typical approaches of the epic and the drama to reality and to life experience put into artistic form and to reveal the typical reactions of an audience hearing an epic and attending a drama. Having established the typical norms for these two modes of audience reaction, he is able to deduce without difficulty the basic laws for the epic and the drama.

Do Goethe's mimes and rhapsodists actually exist? Yes and no. Goethe derived every stroke of his picture from reality;

his synthesis, however, reaches beyond empirical reality, especially since he derives in each detail a functional relationship and a motif of development that becomes immediately apparent through his elimination of everything purely individual or accidental. His mime and rhapsodist are as real or as unreal as his "Urflanze" (archetypal plants). Goethe employs "Urphaenomen" as much in his studies of literary forms as in his scientific studies in evolution.

Such methodological consistency is not distinctive to Goethe, but it is a vivid exemplification of the essence of the literary and artistic approach to the phenomena of life. Goethe is the most consequent philosopher among the poets of all time. By consciously avoiding the most abstruse generalizations, the specific area of the philosophers, and by assuming as the alpha and omega of his thinking the "intermediate zone" of the "archetypes", the specific area of the writer-critic, he shows that this mode of thinking is more than a mere expedient by which great artists achieve philosophic orientation and more than a simple auxiliary for clarifying the premises of a creative effort. It is an important and constructive, peculiar and independent conceptual apprehension of the world of phenomena. In his "Urphaenomen" Goethe consciously created a methodological model for the philosophical speculation of the writer-critic.

This illumination had an extraordinary impact on contemporary thinkers. Schiller did indeed reduce Goethe's intellectual achievement to mere Kantianism at his first encounter with the "Urphaenomen", declaring: "This is not an experience but an idea" [in the Kantian sense—G.L.]. But this crass contrast of experience and generalizing reveals Schiller's failure to comprehend the essence of Goethe's method. But in the course of the collaboration of the two poets, Schiller learned more and more to appreciate the productiveness of Goethe's concept; and the figures of the "elegaic", the "idyllic" and the "satirical" poets in the essay "On Naïve and Sentimental Poetry" are as much "Urphaenomen" as Goethe's rhapsodist and mime, even though Schiller never succeeded in incorporating "archetypes" organically into his own philosophy.

Hegel, who perfected idealistic dialectic, was the first to appraise the methodology of Goethe the theoretician accurately and without reservations. He saw in Goethe's methodology a relatively independent, uncommonly important precursor to a fully evolved dialectic: the unconcentrated motion with inner contradiction of the particular phenomena perceived by the senses but not fully apprehended intellectually, still in bud, so to speak, and precisely for that reason most effectively expanding the general, universal, philosophical dialectic, which is more developed and consequently further divorced from life and from the senses. Regarding the "Urphaenomen", Hegel wrote to Goethe: ". . . in this twilight, so spiritual and lucid in its simplicity and so visible and perceptible to the senses, the two worlds salute each other—that is, the dialectic of absolute idealism and perceptible phenomenal existence." We know how Goethe rejoiced at Hegel's appreciation, and anyone who has studied Hegel's *Aesthetics* attentively recognizes the decisive impact the "Urphaenomene" of Goethe's aesthetics and creative practice had for this work.

But the "Urphaenomene" undergo an essential transformation when incorporated into a philosophical system. If what is decisive for the writer-critic is their autonomy, the concrete embodiment of particular laws of a group of phenomena illuminating the creative elaboration of individual impressions and expressions; what is primary for the philosopher is the synthesis and integration into the totality of life. The "intermediate zone" therefore is the area of transition from what is obscure but immediately at hand into illuminated life. The difference, the contrast and the complementary extension depend on whether this final illumination, this return into actual life, is accomplished poetically or philosophically, whether the "intermediate zone" leads to *Faust* or to the *Phenomenology of the Spirit*.

The "forms" whose transformation from one to another in the movement of the "spirit" provides the primary concept of Hegelian philosophy are intimately related methodologically to Goethe's mime and rhapsodist. But while the theoretician Goethe considered these as ultimates, as the actual exemplifications of the "Urphaenomene", Hegel saw them as aspects of the total process, aspects to be resolved, resolving or already resolved. Each appears as the historical and philosophical displacement of a preceding "form", lives out its life by disclosing the potentials latent within it and then is transformed into a succeeding "form". As forms, the epic and the drama participate in this dance of life and death of "forms". And the substantial agreement in Goethe's and Hegel's aesthetic conceptions of the epic and drama is striking.

In a philosophical system, however, the "Urphaenomene", the "forms", lose the apparent stability and definition they possess for the writer-critic, for the reasons we have just noted. Before our eyes they emerge out of a life-totality not yet conceptualized and as their components become conceptually clear and their individual dialectic unfolds and their autonomous existence, their stability and their definition are affirmed, they submerge within the totality of life now apprehended. Aristotle followed such an approach in elaborating his theory of the drama. In the *Phenomenology of the Spirit*, the framework for the conceptual synthesis is the historical evolution of mankind. The necessity and particularity of the epic and the dramatic, the progression of epic, tragedy and comedy is seen as a reflection of the historical destiny of a people. The external and internal structure in the life of a people provides the motive force for the dialectic of birth and death. The "Urphaenomen" has its origin and history, its birth and death, within this process.

Thus we seem to have reached the opposite pole to Goethe's methodology. But only apparently. The Hegelian "forms" of the epic and the dramatic maintain and unfold the special laws of their particular character like Goethe's mime and rhapsodist but on a broader base in life, more obvious, more mobile; thus, and in apparent paradox, they are less abstract than Goethe's, and the genesis and demise of all forms of being and consciousness is not a concept foreign to Goethe. The lines of the "West-East Divan" could certainly provide the epigraph to the *Phenomenology of the Spirit* :

And as long as thou hast not
This "Die and Become!"
Thou art but a gloomy guest
On the dark earth.
(Und so lang du das nicht hast,
Dieses : Stirb und werde!
Bist du nur ein trueber Gast
Auf der dunkeln Erde.)

The contrast thus implies a complementary extension. For the philosophic critic the "intermediate zone" is clearly just an aspect of the dialectical process. For the writer-critic, on the other hand, it possesses an apparent stability and autonomy. Only apparent, however, for it dissolves when conceived and extended philosophically—without losing validity in content or productiveness for theory or art—as an organic aspect in the dialectical system; for the writer it is really only an "intermediate zone" for realizing in his literary work the proper contact with illuminated life.

The normal relationship between writer and critic is to be found in their encounter within this "intermediate zone": in the cognition and grounding of objectivity in the creative process. On his side the writer rises to the objective relationship between his own creative problems, inevitably subjective in origin, and the laws of reality and their representation in art; on the other side, in the normative aspects of concrete and particular phenomena, the philosopher confirms whether and to what extent he has understood the general relationships in reality and in the forms which mirror them. Thus there is a convergence of Vico's new conception of Homer and Goethe's theory of the epic as genre or the Aristotelian theory of tragedy and Lessing's attempts at raising the struggles of the revolutionary bourgeoisie to the level of tragedy.

With Vico and Hegel and Belinsky, Chernyshevsky and Dobrolyubov this general interrelationship becomes conscious and historical. The theory of genres in Hegel's *Aesthetics* develops into a history of world art; and the great democratic revolutionary critics show how the evolution of the Russian people is mirrored in the artistic transformations and turning points of their literature. The integration of philosophy, literary history and criticism (consequently, concretely a *philosophy* of art) must be emphasized if we are to comprehend fully what the philosophic critic is and what his normal relationship with the creative artist is. The division of labour under capitalism has led to the disintegration, as we have seen, of the organic integrity of the various modes (invalid when isolated) of the scientific approach to art, and has transformed them mechanically into circumscribed "fields" of specialization and turned them over to "specialists", who become increasingly isolated from each other in their activity.

The result is the sterility and loss of principle we have already observed in modern literary history and criticism and consequently their abnormal relationship to literature. Both operate on purely subjective judgments of taste. For when one rejects a work of art simply on abstract political considerations (as did the German Kaiser when still in his glory with his "the entire direction does not suit us") and not because of an aesthetic distortion of reality or a distortion in the representation of reality, then one is only blinding oneself in thinking one has risen above the unprincipled judgments of the pure esthete.

Of course in literary history one also finds the ideal of the "pure historian", who pretends to investigate and describe only historical relationships (ignoring economic and social factors). That with such (with all respect) "methods" no judgments are possible but only unconscious, superficial, absolutely unprincipled, relativistic evaluations, lacking criteria or standards, requires no demonstration.

To complete the picture we must point to the counterpart of this type, the modern critic who boasts of his anti-historicism. In his view, the "old world" of art, which is defined variously according to the need of the moment as extending from Homer to naturalism or to impressionism, has finally petered out. A "radically new" art has supposedly replaced it. Out of the rubble heaps of the meaningless past, indeed, one may arbitrarily pick out, like raisins in a cake, whatever scraps suit the fad of the moment, Negro sculpture or German baroque drama.

We have already analysed the consequences of such criticism. Let us glance at the developments in literary history. I will illustrate the state of affairs with the Germans. Most of their critical concepts (orders of importance, historical periods, etc.) were established by the leading critics of the turn of the nineteenth century, Herder, Goethe, Schiller and the Schlegel brothers, only to be watered down later by liberal political historians like Gervinus. Heine's conception of literature, based on Hegelian philosophy, represented a step forwards, but because of the reactionary turn in German politics, his contribution had little lasting effect. After his time only the philosophic critic and publicist Franz Mehring added anything new to German literary history.

The "specialists" in literary history have merely mouthed the old ideas with or without a note of individuality. One can hardly consider as new ideas grouping writers according to their years of birth (R. M. Meyer) or according to their place of birth (Nadler), or consider these as ideas at all. The "specialists" emerging under the capitalist division of labour can make no contributions of significance even within their circumscribed fields. (We are not speaking here of pure philology, the emendation of texts, etc.)

Indeed, one can go further. Even where German literary history is pursued on false premises, the impulse is not from the "professionals" but from the writers and the philosophers. Anyone who has followed the recent development of German literary history can see that it has been determined by Nietzsche, Dilthey, Simmel and Stefan George. The theoretical views which they introduced are absolutely erroneous, twisted and reactionary and have brought further distortion to literary history. The "specialists" in literary history cannot even exhibit any originality in distortion; here, too, they mechanically reproduce scraps of ideas the winds scatter to them.

With these negative observations we complete our picture of the philosophic critic. The unity of the philosophic cognition of general contexts, of probing investigation of the concrete historical development based on a recognition that decisive changes in art are related to turns in human history, of objective criteria for aesthetic evaluation, criteria based on an historical and systematic understanding of the nature of art and the decisive significance of the individual artist of genius and of the individual work of genius within this evolution makes for a philosophic literary critic.

Only when such critics can co-operate with writers who have become genuine judges of their own and others' art as a result of their own subjective probing, does there arise a normal relationship between the writer and critic. Such was the situation during the Enlightenment, the German Classical period, the great upsurge of realism in the first half of the nineteenth century and during the democratic revolutionary period of Russian literature and criticism.

Of course such a situation does not exclude struggles over principles. In class society literary movements are the inevitable, if not automatic, outgrowth of class struggles, of conflicts among social and political directions. The contradictions in Germany at the time of the French Revolution and Napoleon, the many crises in the evolution of France from 1789 to 1848, the ideological differentiation of democracy from liberalism in Russia, to present only a few examples, are mirrored in literature and criticism. Understandably, there is no less intensity in these struggles and no less vehemence in the antagonisms in literature than in politics itself.

Understandably, too, such struggles, carried out in real life conditions among men living in class societies, are not without elements of personal vindictiveness and malice, pettiness, gossip or rancour. Bourgeois literary historians gleefully detail the squabbling and thus obscure the political significance and aesthetic consequences of such conflicts, falsifying them by making analogies between them and the unprincipled literary wrangling of their own times. What is important is the level and content of these struggles. In setting the social and aesthetic direction of Russian literary history on a scientific basis, Belinsky, Dobrolyubov and Chernyshevski sought to hasten the political clarification of the democratic revolutionary movement and to liberate it from supine liberalism. Anecdotes about "insulted" authors reveal nothing of the significance these quarrels have in the ideological and aesthetic evolution of literature. The political presupposition behind this situation will be apparent to most readers today without any further explanation. Harder to grasp (since it runs counter to the clichés of modern thinking) is that rising above the pettiness of literary brawls means rising to aesthetic objectivity, rising above mere subjective problems of craft to an objective aesthetic. With envy the contemporary reader reads Balzac's critique of Stendhal's *Charterhouse of Parma*—the fiercest conflicts on every issue, whether of social life, politics or literature—and yet (or rather, on that account) the pure, free air of genuine and mighty history: the fundamental issues of life viewed dialectically, the kind of conflicts which promote progress.

We breathe this pure atmosphere in the aesthetic statements of the writer-critics as much as in the philosophic critics. This tradition continues into our time in Maxim Gorki, who carries this heritage into the socialist examination of art. That is why he makes so many modern writers uncomfortable. For in his *Conversations about Craft* he propounds a conception of the writer's task qualitatively different from that dominant today. His approach has nothing to do with the virtuosity of contrived effects. He calls for mining the rich source material of life itself to wrench out what is typical and to crystallize out of it the loftiest spiritual, the most significant social and the most appropriate aesthetic content.

His great contemporary in philosophical criticism, Lenin, precisely appreciated the significance of Gorki's ideological struggles for socialist culture. Between the writer of the critiques of Tolstoy and Herzen and the author of *Mother* and the *Karamasovshchina* there existed normal relations.

Writers and critics alike must rediscover and regain for themselves the loftiest ideal in the tradition of their vocations in order to re-establish normal, fruitful, complementary relations.

Pushkin's Place in World Literature

E v e n outside Russia Pushkin has long been well-known and a popular poet of great influence. And yet can we say that we really know him? I am not thinking primarily whether we know his total life work insofar as many of his most important works have not yet been translated, but whether we really know who Pushkin was and what he represents in the development of world literature. The fact that many readers and writers have taken delight in the perfection of his verse and have succumbed to the moods evoked by scenes of *Eugene Onegin*, does not signify a step in this direction. On the contrary, as long as the picture of Pushkin is associated so closely with the radically false and mystical conception of the development of Russian society and its literature that prevails outside Russia, these impressions can in many respects hinder the appreciation and understanding of Pushkin's place in world literature.

It is to this question that this essay is addressed.

I

Russian literature and Pushkin's significance in it can only be grasped from the perspective of 1917. Only thus can one view the main current, the total development and the place and importance of the major figures from a proper vantage. Contemporaries, including the early champions of democracy, could not properly assess the role of individual writers in world history, especially Pushkin's, since they could not foresee the end to which this road was leading. Despite the enthusiasm which Pushkin aroused in Gogol and Belinsky and later in Tolstoy and Dostoyevsky, each of these men of necessity underestimated to a certain degree his significance in world history, for the role of Russian literature generally in world history and world literature could not be foreseen at that time. Only after October 1917 was there the perspective for such an assessment, a perspective provided by the event itself and by its consequences for the Russian people and for all the peoples of the world. The greatness of Russian literature, which many had previously merely sensed, now emerged in full clarity. One might say that no matter how broad and deep the national and international impact of Russian literature had been until then, its effective role in world history really began only with this event.

The October Revolution exposed the normal, classical quality in the Russian development. What does this mean?

In previous cultural history we know only three developments of this type. The first was the Greek experience, from Homer to the collapse of the democratic polis. Winckelmann and his followers established that the objectifications of cultural life, above all, the artistic objectifications, develop in an organic sequence and dialectic conforming to an inner logic. Even the outstanding progressive bourgeois thinkers, however, were not able to confirm this fact scientifically. Marxism first demonstrated that the logical sequence of categories coincides with historical necessity, of course with the difference that logic does not take into account the accidents which inevitably accompany historical developments and can disturb their course. The classicism and normality of the Greek development arise from the fact that accidents play a lesser role and have a less disturbing effect on the inner dialectic than in other historical developments. Engels emphasized this fact sharply in his treatment of the fall of the Athenian aristocracy and the rise of the Athenian polis. Thus Marx could characterize the period of the Homeric epics as the "normal childhood" of humanity.

The second similar development is the French, from the collapse of feudalism to the French Revolution. (Balzac and Stendhal are in the aftermath, the concluding phase, of this development as Plato and Aristotle were of the Greek.) In a letter to Mehring, Engels draws a parallel in this connection between German and French history in which he shows that all questions arising of necessity in the life of both peoples were resolved by the French, while the Germans never succeeded in finding an organic transition from a lower stage of development to a higher.

The third classical development is the Russian. For a long time this quality of Russian history was not apparent. Before Lenin scarcely anyone understood concretely how the democratic revolutionary movement, consistently becoming more and more democratic, had blossomed at last into a proletarian revolution. While in Europe after 1789 the bourgeois democratic movements experienced a constant deterioration, and the traditions of the French Revolution grew fainter and fainter or turned into caricatures, the Russian development achieved a classical conjunction of revolutionary democracy with liberalism and then on a higher level of development, a classical achievement of the revolutionary leadership of the proletariat and a creation of a workers' party of a new type, the classical form of worker-peasant soviets. (A repetition of 1793 on a higher level in which the class-conscious proletariat led by the party of the new type took the place of the Jacobin plebs.) The Russian counterpart to the European revolution of 1848 is 1905. But the failure of the democratic revolution in this case proved to be merely a dress rehearsal for the victory in the proletariat revolution. Although the defeat in 1905 inspired such aspirations, there was not sufficient time for the bourgeoisie to establish the hegemony of its own ideology, an ideology already in full decadence. In 1917 the Russian people —the first in the world—marched out of pre-history and began true history : socialism.

But with the achievement of socialism the Russian development assumed a significantly different place in history from the previous classical types of development. Greek history from the cultural point of view offers an exceptionally fortunate instance of the dissolution of a primitive communist society. But its short flowering, no matter how magnificent, was trapped in the economic cul-de-sac of a slave-owning society. And the French development following the victory of the bourgeois revolution created a capitalist nation which through its own inner economic dialectic nullified the heroic illusions with which it was born.

The Russian development, on the other hand, brought to an end the "pre-history" of mankind, liquidating class society and making the peoples of the Soviet Union the leaders of mankind on the road to the final liberation, to the one true freedom : the elimination of exploitation in a classless society. The Russian development toward this goal is decisively of a different quality from any that preceded it.

The development of Russian literature has to be surveyed from this viewpoint, retrospectively, if Pushkin's significance in world literature is to be appreciated.

II

Belinsky recognized precisely that with Pushkin a new phase was introduced in Russian literary history. And he saw, too, that after Pushkin a literature arose that was qualitatively different. In the development of literature, Pushkin comes after the Enlightenment and before critical realism (the Gogol period).

These limits cannot be drawn with metaphysical nicety, but on a national or international scale such demarcations between periods can be recognized. When we think of Hölderlin and Goethe and Keats and Shelley alongside Pushkin, then we can observe from the point of view of world history a short-lived but fresh and monumental renewal of the classical ideal of beauty, a consequence of the changes which the French Revolution and Napoleon had impressed upon the face of Europe. This period and the simultaneous English industrial revolution saw the rise of capitalist production and the establishment of bourgeois domination of society, achievements providing perspectives to be realized in Central and Eastern Europe. This period is distinguished from the Enlightenment, which paved the way to the Revolution, by the fact that the basic inner contradictions of the new society had already become apparent, even if not fully obvious—especially the economic contradictions when viewed from a class standpoint. On the other hand, the exposure of these contradictions is not yet sufficiently intensive as to become the immediate centre of all expressions of cultural life. This exposure was accomplished after the July Revolution in the wave of critical realism. As we have already noted, this division into periods is not fully relevant to Russia, but there is no doubt that the transition in style in Russian literature to the Gogol or critical period had already begun during Pushkin's lifetime.

In speaking of a wave of realism, we were thinking of Balzac, Stendhal, Dickens and Gogol. In that case, are the great writers of the earlier period, Goethe and Pushkin, not realists? This is the crucial problem for literary history. The decisive change of style is to be understood and defined as a change within realism. For realism is not a style but the social basis of every truly great literature.

The international impact of the French Revolution, which transformed the world and mankind, would have been impossible without heroic illusions. These illusions were, of course, intimately related to the new reality with all its contradictions and to the birth of a new kind of man. In the time of the Enlightenment these heroic illusions were closely associated with antiquity, with the ancient ideal of beauty. If it had been, however, exclusively a question of illusions, even though socially and objectively determined, then it would have been impossible for a great realistic art to arise on this base. The yearning for beauty of the era, though different in content and form according to nation and class, corresponded to the actual problems of the new world in birth.

In discussing Feuerbach and Chernyshevski, Lenin emphasized that the ideal of realizing the totality of man was one of the chief aspirations of revolutionary democracy. In the following paragraphs we will attempt to concretize how the ideal of beauty of the era is related to this problem. Since, however, such a relationship doubtless does exist, we can state in advance that the longing for beauty, the attempt from Hölderlin to Shelley to realize beauty in art, represents far less a renewal of something past than a call to a future still unborn, a rousing of the energies in contemporary reality striving toward this vision.

Thus our key aesthetic question is : what is this beauty? The answer is not simple by any means. Let us first attempt a negative limitation. Many people confuse beauty with artistic perfection, with the fulfilment of universal formal requirements appropriate to all the arts. If, however, both Raphael and Daumier are said to have created "beauty", then beauty loses all meaning as a specific aesthetic term : it becomes simply a synonym for artistic perfection. Then there is the academic misconception regarding artistic content according to which art should represent only "beautiful" people, objects, etc., beautiful according to conventions of the time determined by class outlooks. It is clearly unnecessary to examine this error.

Is there any sense at all in speaking of beauty as a specific category in aesthetics?

We think so. And Pushkin's poetry, tales and *Eugene Onegin* pose this question sharply. If we compare Pushkin's *Eugene Onegin* with a novel by Saltykov-Shchedrin or Pushkin's "Dubrovsky" with Kleist's "Michael Kohlhaas", we instinctively sense that there is an objective and justified question regarding beauty involved, one that demands an answer.

Perhaps it is easier to deal with this question in relation to the latter comparison since the themes of the two tales are similar. In what respect is Pushkin's tale beautiful in the concrete aesthetic sense of the word? And how is it that Kleist's is merely an outstanding work of art?

The subject matter in both treats of injustice in the social class structure (concretely the declining feudal society), an injustice for which apparently there is no ray of hope for a solution. Whatever a powerful individual with important connections wants to do, he can accomplish even without the slightest legal sanction for his action. A victim who does not submit in silence and even attempts serious resistance, inevitably, despite the justice of his cause—we might better say, because of the justice of his cause—comes into conflict with law and order in the clash. Society will hound him, for all his sensitivity and decency, into committing crimes.

Both Pushkin and Kleist depict with verisimilitude such a society and the spiritual reactions that it inspires. In Kleist, however, greater, more profound, more pathological disturbances emerge in the psyche of the rebel who has been driven to sin than are required by the thematic material, disturbances so profound that they affect the flow of the narrative. Pushkin never goes beyond the depiction of a "normal" man. His rebel never exhibits warped characteristics; on the contrary, in each of his actions he demonstrates an intellectual and moral superiority and thus exposes more acutely the rot within the decaying society. The warping is in those who conspire to commit injustice, a warping carefully balanced, without exaggeration and true to the reality of the social conditions. Thus it is a question of a typical social disorder rather than of a pathological disturbance in an individual.

The styles in the two tales reflect the contrasting artistic approaches. (We must call attention again to the similarity of the point of departure.) Both Pushkin and Kleist achieve the concentration, the unadorned simplicity of good short stories. But only Pushkin's narrative maintains the deftness and lightness of tone and the serenity of the classical novella —even when relating horrors. Formally this is the consequence of Pushkin's depicting men and situations and setting them vividly before us with far less analysis than Kleist employs. This difference in style reflects what we have sketched above. Normal people or disturbances in people can be depicted through direct life experiences and without detailed analysis when these people or these disturbances arise objectively out of the structure of society and are obviously socially determined. Pathological disturbances in an individual, on the other hand, must always be explained and analysed (or set against a romantic, fantastic and exotic backdrop) for the representation to be at all convincing.

The most important basis for the contrast, however, is Pushkin's optimistic perspective. Although Kleist sets his tale in the period of the Reformation, he makes the reader feel the terrors of the decaying feudal society as the oppressive atmosphere of the present, and one sees no way out. (This is the inevitable effect of the German development on a modern romantic poet like Kleist.) Pushkin does not set his tale in the distant past and certainly does not underplay the horror of the events; he himself does not preach, directly or indirectly, but the poetic atmosphere permeating the work and the epic line of the narrative proclaim loud and clear: this cannot continue! (We will return to the significance of the stylistic problem involved here.)

Does he achieve harmony? Yes, insofar as harmony is the artistic resolution of existing social dissonances and not, as with the academic classicists, a purely formal "harmony" excluding all dissonances, providing ready-made resolutions or suppressing the dissonances until they become unrecognizable. Pushkin sees everything and speaks out. One small example. Tatyana is waiting for Onegin; the beautiful poetic singing of the peasant girls is heard from the garden; the atmosphere is haunting. But Pushkin does not hesitate to add that the servant girls are singing at the master's orders so that they will not be nibbling at the berries while they are picking.

But the harmonious resolution of dissonances, the most generalized manifestation of beauty, leads us back to our principal question: first, if what we have said is so, how then does this harmony differ from the ordinary aesthetic resolution of social dissonances indispensable to every self-contained work of art. Once again: is there really a difference between beauty and artistic perfection? Second, is it possible to represent harmony in art as long as art is the reflection of the reality of a class society?

The two questions are intimately related. Let us take them one at a time. *Aesthetically of value*, or beauty considered in relation to abstract form: the unresolved social or personal disharmony in the subject matter can indeed be resolved when the social issue and its solution are correctly posed; when, accordingly, the form has not been damaged, that is, when the deformation caused by a class society merely provides the subject matter of the work and does not affect the formative principle. (We can merely note the extremes in this problem; in reality these extremes merge into each other and separate from

each other over a great many intermediary stages.) Such a solution must be based on a humanistic view for the author's social
and moral sense to be healthy enough for him to be able to
judge with reasonable accuracy what is good and what is bad
and what is healthy and what is diseased.

Beauty differs qualitatively from such an attitude, even at
its highest level. Truth of social content and its clear exposure
in an artistic representation is once again the first prerequisite.
But the fundamental goal is to save the ideal of the totality of
the individual in the midst of the distortions inevitably arising
in class society (always keeping to the truth and defending it).
The second solution, to follow Schiller's striking formulation,
is to take poetic revenge for these distortions.

This antithesis permits the answer to the second question.
If we simply generalize and consider the individual, particular
poetic solution from the start as being typical, then doubtless
it is impossible to represent harmony clearly in the artistic
reflection of class society. But this by no means implies that it
is aesthetically impossible in the representation of an individual
instance, too, as the case of Dubrovsky demonstrates. That
Pushkin does not let the rebel Dubrovsky break down as an
individual certainly does not mean that Pushkin considered
the optimistic outcome socially typical. In this instance, Pushkin undoubtedly chose the short-story form as the one best
suited aesthetically for exposing in the very exceptionality of
the case an optimistic view of the future; for this purpose the
novel or the drama would have been far less appropriate.
Indeed the exceptionality ought not to be taken literally; for
absolute exceptionality would go beyond the bounds of literature which offers a truthful reflection of reality, and would
mean an embellishment of the social dissonances represented.
The exception, the exceptional individual and situation, always
mirrors, when exposed artistically, an actual social direction,
even a direction not absolutely dominant or at least not
obviously so. The truth in the artistic representation need not
follow word for word the *direct* sense of the resolution of the
action represented : thus the suicide of the heroine in
Ostrovsky's "Storm" and the arrest of the heroine in Gorki's

Mother proclaim without any commentary the optimistic perspective, despite the tragic gloom of the moment.

Thus, too, in Pushkin's short story the rebellious hero driven to crime by corrupt feudalism does not triumph. The beauty in this story merely demonstrates that in an accurate representation of the actual dynamics of the social relationship of forces the author can show that decadent feudal society does not succeed in corrupting the hero's humanity or undermining his human decency. Such an outcome is closely related to Pushkin's revolutionary optimism : he depicts the individual and popular forces which in the future will overthrow the rotten social order. The rescue of the human totality in realistic representation provides the basis for the spare beauty of the epic line; this beauty derives, however, from the social perspective and social attitude of the poet.

This perspective and attitude in Pushkin's case is confidence in the revolutionary aspiration to overthrow the society of the day which inspired the best elements of the nobility. The mass of Russian aristocrats, of course, provided support for czarism, which had established itself on the vestiges of feudalism and now stood at the threshold of capitalism. Only a tiny vanguard, influenced by the French Revolution, the Napoleonic wars and above all by the glorious patriotic struggle of 1812, not only perceived that Russian society had to be transformed but also were prepared for deeds to accomplish this transformation.

The question is further illuminated when we think of Kleist's short story. Here the basis for the hero's crippling and consequent pathology and for the narrative's wandering off into grotesque and fantastic romanticism is first to be sought in Kleist's incapacity seriously to criticize the feudal society with which he himself was in close sympathy because of his own Prussian Junker ideology. As a skilled writer, he was often able through his incisive observations of life to transcend the limitations of his ideology and even to oppose his ideology, but in the last analysis Kleist remained in this, as in most of his other works, in the grip of his Junker prejudices. On the other hand, his pessimism and propensity to decadent emotions arise out of the persistence of this insoluble conflict and propel the inner life of his hero into the deformations of a feudal society in dissolution. The pessimism of Kleist's tales is exemplified also— in contrast to Pushkin's works—by the spiritual incapacity of his characters to oppose the forces destroying humanity.

III

Having clarified these questions, we can advance to a closer and more concrete definition of Pushkin's beauty. We should point out first of all the accurate proportionality of emotions, experiences, character qualities and events. This is not primarily a question of formal balance or polish. We do find careful balance in all of Pushkin's works, but formal perfection is an ultimate artistic consequence, the social and artistic bases of which must first be investigated. To summarize briefly, Pushkin's formal balance arises out of his special creative approach; whatever he creates, whether representing an emotion or an event, conforms precisely in content and form quantitatively and qualitatively to the most profound, real tendencies in objective social reality, to the proportions of movement, change or transformation in the direction of the future, of progress, even when these tendencies appeared only intermittently and vaguely in Pushkin's day.

Of course all these manifestations are time-bound and evolve with the times; such changes occur within Pushkin's own life. But what remains important is that the poet's creative view, which determines these proper proportions, always reaches beyond his day and beyond superficial prejudices and constantly corrects these proportions from the perspective of the future and of progress.

There is far more involved here than in the problem of deformation discussed earlier. For the proper proportionality about which we are now speaking encompasses the healthy as well as the deformed and the sick, the emergent as well as the dying. The question is whether the poet correctly grasps and represents the proper social and historical proportions of *all* these phenomena. Literary history offers many contrary examples of illuminating failures, particularly glaring for our discussion. In every period many new phenomena emerge that are genuinely new, much that is new and interesting, which even outstanding writers underestimate or, more often, overestimate out of the enthusiasm of discovery, the preconceptions of the time, or out of class prejudice.

Such under or overestimation in reaction to decisive historical changes is one of the most important factors in the outmoding of literary works. With the passage of time, the historical development of society makes both the proper proportions in particular aspects of social developments and the advance or degeneration in these developments obvious even to the ordinary man. No matter how talented a writer without this insight may be, the succeeding generation inevitably fails to understand him and coldly rejects many details in his work. This is what it means to become out of date. (Ibsen's dramas are an especially clear example in view of his great talent and staunch honesty.)

The reason why beauty never becomes dated is intimately related to the fulfilment of fundamental aesthetic (compositional, representational, etc.) principles and to the personal and social bases of these aesthetic principles. The basis for lasting beauty is the grasp and representation of content in proper proportion. This gives Priam's embassy to Achilles its unfailing beauty; on this rests the greatness of Sophocles and Shakespeare.

In dealing with this question, bourgeois aesthetics speaks of the representation of the "eternally human". This is, of course, an idealistic distortion of the problem. What bourgeois aesthetics during the progressive period evaluated on this basis —in many concrete instances correctly—historical materialism can assess accurately today: it is a question of distinguishing what are persistent values from what are persistent threats to civilization and the proportion between these, a proportion time-limited but exposing the enduring values or threats. The aesthetics of historical materialism oppose not only the metaphysical "eternally human" but also the relativism of decadent bourgeois aesthetics, which holds that "eternal human nature" does not exist and then goes on to deny any human progress and to see every emotion and experience only in connection with the immediate moment of their origin and to dismiss everything else as cobwebs in the brain.

Let us attempt to clarify what we are now discussing with a look at Pushkin's "Queen of Spades". We choose this example since in this work Pushkin came very close to the critical realism which followed his own period and very close, too, to the subsequent period of decline. The characterization and career of the hero resemble those of the heroic types of his great realist contemporaries, Balzac and Stendhal; and he even anticipates much of Dostoyevsky, Pontoppidan and other modern writers. If one can say that later Russian literature stems from Gogol's "Overcoat", one can say the same of Pushkin's "Queen of Spades", as Dostoyevsky noted in his famous eulogy of Pushkin.

Yet out of this subject Pushkin composed a short story of spare line, classical in concentration and free from the fantastic "apparatus" of a Hoffmann or Poe, in sharp contrast to the best modern critical and analytical novels. The contrast is not primarily formal and aesthetic. Pushkin saw his hero as clearly as his great realist contemporaries or successors; he examined him inside and out just as realistically and saw what was typical in this kind of man from the point of view of the bourgeois society of his time. If Pushkin depicted all this in a lean, brief tale and did not make his hero the protagonist of a mighty novel, the main reason is that he does not make Herman, the hero, a "fallen angel", a tragic hero like Dostoyevsky's in *Crime and Punishment*, but only the victim of a fantastic catastrophe for which he himself is to blame, a catastrophe which ends prosaically and without any ado in a madhouse. Behind this difference is the fact that Pushkin sensed, whether consciously or unconsciously, in this kind of figure not only what was typical for his own times but also what would recur in the future.

In the course of the nineteenth century no one was fully aware of the extent to which, through his perspicacity, Pushkin had provided an accurate delineation of this type; yet the

violent struggles had already emerged which determine the
destiny of such a type, struggles in which most leading writers
were deeply involved; the destinies of Rastignac, Julien Sorel
and above all Raskolnikov were related closely to the intimate
personal problems of Balzac, Stendhal and Dostoyevsky. But
Pushkin looked at Herman from the outside as a certain
interesting and significant type, one with whom, however, he
himself had nothing in common.

This difference in viewpoint reveals where and how we must
refute certain generally accepted evaluations of Pushkin. We
have already mentioned Dostoyevsky's famous speech on
Pushkin. Dostoyevsky properly recognized the "Petersburger",
that is, the big-city character of certain Pushkin heroes, products of developing capitalistic culture (Onegin, Aleko,
Herman). At the same time, however, he entirely misunder-
stood Pushkin's attitude toward these heroes. It is known that
Aleko ("Gypsies"), the new man of a Russian society that had
not reached maturity and was far from freeing itself from
feudal institutions, seeks refuge from the aesthetic and moral
ugliness of his time among "natural", primitive people. (Later,
Tolstoy was often to treat this same theme.) The attempt ends,
of course, in tragic failure. Dostoyevsky drew the following
lesson in his Pushkin speech: "Bow, proud man, humble your
pride!" He passionately rejected the accurate statement of his
contemporaries that Aleko had fled to the gypsies from Gogol's
police and civil authorities, that is, from a feudal absolutism
on the way to becoming capitalistic. Thus he reversed and rejected the profound social criticism in Pushkin's work. Dostoyevsky would have eliminated any sharp condemnation of the
aristocracy, who in Pushkin's day were moving toward capitalism. But Pushkin's old gypsy declares with Shakespearean
pungency after Aleko's catastrophe:

> You were not born for a wild existence—
> You chose freedom for yourself alone.

Pushkin was criticizing the capitalistic, anarchistic and
selfish aspects of the rebellion against a feudal society moving
towards capitalism, a rebellion which he considered objectively

and subjectively justified. He recognized that this quality of the rebellion was an inevitable outgrowth of the social conditions of his time, that it could not be justified and did not in fact point the way to the future.

On this account, in his representation of this type, he surpasses in artistry many of his outstanding and even great successors. On this account, we can call the artistry in his creative representation—beauty. We can see now what complicated social issues underlie the aesthetic beauty of a slight, spare, lightly sketched tale.

We can appreciate the artistic and social distinction in this beauty more concretely in the fundamental principle of Pushkin's composition: briefly speaking, the concentrated, unadorned representation of individual details in integration with the polyphony of the total work. That capitalist society does not afford a favourable environment for art and especially for great literature is evidenced, among other things, by the ever-increasing complexity of the social relationships and class divisions and the consequent spiritual effects and spiritual developments. Writers are compelled to attempt to elaborate all details polyphonically and to compress all viewpoints within each detail in order to make the totality of the fictional world true to life and understandable.

But the polyphonic elaboration of details for artistic reasons concentrates all parts too much and thus renders formal, representational contrasts (no matter how important to the social content) difficult and establishes a uniformity in the entire compositional structure. This weakness results from the fact that in the truthful mirroring of modern life of critical realism, narrative and characterization become more and more encumbered with expository analysis. Consequently, the artistic differentiation of the components in the great genres becomes more and more difficult; hence the great battles over style of the nineteenth century and the loss of artistic plasticity in a great portion of the literature of the twentieth century. We recognize this conflict as early as Balzac; Flaubert is already fully conscious of the repressive monotony that is the inevitable outcome of this development. The closer we come to our own day, the more difficult and ineffectual this struggle becomes, and the more writers surrender in advance in the struggle and develop a supposed artistic rationale out of this effect of capitalist philistinism.

Pushkin stands on the threshold of this basic problem of modern literature. Of course, this question may not be approached from the point of view of abstract form or of so-called "pure" art. The very social and personal reasons why Pushkin never succumbed to the capitalist deformation he portrays, account for the unadorned simplicity of detail in his style—a quality that is characteristic of folk literature. Such stylistic simplicity has been introduced artistic-ally, especially since romanticism, without any integrated work of art ever resulting. For analytic polyphonic fullness of detail, the modern capitalist principle of artistic representation, is in such constant opposition to this folk "colouring" that the artificiality in the total effect and the fundamental antagonism to folk literature further destroy the compositional integrity of a work. (Such a disintegrating tendency can be seen most clearly in the short stories of the German romantics, Tieck, Arnim and Brentano.) There is even less chance of artistic success when, as is often the case in the imperialist period, writers strive to imitate the unadorned simplicity of folk litera-ture without adapting their characters inwardly or contextually to the folk spirit; the absence of analysis or the artificial exclusion of analysis introduces an impoverishment of content without achieving the concentrated self-containment of folk art.

Like his older contemporary Goethe, Pushkin considered this unadorned simplicity a fundamental element of folk poetry, but he also realized that this manner of expression could only be fruitful in poetry when it was an organic expression of the poet's view and when the poet regarded all literary forms as the highest modes of expression of the national life; when the entire way of feeling and thinking and posing problems, etc., had become an indirect or direct echo of the joys and sorrows of the nation. "What is tragedy supposed to express?" Pushkin asked. "What is the purpose of tragedy?

The individual and the nation, the fate of the individual and the destiny of the nation."

It is not possible to represent the many-levelled reality created by modern society through a mode of representation in which each individual event explicitly and in all its ramifications exposes the totality of its motivating factors; this totality can emerge only through the whole of a work. In the latter approach, each particular event is, however, not only complicated in content and form but also contains a dominant, decisive and ultimately characteristic quality. The simple mode of representation adopted by great writers from folk art provides in each individual event the plasticity to this decisive quality, a plasticity in the complete perceptual abundance of its manifestations; it provides this plasticity precisely where life itself, bursting into this decisive and characteristic quality, brings it before our eyes; thus this quality can be represented with simple palpable plasticity. The polyphony and spareness of composition achieved through the simple narrative line is the expression of a profound creative approach and methodology; all the components so varied in colour, tone and value are creatively summed up in an ideal, artistic unity, and each detail is accorded its appropriate place, its proper weight and precise proportions in accurate conformity to reality.

It is clear that such balance is not primarily a question of artistic representation : proportions can only be properly adjudged, as we have already noted, by a writer who perceives them within the social conditions of his own time, in relation to the future perspectives of society. With its direct plasticity, such a mode of representation exposes immediately an error in judgment, whereas with the modern analytical representation a distortion or misapprehension of the proportions in historical development can escape notice for a brief period.

Pushkin's method of representation thus rests on the classical side in this basic question, a question that is one of the most crucial in modern art. If one may use a musical analogy: Pushkin pursues Mozart's path and not Wagner's, still less that of the post-Wagnerians.

Think of *Boris Godunov*. In a variegated, Shakespearean

representation of history Pushkin shows us how in the decay of feudalism the difficult birth of Russian absolutism took place. Here we can draw attention to only one factor in Pushkin's mode of composition to illuminate his method. In his drama Pushkin shows, among other things, how, since the people themselves were not yet capable of playing an active and leading role in determining society, in the transformation both the mighty and lowly were crippled and deformed. This theme emerges everywhere in the drama as an obvious effect on and motivation for the characters. But it appears explicitly only in two scenes that are qualitatively different in tone and character. The old monk Pimen has retired from life to become a chronicler in an attempt to maintain his integrity. The false Dmitri, like the other active characters, falls victim to history. Only in one scene does he try to break his bonds and preserve his human dignity despite the historical role which deforms his humanity. He attempts to disclose his true self to the one person he loves, Marina, but she, ambitious for the crown of the czars, haughtily rebuffs him, and he can fulfil his lofty ambitions only by redoubling the comedy and surrendering absolutely to his role. Thus in a powerfully dramatic scene he is thrust back into the hypocrisy which thoroughly deforms him.

These two important scenes lend a particular light and colour to every detail in the drama so that Pushkin does not have to overload, complicate or make the remaining scenes and historical aspects superfluously polyphonic; he can present them with the same simple and unadorned power and plasticity. He can provide them with full artistic expression and life in qualitatively different ways. The entire drama becomes more colourful and polyphonic than modern dramas precisely through this unadorned simplicity and direct plasticity.

As a result, the totality in any of Pushkin's compositions is neither so homogeneously simple as that in academic classical works nor so homogeneously polyphonic as that in modern bourgeois works. As a result, too, the totality does not disintegrate into disparate elements pulling in different directions, as happens in a significant portion of modern literature. From the briefest verse to the weightiest novel and drama the plasticity and variegation in each detail derive their meaning from the total conception.

Without formal composition there can certainly be no work of art, and who would deny that the great critical realists of the nineteenth century also structured their work? But for the reasons noted, what is peculiar to Pushkin are the ease with which the components fit together, without artifice, without exposition and analysis; and the comprehensive social, intellectual and artistic atmosphere provided by the sharply contrasting elements as a result of this direct representation.

Significant also is the fact that Pushkin approaches form anew in each of his works. Many outstanding modern realists, in contrast, in keeping with the problem of polyphony just discussed, actually construct in advance (perhaps for a stage of the development) the general form of their dramas, novels, poems, etc., underlining first of all in regard to the aspect of life in their representation that very polyphonic unitary principle which they think is made possible through analysis.

Even with great writers such an artistic approach inevitably tends to a certain mannerism; we are thinking of Heine, who was fully aware of this danger threatening his solutions to problems of style.

Extraordinarily important in Pushkin's tremendous creative power is his fine sensitivity for the distinctive quality in every aspect of experience, the exemplification, of course, of what is distinctive in the society, the history and the development; this sensitivity includes his affording each specific aspect of life its appropriate artistic form. In this creative approach Pushkin and Goethe concur, but in this respect Pushkin distinguishes himself decisively from the great critical realists who follow after him. For the striving after artistic beauty and the creative realization of artistic beauty preclude any mannerism or any exaggerated display of a purely individualistic writing style. The striving after purely aesthetic unity and perfection is more readily compatible with mannerism; the toleration and indulgence of mannerism in this endeavour demonstrate that mere aesthetic perfection stands on a lower level artistically than actually realized beauty.

IV

Now we are led back to the questions of literary history and of history we posed initially. We have become accustomed, and properly, to see in Goethe the representative world figure of this transitional period we have sketched. For this reason we must speak briefly about him, too, especially since the questions of beauty we are treating were central to his aesthetics; and since he first introduced many of these questions into modern literary theory and practice—though Pushkin's investigations of the same pivotal questions, conducted in the same spirit, did not develop under Goethe's influence but were a product of contemporary Russian society and Pushkin's own creative personality. Furthermore, only in Goethe can we find a standard by which to assess Pushkin's position in world history.

In short, understanding Pushkin properly means seeing him as a poet of Goethe's rank and, in certain respects, as we shall now discuss, even of a higher rank.

We are not attempting a comparison of talents—always a fruitless task—nor a comparative assessment of their life work —an impossibility, for if Goethe had died at Pushkin's age, only *Iphigenie* and *Egmont*, among his mature works, would remain; *Tasso* would have been still in a prose draft; of *Wilhelm Meister* we would possess only the initial, in some respects, immature sketch; of *Faust* only the brilliant scenes written in his youth, a long way from the ultimate world masterpiece; *Hermann and Dorothea*, the *Roman Elegies* and much else would be missing.

The only meaningful comparison possible is on the key aesthetic question of the time, especially since it is a question relevant to both : beauty. How do they compare in this respect? (We repeat that both poets pose the problem according to their national traditions; and, in accordance with the particular development of their own people, both created their own national traditions as well.)

We stated that beauty rescues man from the dehumanization of capitalist society and class domination and does so by portraying the whole personality with immediacy and not by implication, that is, not by arousing pity for the man being destroyed, or by an elegiac bemoaning of this destruction, or by taking artistic revenge (through irony, for example) for this destruction—common practice in modern bourgeois literature—a reaction anticipated theoretically by Goethe's contemporary, Schiller.

Goethe perceived this problem very clearly in the difficulties within bourgeois society generally and within contemporary German society specifically. Regarding the possibility of creating a modern classical literature he declared: "When and where does a classical national writer emerge? When in the history of his nation he finds great events whose consequences result in a fortunate and meaningful unity; when he does not fail to capture the greatness in his countrymen's convictions and the intensity in their sentiments and the impact and consequences of their actions; when imbued with national spirit he feels an inner capacity to sympathize with the past as well as the present. . . ." Then surveying the German situation in his own day, Goethe adds in resignation: "We would prefer not to wish for the revolutionary upheavals which could prepare the way for classical works in Germany."

This ambivalence is decisive for Goethe as artist and as man. He sees that a democratic revolution is absolutely essential for a genuine renewal of German culture; simultaneously he not only considered it an impossibility in his own time but even shrank spiritually before such a prospect. From this ambiguous attitude toward revolution seeps as through a fissure all the inconsequentiality, vacillation and equivocation in Goethe's artistic theory and practice—weaknesses of which Pushkin's art is entirely free.

Goethe thus seeks to grasp the classical ideal of beauty from two different sides. On the one road, the study of ancient art and the Greek model of beauty was to help provide or at least approximate real beauty for the specific content and form in the representation of contemporary life. That is, the study of antiquity was to point the way to a representation of contemporary life in a manner appropriate to the modern world and directed to fulfilling the ideal of beauty. On the other road, using the example and model of ancient beauty, the poet was to seek to overcome the ugliness, decadence and deformation, formlessness (in the aesthetic sense) and the absence of an artistic immediacy in modern life, by appropriately transforming the content of life. In this attitude Goethe came close to the artistic approach to beauty, restyling modern life to a certain degree in the sense of ancient beauty.

To sum up, in Goethe's life work, *Wilhelm Meister* represents the former approach; *Hermann and Dorothea*, the latter.

Goethe himself often decided in favour of the second road as the true road for poetry, opining that the great modern novel, his own included, could be no more than half poetry, an imperfect and problematic realization of beauty. The price of such a decision inevitably was the limitation of social content in his work. With such an approach no modern counterpart to the beauty of the ancient epic could be found, but at best an idyll, even if, as in the case of Goethe, an idyll set in a background of world and historical significance.

On the other hand, with Goethe such decisions are never definitive, and for that reason he remains an epoch-making writer. He often speaks of the "barbarous advantages" the modern epoch afforded and promoted, which a writer of the times could not and might not shrink from exploiting. It was no accident that in his correspondence with Schiller regarding *Faust*, this question attained greatest theoretical acuity.

Pushkin did not know Goethe's dilemma, and had he known it, he would not have acknowledged it. Why? Because the social prerequisites for producing classical literature in his time were not so terrifying to him as to Goethe. Everyone knows that Pushkin was closely associated with the Decembrist movement and that his support for the Decembrists, even under the most difficult circumstances, never wavered after they were crushed and that his confidence in the rebirth of his country in the spirit of freedom never flagged. When Pushkin spoke of what would make his poetry immortal, he pointed to the social basis for its immortality :

And I will long be dear to my people
For I roused with my lyre good sentiments,
For in my cruel time I praised freedom
And brought comfort to the fallen.

The contrast in attitude between Pushkin and Goethe was conditioned, of course, by the difference between the Russian and German historical developments. We certainly do not have to look far back into the past : with the collapse of feudalism Russia achieved national unification albeit under absolutism; in Germany the result of that collapse was a splintering of the nation into petty states. It is sufficient to glance back at the Napoleonic era—the glorious patriotic war of 1812 in Russia and the disgraceful disaster at Jena in Germany. The contrast between the two poets is reflected clearly in their different conceptions and representations of their times. Without the slightest reflection the youthful Goethe simply ignores the peasants' revolt in *Goetz von Berlichingen*. But Pushkin commemorated the Pugachev uprising and became its historian; earlier he had called the other leader of the peasants' revolt, Stenka Razin, the only poetic figure in Russian history.

With such an approach Pushkin was able to achieve in *Eugene Onegin* an integration of the aspirations for beauty of his own time, whereas Goethe vacillated between two contradictory positions. Belinsky correctly said of *Eugene Onegin* that it was a novel and not an epic, not even a so-called modern epic. It is a novel encompassing the totality of Russian life of the day; of it Belinsky again correctly remarked that it was an encyclopaedia of Russian life. It is a novel, and indeed an epoch-making novel, of the first order; in it Pushkin grasped and depicted the important types of his time in such depth that they emerge as the types that were to remain significant for the next century of Russian development. Dobrolyubov particularly emphasized this excellence of Pushkin's novel. Thus the style of *Eugene Onegin* is not to be associated with the attempts by Goethe, Byron and other contemporary poets—whether with classical or romantic means

—to surmount the prose of capitalist life. *Eugene Onegin* is a novel, but in its very form, a unique phenomenon in the entire history of the novel. Elsewhere I have pointed out that Hungarian literature also possesses similar unique phenomena in Petofi's *Hary Janos* and the first section of Aranys' *Toldi*. But because of the social backwardness of Hungary in that time, these works could not, of course, be novels.

The playfully winged verse and the untrammelled lyrical expression of personal attitudes do not detract for a moment from the classic plasticity of the characters and situations in *Eugene Onegin*. On the contrary, because of them the unadorned simplicity in the individual elements we have noted comes forth. Each character is plastic and vivid, yet if we examine the entire novel closely we see that only a few decisive crises in the lives of the protagonists are depicted; and these are further concentrated by being restricted merely to the essential. It is no accident that the most important inner crisis for Onegin and for Tatyana is presented through letters.

Thus in its fundamental construction, *Eugene Onegin* is a novel not only in the general sense, but it is also one of the typical novels of the nineteenth century, one which already contains dramatic elements. (Compare Walter Scott, Balzac, etc.) But the spare infusion of the dramatic element is never dull or a mere outline as in the writers who seek to achieve artificially the spare style of the old storytellers. And still less is the novel drowned in the personal lyric, which hovers over the narrative, accompanies it and comments upon it, as is often the case with Byron and still more often with Byron's successors.

On the contrary, this very personal lyric—and the inherent irony and self-irony—gives the characters, the events and the scenes their delicate, airy and yet definite contours. Pushkin knew it was no longer possible as it had been from the Renaissance to the Enlightenment to characterize a figure or to integrate him into the plot simply by stating his position in society or his class. The lyrical verse shading into irony adduces so many concrete social motivations and contributes so much to the concrete illumination of the personal and typical qualities of the characters and to the interweaving of situations which bring to life the social and individual development that, in apparent paradox, this very lyricism provides the basis for the epic objectivity and for the representation of the totality and thus, in an unparalleled and unique fashion, subdues the prose of modern life and affords beauty to the accurate reflection of reality.

Pushkin here, and not only here, surmounts Goethe's dilemma between *Wilhelm Meister* and *Hermann and Dorothea*.

But this is accomplished not merely in form and artistry but also in content. Goethe was perhaps the greatest creator of women characters since Shakespeare. But in his work we encounter by and large two extreme types: the instinctive woman of the people (Gretchen, Klaerchen, Dorothea, Philine) and the spiritual and highly moral, thoroughly cultivated lady who epitomizes the totality of society and its conscious morality (the Duchess Leonore and Natalie). The latter characters are often bloodless and divorced from life, and their characterization is by and large merely intellectual and moral and thus often pale and indistinct.

Tatyana in *Eugene Onegin* is alien to both of Goethe's extremes. Her dignity, her increasing nobility, her maturing awareness and her fine moral balance are the results of her inner attachment to the people, of her being rooted in them. Belinsky was right in defending the folk quality of Pushkin's novel against the superficial reproaches masked under the guise of championing the plebeians.

Pushkin's stand toward revolution and its champions, the Decembrists, illuminates most clearly the contrast between him and Goethe. How much Pushkin participated in an organized fashion in the preparation of the Decembrist uprising is not decisive. One thing is sure: he was not only bound to the leading Decembrists through ties of friendship and conviction, but his poems, too, both those published and those circulated in manuscript because of czarist censorship, played a leading role in the development of Decembrist ideology and social criticism. And Pushkin never denied his sympathies even after the bloody suppression of the uprising. The repressive measures and humiliations Pushkin had to endure from Nicholas I are to be traced to this refusal to compromise; this is also the reason for the complicity of the Czar's court in Pushkin's premature death.

The establishing of all these relationships still does not exhaust the question. Lenin, who had high praise for the progressive heroism of the Decembrists, frequently criticized the movement because it was not rooted in the people, hardly fought for the interests of the people and had no real association with them. Pushkin, the poet, saw further and explored more deeply than his revolutionary comrades. His personal actions and his poetic theory and practice testify to the decisive significance he ascribed to his connection with the people, to his being rooted in them. And it does not detract from his merit that he could not provide any clear social content and political direction to the new relationships he saw, confirmed and depicted. He enriched "only" his artistry with such insight. This "only", however, was of decisive significance for all subsequent Russian literature, and for Russian culture in general.

The complicated picture sketched above, not to be divorced from social, historical and artistic factors, makes Pushkin, to use Belinsky's words, the "artist poet". Even in Pushkin's lifetime a new period of Russian literature was beginning, the Gogol period. And it is no accident, but an acute historical insight that impelled Heine to declare that Goethe's death denoted the end of "the artistic era".

This dividing line was historically determined, and it represents a demarcation in the objective social development. For in Pushkin the people and the noblest intellectual aspirations could as yet unite only in a spontaneous, artistic synthesis. But as the class struggle became more concrete and sharper and the search for a real social and practical unity more intense, the revolutionary struggle for this integration and for surmounting the weaknesses of Decembrism took place on an ever higher level. The alienation that developed historically between the people and these intellectual aspirations was reflected in the literature of critical realism as condemnation of and complaint or irony about this alienation, as a striving after integration (not uncommonly despairing and ineffectual), as the unfolding of the tragic struggle for the achievement of this integration.

Such a reaction was socially determined. It required the coming of a Lenin and of the Bolshevik Party to weld the highest intellectuality, Marxism, in struggle and practice with the most profound passions, aspirations and yearnings of the working people and to raise the popular progressive traditions to a higher level.

This discussion brings us back to our original question, to the classic quality of the Russian social and cultural development. After the French Revolution two lines of development emerge in Europe : the first, the bourgeois, leads from the heroic illusions of the French Revolution to Balzac's Crevels and Popinots and to Flaubert's Homais and later to the baser types of our own day; the starting point of the second line of development is the Babeuf uprising; from it a road of heroic proletarian struggle leads to the Paris Commune and to the present. In Western Europe this line achieves no real victory and no real liberation.

The road of Russian development is quite different : it leads from the Decembrists to the October Revolution and thence to the full, victorious emergence of socialist society.

Pushkin's unique position in world literature rests on the fact that he stands at the outset of this development. One might say that his style is a synthesis *ante rem*, that is, that at the starting point of this process he provides a spontaneous unity of the tendencies which resolve themselves dialectically in the subsequent development only to reappear in a dialectical synthesis on a higher level. The future victory of the liberation of the Russian people is the social basis of Pushkin's beauty.

The statement sounds paradoxical at first. But the paradox is merely an apparent one. For in establishing these relationships we are not asserting that Pushkin could foretell the future event at all or that it could have been determined objectively and fatalistically in advance. One merely has to note the innumerable turns in the road or simply Lenin's passionate individual contribution on the threshold of the October Revolution, and his vigilance lest the party miss any chance for a decision in the struggle, a chance that might never recur.

Yet even if we accept all this and include in our calculations the many other factors—individuals, favourable or unfavourable international situations, etc., and all the accidents possible in the course of a development—we still cannot consider it an accident that the Russian development from its beginning in 1825 or rather somewhat earlier to 1917 proceeds in such fundamental contrast to the German, French and English developments during the same period (no matter how different these may appear among themselves).

No one denies the role of chance. But chance events occur only within objectively determined economic and social tendencies and within the social and ideological currents that result from them. The inclusion of chance thus cannot obscure the basic directions of social development or prevent an understanding of their character, admittedly very complicated. The possibility therefore of the consistent progress of the Russian workers along the road to liberation from the Decembrists through Chernyshevski to Lenin and Stalin was determined by the objective structure of Russian society as it developed historically and by the inner dynamics in the transformation of this structure.

We spoke merely of a possibility since the achievement is not fatalistically determined. *Hary Janos* and *Toldi* also mirror a social potential for a rebirth of the Hungarian working people. That this rebirth was not achieved in 1848 does not mean that the social basis for the potentiality had not really existed, nor does it mean a denial of the realistic character of Petofi's epic and that of the young Arany, both of which reflected this basis. It was only a change in the direction in society's advance that caused the break in this line of development in literature. The defeat of 1848 and more particularly the events of 1867 did not permit the continuation of the great beginning initiated by Petofi and Arany. And when a century later the Hungarian working people achieved their liberation, it was under social conditions of such a higher level that the literature between the two periods could not afford a link between them; thus this great beginning within Hungarian literature had no direct influence on the recent liberation. The contrast of the roles of Onegin and Toldi in literature illuminates from another side, the negative side, the classicism of the Russian development.

Any potentialities for social rebirth, however, which are latent in the world mirrored in Pushkin's poetry would be achieved in class struggles over a period of a century. Not by chance, but of necessity. We repeat that we can recognize this necessity within the dialectic of necessity and chance only *a posteriori*, only from the perspective of the October Revolution.

The fact that we can only now survey these relationships does not mean that those social forces whose true proportions only now are fully apparent did not influence social conditions and ideologies before October 1917 had provided the key to understanding them.

After all that has been presented we hope it will sound less paradoxical to say that the reality which led in the course of time to 1917 without anyone's being aware of it was mirrored in Pushkin's writing and determined its content and form and provided the basis for its beauty. Thus we can see something more in Pushkin's works today than Pushkin's most penetrating critics before the October Revolution. In retrospect the completed process illuminates its origin. . . .

Pushkin's meaning for today paradoxically is future-oriented: the artistic attitude and its expression in artistic form of the great poet born a hundred and fifty years ago and its social and human background stand before us as a goal still to be achieved.

Not in the sense of imitation. Pushkin too is a child of his time. And the social content of his time and the forms for representing this content disappeared, of course, together with his time. But, as Lenin recognized, certain conceptions of the great utopian socialists achieved a new actuality a century later, in socialism; so it is with Pushkin's beauty and its human core, its meaning for humanity. We must therefore direct our view not only to the great past but also to the much greater future in commemorating Pushkin, who came into the world a hundred and fifty years ago.

1949